DENIS JOHNSON

FISKADORO

"A remarkable novel."

— NEWSWEEK

"A startlingly original book....It affects one like a feverish dream whose symbols and images demand interpretation....*Fiskadoro* has an allusive grandeur and depth...and its intensity is heightened by Mr. Johnson's ability to release language like a full-throated, many-voiced choir."

— THE NEW YORK TIMES BOOK REVIEW

"A fully realized fantasy of the future [that] has important lessons for contemporary life."

— THE SAN FRANCISCO CHRONICLE

"An ambitious book, both in its methods and in its subject—the end of the world. ...[Johnson] revives the frightening sense of mystery that is blunted by reliable experience and predictable turns of phrase."

— THE NEW YORKER

"A risky, ambitious, exhilarating book propelled by the kind of mad excess energy we detect in writers like Melville and D.H. Lawrence. The post-nuclear world it explores is rendered in intense and memorable detail...evidence, everywhere we look, of a truly creative imagination excitedly inventing, describing, characterizing, plotting. It's a remarkable performance."

— THE CHRISTIAN SCIENCE MONITOR

"Extraordinarily beautiful and inventive....You must read *Fiskadoro* f
beauty, power and originality, for its cornering of life's mysteries into w
page."

— NEWSDAY

ALSO BY DENIS JOHNSON

Fiction

Angels

Poetry

The Man Among the Seals
Inner Weather
The Incognito Lounge

DENIS JOHNSON

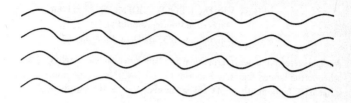

FISKA-
DORO

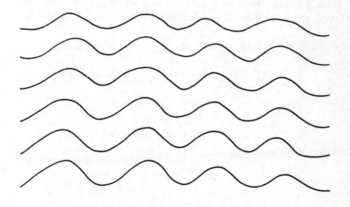

VINTAGE CONTEMPORARIES

VINTAGE BOOKS
A DIVISION OF RANDOM HOUSE   NEW YORK

FIRST VINTAGE BOOKS EDITION, April 1986
Second Printing, April 1986
Copyright © 1985 by Denis Johnson

Grateful acknowledgment is made to the following for permission to reprint previously published material: ABKCO MUSIC INC.: Excerpt from lyrics to "Sweet Virginia" by M. Jagger and K. Richards. © 1972 by ABKCO Music, Inc. All rights reserved. Reprinted by permission. COLGEMS-EMI MUSIC INC.: Lyrics from "Torn and Frayed" by Mick Jagger and Keith Richards. Copyright © 1972 by Cansel Ltd. All rights for the U.S. and Canada controlled by Colgems-EMI Music, Inc. Used by permission. All rights reserved. ISLAND MUSIC INC.: Excerpt from lyrics to "Struggling Man" by Jimmy Cliff. © 1972 Island Music, Ltd. All rights for the U.S.A. and Canada controlled by Island Music, Inc. (BMI) All rights reserved. Reprinted by permission. NORMAL MUSIC: Excerpt from lyrics to "Lo Siento Mi Vida" by Linda and Gilbert Ronstadt, and Kenny Edwards. © 1976 Normal Music. SPECIAL RIDER MUSIC: Excerpt from lyrics to "Man of Peace" by Bob Dylan. © 1983 by Special Rider Music. All rights reserved. International copyright secured. Reprinted by permission.

Author photo copyright © Vincent McGroary

Library of Congress Cataloging-in-Publication Data

Johnson, Denis, 1949-
Fiskadoro.
(Vintage contemporaries)
I. Title.
[PS3560.03745F5 1986]   813'.54   85-40874
ISBN 0-394-74367-9 (pbk.)

Manufactured in the United States of America

for Morgan Johnson

pescador, ra, *n.* fisherman (-woman).

fisgador, ra, *n.* harpooner . . .

—*Appleton's New Cuyas Dictionary*

ACKNOWLEDGMENTS

A good deal of the inspiration for this story came from the works of Ernest Becker, Bruno Bettelheim, Joseph Campbell, Marcel Griaule, Alfred Metraux, Oliver Sacks, and Victor W. Turner. With the caution that this book doesn't offer to represent their thinking, I want to acknowledge my debt to these students and teachers of humankind.

The quotes on pages 45–6 come from *All About Dinosaurs* by Roy Chapman Andrews (Random House, 1953). Those on pages 152–3 come from *Nagasaki: The Forgotten Bomb* by Frank W. Chinnock (The World Publishing Company, A New American Library Book, 1969). Phrases from the Koran are quoted from the Penguin Classics edition of the N. J. Dawood translation.

It is a pleasure to thank the National Endowment for the Arts and the Massachusetts Arts Council for grants that made this writing possible; and Bill and Nancy Webb for a gift of space and privacy.

FISKADORO

ONE

Here, and also south of us, the beaches have a yellow tint, but along the Keys of Florida the sand is like shattered ivory. In the shallows the white of it turns the water such an ideal sea-blue that looking at it you think you must be dead, and the rice paddies, in some seasons, are profoundly emerald. The people who inhabit these colors, thanked be the compassion and mercy of Allah, have nothing much to trouble them. It's true that starting a little ways north of them the bodies still just go on and on, and the Lord, as foretold, has crushed the mountains; but it's hard to imagine that such things ever went on in the same universe that holds up the Keys of Florida. It strains all belief to think that these are the places the god Quetzalcoatl, the god Bob Marley, the god Jesus, promised to come back to and build their kingdoms. On island after island, except for the fields of cane popping in the wind, everything seems to be asleep.

In our day sugar is a major crop of the Keys. In Fisk-adoro's time, during the Quarantine, whole islands were given over to the cultivation of rice, while sugar cane was a product only of patient neighborhood gardeners like Mr. Cheung.

On the day they met, Mr. Cheung happened to be tending his garden. The gritty earth stung his bare knees where he knelt in his underwear behind the house planting two rows of cane parallel to the wall. He put his feet under himself, trying to squat on his haunches, but he was getting such a belly these days it got between him and his knees and un-balanced him onto his rump. Grandmother Wright, in her—very heavy, he'd moved it himself—red plush rocking chair, was making noises deep in her throat. Once she'd been quite a talker, but now she was a hundred years old. She was trying to soak up the heat of the day, to loosen the icy marrow. How could a person sit fully dressed and draped with a black shawl in heat like today's? Mr. Cheung blotted his face with his denim bag of seeds. Its dust turned the sweat on his forehead into mud.

In planting his cane, Mr. Cheung found it advisable always to get help from the neighborhood children. They came, all of them who happened to be playing in the road, when his six-year-old daughter Fidelia called them to the cane. But Fidelia didn't want to help. She sat in Grandmother's lap sucking on the two middle fingers of her left hand.

"We'll put two extra rows of cane," Mr. Cheung told the children. "Do you see this magic ribbon?" He held out a brief length of pink ribbon that had an unearthly brightness about it. "We'll make a border of magic ribbon on two rows. You see? I've scratched out two rows. We'll dig two more. Do you know what the magic ribbon does?"

They jostled one another and smiled speechlessly.

"It keeps away the little thieves."

In confusion they avoided his eyes. One boy crouched behind his younger brother and sighted along the brother's ear at Grandmother Wright and cast sidelong glances at Mr. Cheung, who staked off the planted rows with bamboo shards and ringed them around with fishing twine, flagging the twine at short intervals with knots of ribbon.

"Magic ribbon, very precious, very hard to find. And anything that's growing outside the magic ribbon can be stolen. The magic ribbon won't protect it from tiny thieves."

He started digging a third row, and then a fourth one, for the neighborhood thieves. "I don't mention any particular people," he said.

"How long to grow?"

"Oh, maybe six months."

"How long is six month? Ten years?"

"Until after the rain is over."

"Will there gonna be hurricanes in the rain?"

"No."

"One hurricane?"

"Okay. One hurricane. Blow the cane down. Blow the water off the rice paddies."

"But not the cane with the magic ribbon," they said. And they stood with their navels offered blatantly to the world by round bellies, their little penises and vaginas loitering incidentally beneath, and the greed shining in their eyes. There were five of them, two girls and three boys. They all lived here in the neighborhood but one, a fellow who looked twelve or thirteen, big enough to wear pants.

Mr. Cheung knew by the faded military olive of this little boy's shorts that he'd come from the village of wrecked quonset huts several miles east, a deteriorating shantytown once the dwelling place of sailors, and then marines, and still inhabited mainly by their grandchildren and great-grandchildren and generally known as the Army. "We're planting cane," Mr. Cheung told the boy.

Like most of them up there in the Army, this one had curly, rusty hair and black eyes. He appeared to be shivering even in the heat.

"Do you know what cane is?"

The boy's mouth came open, but he said not a word, only stood there.

"A home for the flies." Mr. Cheung gestured as if to put his finger into the boy's open mouth. "Cane is the plant that gives sugar. Do you speak English? Are you an American? Cane is the plant that gives sugar."

"Sugar es por la candy," the boy said.

"What is your name, young Army boy? Are you from the Army?"

"My name Fiskadoro," the boy said, "from over the Army. Mi father es Jimmy Hidalgo."

"Pescadero? The Fisherman?"

"Fiskadoro. Fiskadoro es ain't a fish-man. Fiskadoro es only me."

"Help us plant some cane, Mr. Fiskadoro Hidalgo, and then put ribbon for the thieves."

But the boy Fiskadoro only rose up and down on the balls of his feet and spanked his thighs nervously, as if his shyness would make him take wing.

With his seeds Mr. Cheung walked from one child to the next, reaching down into the bag and letting these tiny sparks that would someday flourish into cane fall out of his fist onto each one's head. "Don't let the wind take them!" he said, and they clapped their hands over their heads to save the seeds. "Walk. Keep your toes on either side of the row—see where I've dug? Plant it from your hair." He demonstrated by wagging his head.

They took careful steps, all five of them, with their hands on top of their heads.

As they stood above the rows shaking the seeds from their hair onto the earth, Mr. Cheung said, "Don't let the wind take your cane!"

He helped them put a blanket of soil over the seeds, and then he stood for a while watching the sand blow across the parking lot beyond his back yard. Someday the sand would rise up and cover the old high school, and then the slowly collapsing church next to it, the Key West Baptist Church of Fire.

The children stood around, too, waiting hungrily for their seeds to sprout into tall stalks of sugar cane.

"Little thieves going to come for this cane someday," Mr. Cheung said to them, "but that's all right. They won't take the cane from inside the magic ribbon."

"How long till it grow?"

"I told you. Maybe six months."

"Still six month?" Their faces told how they'd been made fools of again by the counting and measuring of things.

In a minute the children were gone, and in another minute, Mr. Cheung sensed, everything that had just happened to them would be forgotten. Fidelia was climbing too roughly from Grandmother's lap, and Grandmother complained without quite managing to make words. The parking lot in back of the house lay under a mirage of water on whose other shore the old Key West Baptist Church of Fire blurred and shifted. And the Army boy, Fiskadoro, was still here.

"Business now," Fiskadoro told him.

"Who business?"

"I got a business for you," the boy said.

"A business for me?" Mr. Cheung asked.

"All you say he like what I say. Why you don't say what *you* say?"

"Excuse me," Mr. Cheung said. "What I have to say is this: What the hell are you talking about?"

"Let's go come on now la street door. I got a business for you, Manager."

Mr. Cheung imagined that business must be a thing conducted on the front stoops over there in the Army. "All right," he told Fiskadoro. He splashed some rainwater on his face from the barrel by the kitchen door. "I'm going for one minute, Grandmother."

Grandmother Wright moved a word around on her lips and scowled at the distances before her. Mr. Cheung and Fiskadoro went around to the front of the Cheung house.

Mr. Cheung commanded the esteem of his neighbors, though like anyone else along the Keys he couldn't have been called wealthy. His house was one of the fairly new ones here in Twicetown, built a few years before when the group known as the Alliance for Trading, in its brief golden era, had moved freight and revitalized some industrial areas north of the terrifying city.

The house was set down on a floor of tabletops from the cafeteria of the school across the parking lot and had no foundation. Where a concrete slab might have been poured for a front porch, damp boards of driftwood lay on the ground. On the door were pasted shiny letters saying MIAMI SYMPHONY ORCHESTRA, and beneath them letters spelling out his name, A. T. CHEUNG. Under his name a sign of plastic wood affixed to the door said MANAGER.

Mr. Cheung bent over to examine an old briefcase labeled Samsonite, with a metal clasp and lock on it, which sat upright on one of the boards. The briefcase lacked a handle.

Fiskadoro reached around him and picked up the briefcase, holding it in both hands. The contents rattled as he moved it.

The Manager of The Miami Symphony Orchestra knew instantly, just by the sound of it, what was inside. "What do you have there?" he asked Fiskadoro. His mouth was dry, and he felt the tears coming into his eyes.

Fiskadoro set the briefcase on the ground, squatted before it, and began to fiddle with the clasp.

"Here, I'll be the one," Mr. Cheung said, but the child hunched his shoulders protectively and managed, apparently by sheer force, to undo the clasp. He raised the lid and Mr. Cheung looked at just what he'd expected to see, the five pieces of a disassembled clarinet.

"Where did you get this?" Mr. Cheung asked, not making a move. "I knew that sound. I knew you had one."

"He belong mi father Jimmy Hidalgo. From a long time"—Fiskadoro gestured backward over his shoulder—"grandfather, grandfather, grandfather, like that."

"May I see this clarinet?"

"Let's talk business," Fiskadoro said.

"Is your clarinet for sale?"

"Never happen no way," Fiskadoro said. "I gone buy a lesson off you."

"You want me to give you lessons?"

"I gone *pay* you."

"How much?"

"Ten million," Fiskadoro said.

"Ten million?" Mr. Cheung repeated.

"Ten million es I just said."

"I heard you, Mr. Hidalgo. Ten million what?"

"Ten *million*. Ten million *dollar*."

Mr. Cheung smiled broadly with understanding. "Paper!"

"Yeah paper! How could I gone carry ten million change down here aqui to Twicetown, Manager Cheung?"

"Do you have ten million in change, even if you could carry it?"

"Not today," Fiskadoro said.

Looking at the clarinet, Mr. Cheung felt something like

thirst. "I'll give you a counter-proposal, Señor Fiskadoro Hidalgo. I'll offer you free lessons—no money, no pay—free lessons if you let me keep your clarinet here in my house, where I'll know it's safe."

"Never happen no way," Fiskadoro said. "Chance in hell."

"That's nice and definite," Mr. Cheung said.

The boy shut the briefcase and held it to his chest.

"Ten million?" Mr. Cheung asked.

"But I don't go pay you today," Fiskadoro said. "Later on, maybe tomorrow."

"I agree," Mr. Cheung said without hesitation.

When the boy had gone, Mr. Cheung went back to collect his seeds and his grandmother from his yard where the dirt still held the heat. He took off his white Jockey shorts and splashed water from the barrel all over himself.

Grandmother Wright was shifting in her chair with a fragile laboriousness that tugged at his heart. He could remember when she'd been active and impatient and sharp with little children. I would like to be where you are, he thought, to see what you're seeing. I wish I could remember your memories.

Mr. Cheung believed in the importance of remembering. He could recite but couldn't quite explain the texts of several famous speeches and documents. He kept up his repertoire by various mnemonic devices. For instance, although she meant nothing to him anymore and he would never see her again, he generally spent a little time each day remembering his first love, a young girl whom he now thought of as "The Fifty States in Alphabetical Order," fixing in his mind the blurry image of her face and telling himself, It just went *blam!* And then he saw himself falling on his knees before her, which brought to mind the phrase

I'll ask her, and he saw in his mind's eye the track of her footprints leading into *another zone*, a region where there loomed a great *ark* filled with tin *cans*—and in this way Mr. Cheung recalled four states in their alphabetical order: Alabama, Alaska, Arizona, Arkansas. I'm *calling for you* (California), she'd been a *colored* woman (Colorado), but we weren't a good *connection* (Connecticut) . . . Metallic fields of wheat, fat thoughtless cows, angular and greasy cities like big machines—he'd seen pictures of these places that had once marched across all the maps. Grandmother Wright had grown up in them . . . Delaware; their own state Florida; Georgia, Hawaii, Idaho, Illinois, Indiana, Iowa, Kansas, Kentucky, Louisiana, Maine, Maryland, Massachusetts, Michigan, Minnesota, Mississippi, Missouri, Montana, Nebraska, Nevada—New-Hampshire-New-Jersey-New-Mexico-New-York—North Carolina, North Dakota, Ohio, Oklahoma, Oregon, Pennsylvania, Rhode Island, South Carolina, South Dakota, Tennessee, Texas, Utah, Vermont, Virginia . . . all linked, in his memory, to a series of mental pictures, and each picture joined to the next in a chain of imagined sights and sounds reaching back toward the face of his first love, whom he thought of as "The Fifty States in Alphabetical Order" just to get the half-light of memory moving across the chain, name after name . . . Washington, West Virginia, Wisconsin, Wyoming . . . Like almost everybody who'd survived what in those days was called the End of the World, Grandmother Wright had never said much of anything about it. It was Mr. Cheung's understanding that these people had lived because they'd been too far away from the holocaust to witness it.

Now that he was middle-aged and felt that he, himself, was composed more of a past than of a future, he wished he'd asked her, when she'd still been able to talk, to tell him whatever she knew about the other age. Grandmother Wright had told him about some of the things they'd possessed in those days—ferris wheels, elevators, boxing matches, mining operations—but they were only *things*. Now he wanted to hear about the people and places his grandmother had seen, but it was too late: the nearest she came to speech was to form various silences with her lips. She'd fallen asleep, one night, in an inexpensive motel in Key West, and had woken up in a world that had ended, and thenceforth lived her life in the southernmost region of the Quarantine, in a time between civilizations and a place ignored by authority.

Most of our dramas and plays seem to concern themselves with the place she woke up in, the world north of the Twenty-fourth Parallel during the Quarantine, a place and time that were cut off from us for sixty years. That's not entirely healthy. Thinking about the past contributes nothing to the present endeavor, and in fact to concern ourselves too greatly with the past is a sin, because it distracts our minds from the real and current blessing showered down us in every heartbeat out of the compassion and mercy and bounty of Allah. But we are human. Can we help it if sometimes we like to tell stories that want, as their holiest purpose, to excite us with pictures of danger and chaos?—the innumerable stories about Anthony Terrence Cheung, a real person, and about his grandmother, a woman who actually did live to become the oldest person on earth, and, of course, about the boy Fiskadoro, the one known to us best of all, the only one who was ready when we came.

On this day of his contract with Mr. Cheung, Fiskadoro started toward his home in a frenzy and held onto his brief-case with a sense that it gave out shafts of fire that would blind all his relatives and friends. He would be a member of The Miami Symphony Orchestra. This organization hadn't yet "grown up." The orchestra never gave any performances and didn't get together very often, even for rehearsals. It wasn't widely known of. Fiskadoro had heard of it only recently himself. Just the same he'd tell everybody in his village about it and then it would be famous.

It was several kilometers to the Army, and he was asleep on his feet by the time he got there. Now the fact that he was getting home crowded out of his mind the fact that he'd been somewhere, and he forgot all about his new status.

The boats were in. When he entered the shadows of coconut and date palms and felt the silence among the corrugated huts, he knew they'd come in and that everyone, even the dogs and cats, would be down at the water. He heard their cries.

When he reached the shore, he saw they'd already landed the nets. The *Business* and the *El Tigre* and the *Generalissimo* lay twenty meters out on the water of the Gulf, and the nets lay on the beach among all the villagers with a mist rising off the piles of mackerel. His father's boat, the *Los Desechados*, was there. The catch was heavy. Everybody was happy. He ran to get near the nets, and the salt spray from the fish stung his eyes. He was nearly thirteen, he was growing every day, but he still felt smaller than everyone else.

Their olive rags splashed and dangling, the white shifts of the younger women wet and translucent over their dark bodies, bright scarves around their heads, the heavy-footed older women in olive or khaki skirts, without blouses, their breasts swinging as they made merry over the fish or their mouths open and their faces dull as they caught their breath after the work of hauling in the nets, the people of his village, the six names—Hidalgo, Delacorte, Chicago, Wilson, Sanchez, Revere—attended to the tasks of the moment without any thoughts in their heads.

White fish-merchants from Twicetown and Marathon

patrolled the borders of the open nets and kept the naked Army children at bay with threats and hostile gestures, while the children, for their part, harassed the dogs and cats who seemed to be all around them.

Fiskadoro's younger brother Drake found him and stood breathless right in his face, reaching out his hands to the briefcase called Samsonite. Drake said, "You back from Twicetown."

"Bueno. Smart man." Fiskadoro kept the briefcase out of his brother's reach.

"He teach you on that thing, Fiskadoro? You gone play now?"

"I be go play tomorrow," Fiskadoro corrected him. "Not today."

A couple of Billy Chicago's kids braced Drake on either side and put their arms around his shoulders. "He got the music, Drake? Fish-man got the music?"

"He be go play tomorrow," Drake told them. "He gone play"—he began singing—"*Let's seize the time now, let's seize the time, let's seize the time*," and pretty soon a lot of kids were singing the old hymn learned only recently from the Israelites who'd suddenly turned up on the Keys, landed out of nowhere in their big boat, half of them dead:

> *Let's seize the time now*
> *Let's seize the time*
> *Let's make the sys-tem*
> *Pay for its crime . . .*

Fiskadoro could see he was too late. For everybody else, all this happiness was starting to get old. The sun was falling, the merchants had to get back on the road, and the villagers were exhausted. Still trying to keep the party going, the children drummed with professional art on the metal barrels of diesel fuel in the merchants' mule-carts and climbed all over them until banished by Simpson Delacorte of the *Business*, who was taking the lead for the villagers in the negotiations. "We want all five oleo barrils. And you gonna bring us five more barrils tomorrow—*full-up*. Plus also ten million dollar," he told the white merchants.

When the trading was over, the men paraded about with sheaves of money stuck in their knife-belts and gave bills away to the little children. While the women shoveled the carts full of fish, the merchant families hitched up their burros. In a few minutes the two-wheeled carts began inching off toward the Army paths and the road beyond, leaving the treadmarks of their huge rubber auto tires in the sand.

There were plenty of fish left, many of them still flickering and moving on the nets. The villagers had carried home what they could cook, and their animals sat gnawing fish on the beach.

Drake and Fiskadoro found Pressy, their mother's youngest brother, and followed him until he sat down under a tree. Pressy was a small, handsome man, much darker than his sister Belinda, and because of his brownness and also because of his general empty-headedness, Belinda claimed he'd gotten more Cuban blood than she had. Drake and Fiskadoro liked to go here and there with Pressy because he talked to them about sex: not the kind between men and women, but the kind between dogs and dogs. Pressy wanted to breed a variety of dog that would catch fish. If he threw a dead mackerel in the water, his dog Sarge would fetch it back, but Pressy's idea of going after a live fish never got through to Sarge. "He dog ain't have a big mind," Pressy said, laying out all the facts for his two nephews. "I can't gone sit down and explaining it all about fish to a dog. I need one that *know*. Then I get that pescadero dog breeding up on another dog.

That dog be go drop out six puppies—three pescadero puppies, and three just dog puppies." He held up three fingers of one hand, and three fingers of the other. "Now, comprende, comprende—breed up the three fish-dogs on three just-dogs, I be getting *more* and *more* fish-dogs." Confused and elated by the mathematics of breeding, he drew innumerable lines in the dirt. "He oleo gone dry up outa these Keys tomorrow," he said, "but when we can't run the engines no more, we can forget about boats. Don't talk to me about no boats. Custom special breeded *dogs* gone bring in them fish."

In fact Pressy's breeding practices amounted to not much more than a lonelyhearts service for mongrels, and some of the less generous minds—Belinda was among them—referred to him as a silly pimp. But Drake and Fiskadoro were fascinated with certain information Pressy had in his possession about how the talents of one dog got inside another dog and then inside their puppies, things to do with sperm, gene-balls, desechado-molecules, and contamination. "Everything I telling to you es so small you can't gone see it," he told them. "Trust me."

Tonight as the sun disappeared and some of the families got together and built smoky fires in front of their quonset huts to keep away the darkness and cook up a feast of fish, Drake and Fiskadoro waited for Pressy to talk about these microscopic things. He knew what they were waiting for, but he kept quiet and seemed sad. "I get you a fish cooked up, Pressy," Fiskadoro said, but Pressy wanted them to believe he'd gone deaf. Fiskadoro shoved Drake and said, "Get us three fish cooked up pretty good," and Drake slid away from his hands, danced around, and sang, *"Struggling man, struggling man."* Drake looked hypnotized.

"I gone tell Belinda Drake's tired," Fiskadoro said.

"Never happen no way no time tomorrow, shitface boy," Drake said.

"Then why you don't get us three fish?" Fiskadoro said, and Drake went over to Nancy Hidalgo's yard and begged three fish strung on a sword of palm leaf.

But Pressy wouldn't look at the fish.

Fiskadoro was hungry. "Ain't you hungry, Pressy? I gone eat the head. Eyeballs. Hungry." Drake was glad to have his, too, eating it with the same dead face he used to have at Belinda's breast.

But Pressy was building up a resentful silence around his shoulders. At last he said, "I don't wanna talk to no fish. They don't lemme on their boat, and I gone die of it. I gone sink down in the sink-down," he announced.

"Ain't you hungry?" Fiskadoro said.

"That's mi family and I belong on that *Los Desechados*," Pressy said. "But instead they won't never take me out, and now I be gone *die*—the man, me, who I'm inventing the fish-dogs that saved the Army."

Mike was asleep; Drake and Fiskadoro were wandering the compound; and Jimmy Hidalgo, sitting with his wife Belinda on the front step, lifted the calf of her leg in his hand and put his lips to her thigh.

"Dirty man," Belinda said.

Candle flames in the room behind them jerked when a little breeze came off the Gulf. Their quonset hut was close to the water and didn't get the shade, but they had the sea and its lonely company, and they never had to worry about any coconuts crashing through the roof. On either side of the doorless doorway that silhouetted them, a row of three ornamental auto turn-signals blinked crazily.

"Es time I about ready to make some trouble," Jimmy said, reaching his hand up under her shift.

"You ready to make some babies, dirty man. Then I gone

get alla troubles and you go fish. That's how Mikey come around." Mike was their youngest, two years old. But she put her head on Jimmy's shoulder and opened her legs for him.

They kissed a little, and then they heard the boys arguing as they approached. "Here come Mr. Radar and Assistant Mr. Radar," Jimmy said sadly.

"Ma," Fiskadoro said. He had a feeling that maybe whatever he had to say wasn't important enough. He gripped his brother authoritatively by the shoulder. "Drake tired, Ma."

"Oh, don't bother me about Drake," Belinda said.

Jimmy took Fiskadoro by the back of the neck and gave him a shake so his head jumped. "Brains still messing up the machines in there, Mr. Radar?" He took the two boys into his lap, one on each knee. "Moon gone have you looney toons when we sleeping tonight?"

Sitting on Jimmy's knee, Fiskadoro was tall enough now to keep his feet on the ground and take the weight off his father's bones. In the blinking red illumination that turned the moonlight on and off, Fiskadoro looked at the faint whorls of dried sea salt on Jimmy's cheeks and shoulders. These vague signatures of the Gulf had always been decipherable there. Fiskadoro knew by the clenching of his own stomach that he would never go to sea.

When his father released him, he went inside to the radio. "What's on today?" He spun the dial through static and with both hands rattled the auto battery it was hooked up to.

Belinda said, "You know that radio he all lies. Cada palabra de la voz del radio es una mentira," she told him as she always told him—every word of the voice of the radio is a lie.

· · ·

He woke up, and the moon was falling down on him. The moon had him looney toons, a few monster things, a few ghosts, a few *rrrrrrrrr* tiny psycho cyclers. He heard their howling: "Oh, I like that, I like that. Jimmy, Jimmy." It was his mother's voice. Out the window the moon had a rope laid right across the water to the shore. The Gulf was black as grease and the beach wasn't white; it wasn't quite blue; it wasn't grey. The moon had him looney toons. He stood at his parents' doorway and witnessed a thing in their bed, a monster with four legs in the moonlight. But it wasn't a crazy kind of thing, it was familiar, it was Jimmy and Belinda. *Rrrrrrrrr* behind him the tiny psycho cyclers rode the air into his home, and his father made a noise as if a bad thorn were coming out. The tiny motorcycle maniacs made *rrrrrrrrr* boom boom bwa! boom boom bwa! that shot right through Fiskadoro. It wasn't the crying of tiny engines, it was the radio on the windowsill. The radio was playing Jimi Hendrix.

He trembled to hear the radio in the midnight playing things it never played. *"Purpa haze, all through my BRAIN"* —Fiskadoro had heard it a dozen times at sound-shows in Twicetown. Jimi Hendrix on *Cubaradio*—if his mother talked with a man's voice, if the fish danced on dancing legs—Jimi Hendrix on *Cubaradio*. He wanted to play along on his clarinet, but he didn't know the first thing about it. In the dark he took the briefcase from the closet and fitted the instrument's pieces together as best he could and hummed through it with a choked voice, leaning close to the radio and hearing the static from its face and the hiss of the Gulf through the window and Belinda crying, "Ow-ow-ow-ow!" in the other room. Before too long the shadow of his father stood in the doorway saying, "Jesus Christ, Radar-head blasting his music-horn out here. Es she moon gotta be have him looney toons." Fiskadoro sensed the shadow's astonishment when Hendrix's guitar buzzed. "Es Hendrix coming out of the *Cubaradio* tonight," Fiskadoro told his father proudly.

Belinda came to stand behind her husband. Now that his parents seemed worried, Fiskadoro felt sick. Squatting by the window and leaning on his clarinet, he listened to "Purple Haze" with his mother and father.

The radio started clicking, and Jimi Hendrix said the same thing over and over: "Scuse me—scuse me—scuse me—"

"Scuse *me*," the radio said. "Guess what, this ain't the program as usual like you thought it was, this is Junior Staff Sergeant Bud Harmon from Nawtha Nawlins Texas and me and Danny and Rick Ames and the Pork-jumper himself Junior Corporal George Wills caught the typhoon and busted up at I guess approximately thirteen hundred hours on them rocks right down there, I can see 'em from the window, and I can see *you too*, motherfuckers, and *I got rounds left*."

Fiskadoro put down his incorrectly assembled clarinet. "I don't make nothing outa this radio show." He gave the radio a shake. "Play those music again."

"Nawtha Nawlins?" Belinda said.

"I don't know," Jimmy said.

"—blah blah," the white-boy voice was saying, "et cetera" —nothing that made sense. "And we killed six a them and they killed three a us, and I got this radio station and *I love Hendrix!* So phone in your requests, only the phone here don't have a number on it, so fuck you. I'm thirty-six years old and I just believe I'll *rock all night!* My dad was a Staff Sergeant and he made me one, and he *loved* Hendrix, and *his* dad loved Hendrix, and *I* love Hendrix—nobody never told me I was own die in Cuba, but I really don't give a shit, if that's how it is, that's how it is. Because it feels like once the other boys eat it, you know, and you're just the last one left, who cares. All I own do is gepback home. But ain't no way I'm own gepback home. I got this radio station and I got rounds left. Goddamn I have rounds in possession—got two real shiny stainless-steel thirty-round clips and I love Hendrix and *I am going to rock till I die!* Fuck Cuba!"

"Que pasa?" Belinda said.

"Well, sound like he fighting Cubans," Jimmy said. "Sound like he stole *Cubaradio* tonight. I don't know."

Belinda and Jimmy and Fiskadoro listened while the man played two more Hendrix songs all the way through: "Red House," which Fiskadoro knew; and another one, which the man said would be the last one he played before he died, "The Star-Spangled Banner," one that Fiskadoro knew from other records at the sound-shows but had never heard performed by Jimi Hendrix. And the man asked Belinda and Jimmy and Fiskadoro to remember his name, which they'd already forgotten, and asked them to remember him as the man who attacked Cuba.

After that, *Cubaradio* went off the air.

Jimmy said nothing, only sucked the air in over his teeth. Fiskadoro said, "What es, Ma? Why he radio coming on at night now?"

"Oh, don't bother me about that radio," Belinda said. "You know that radio es a big fat lie. Cada palabra de la voz del radio es una mentira," she said.

TWO

Sugar cane rises up out of its own stubble after it is harvested. Mr. Cheung had no need of planting seeds if he wanted another crop, but twice a year he put in a couple of new rows, and each time he brought some of the neighborhood children around to help him lay in the seeds.

Now that Fiskadoro had been his pupil for six months, Mr. Cheung was ready to face the fact that the boy wasn't talented. He had a feeling for music, but he expected it to come out of the clarinet as out of a radio: turn it on, turn it off. The Orchestra Manager had tried to teach him to read words, too, but beyond learning to sound out phrases painfully, Fiskadoro had picked up nothing. Just the same, Mr. Cheung kept on patiently. You never knew. Maybe inside of the boy, two wires were growing toward each other that would eventually make a connection for power. And there wasn't much else to do.

While Fiskadoro spent time with his teacher or wandered up one side of the island and down the other, his mother Belinda stayed in the Army and passed her moments with absolutely anybody who came along, even people she didn't think a lot of, like Lizabeth Sanchez.

Lizabeth Sanchez had been called Lizzie before her husband's boat was lost, but afterward she was known as Lizabeth. She'd been quiet and shy before, but now she laughed too loudly and she'd put on weight and was known to keep company with hard men. She dropped around to Belinda's house nearly every morning. It made Belinda tired.

Though round-faced and sleepy-looking, Lizabeth was a nervous type, rocking from side to side on the rolled and pleated Ford Fairmont seat that was Belinda's most impressive item of furniture, crossing and uncrossing her thick ankles. This morning she was eating fire-dried peanuts one at a time, spitting wet shells into her hand and tossing them out the window. "You keep such a nice house."

"Oh! This house just a big mess," Belinda said politely.

"Oh no, Belinda, the decoration and all like that. You keep a nice house."

"With trying some more, it could be a nice house," Belinda said. "But right now today—es a horrible mess. Blast-crater."

"Donde Fiskadoro? He fetching errands for you?"

Belinda suddenly hopped up and went to the door. "Drake?" she called, parting the bead curtain. "Make sure Mikey stay in a yard with you." When she sat down again, Lizabeth's question was gone from her mind.

Lizabeth remembered not only the question, however, but

the answer also. "I hope you know Fiskadoro he all over these lower Keys," she told Belinda, "all slick-up with skunk-juice and look like he wanna make a big name outa himself, ever since from when he start on that Negro horn."

"I don't mind," Belinda said. "He in a big orchestra."

"I don't think es a orchestra out on that West Beach, Belinda. Too windy," Lizabeth said.

"Too windy?"

"I mean Fiskadoro he too windy. I mean he giving you la big vente." Lizabeth imitated a storm for her hostess, fluttering her hands and blowing air from her fat cheeks and inadvertently dropping peanuts.

"Fiskadoro in a orchestra. A big hand with letric generators."

"In a middle of the night? In a middle of the night, Belinda? In a big band with letric generators in a middle of the night?"

"Miami Symphony Orchestra," Belinda insisted uncomfortably.

Lizabeth stuck out her tongue and picked a bit of shell from its tip. Since her husband's death the veins had started to stand out more and more around her eyes.

Belinda saw that Lizabeth's anger was causing her to eat peanuts all the time and become fat. She would come around for a snack before supper, too, Belinda knew it. It had been months since Lizabeth's husband had disappeared, but they would finish the day by crying loudly together while the late sun laid out planes of violet light across the beaches.

"Gone be some big problem down over West Beach," Lizabeth announced.

"Yeah?" Belinda said.

"Already problem down over there. One of them swamp-boys was on the Marathon beach."

"Yeah? What for was he?"

"For because he was drownded. For because he was swoled up as big as a shark."

Leaning over toward the windowsill to squint at the numbers on the radio, Belinda began slowly turning the dial. But there was nothing on yet.

"They wasn't look at him up close till the next day. They all the people just thought es a shark out there."

Belinda stretched her neck to check on Drake and Mike out the window. She put her hands pertly on her knees and smiled. "Do you remember," she asked Lizabeth, "when alla them seals come down that time? On the Ocean side?"

For an instant Lizabeth looked angry. Then she made her face into an unrippled curtain of decorum. "You pissing me off," she said.

"What you getting your eyes so red about?"

"About you only mess on a radio and talk about seals, when I gone tell you something important."

The weather was funny today, and from where they sat in Belinda's living room on uprooted car seats, the sky looked like something flat and heavy shoved up against the kitchen window. Belinda felt more stifled because of it. "I just remembering the seals, because for you say a shark."

"I didn't say no shark. I say *look* like a shark."

"Oh."

"I say a dead boy."

"Yes, I know that, Lizabeth. A dead boy, I heard you said so exactly in my goddamn face."

"*Now* who getting the red eyes?"

"Me es who," Belinda told her.

"This boy," Lizabeth said, "he one of them all-blacks from over the swamps. Got the—" Lizabeth pointed at her crotch. "Got he Johnny all tore up like they do."

Belinda's dead father and dead mother, all the dead of her

blood and their animals, drew closer in the room. "Oh well," she said. Her flesh stood out in bumps.

Lizabeth left much earlier than usual because a man off her husband's old boat was coming to visit her. Belinda stood at the kitchen window and saw herself trapped in its frame, with the girl she had been and the hag she would become occupying the windows on either side of her. She could walk anytime around this compound and see the young Belinda of a few years ago in the contemptuous single girls carrying their butts like sugar candy down the shade of the dirt paths, their faces as empty of sense as little full moons, their eyelids whitened and the lashes darkened with Kiwi shoe polish; and she could see the sun-blackened, fat-assed future Belinda in the gatherings of hopeless fishwives by the well, resting their water jugs on cocked hips while they talked about nothing that mattered, setting the jugs down to talk some more, wobbling the flab under their arms as they gestured, picking the jugs up and holding them some more and talk, talk, talk.

Belinda was thirty-three. She'd nursed three children and lost a brother to the Gulf, but she still affected the youthful modesty of covering up her breasts like a virgin.

She sliced fish, and the blood ran down the drain. The drain emptied out beneath the quonset hut. The boys tossed sand over the mess down there periodically. It was Belinda's life to clean the fish her husband and sons brought to her, and cook the fish on the wood-stove, and eat the fish and clean the fish and cook the fish. Most people kept their fires outside during the hot months, but Belinda stuck to the old ways. She tended the stove in the kitchen, stirring ashen coals and throwing in pieces of cypress root twice a day. Now and then she fed or punished the baby Mike.

The rest of her time she generally passed on the rotted front stoop, squatting flat on her heels and raking brown shards of coconut across her lower front teeth, scraping the ivory meat from the shell and watching the sea do what the sea always seemed to do, which was to curl its numberless fingers over the land, time after time, and take a little of it away. And the men were out there, combing the sea for fish. And the sea kept some of the men.

She hadn't seen Fiskadoro since noon the day before. It was breakfast time when he got home. He was standing in the middle of the room before she noticed him. "Where you come from? You bring yourself around here with that lying face, look for you mother gone cook you breakfast?"

"I got some fish for you."

"I don't see no fish."

"Es outside."

"Well why you don't get them? You gone leave you head someplace one day."

"I'm so thirsty," he said. "I got a taste of sand in my throat please."

Belinda sat him down at the table. She took the jug and measured him out a few swallows in a shell. "You in the wrong place."

It was hot and steamy in the little hut because the wood-stove was always going. Fiskadoro let the water touch his lips, meaning to drink slowly, but then gulped it all down in mixed despair and pleasure. Savoring the aftertaste, he became aware of the odors that had always meant mother and home to him but now were beginning to signal something else, a deprivation and powerlessness, a feeling of slight shame —the odor of sweat and the smoke of fires baked into everything, a stench of rotting fruit and baby-puke. The smell of fish on his own hands was revolting.

And the things his mother had chosen to get and keep in her life were beginning to seem pointless to him—halfhearted and stupid. Around him, decorating their home, were many of the accoutrements of the cars of the previous century— emergency signal-lights flashing constantly, the radio emitting a low steady wash of static, these things hooked by cables to an auto battery that rested on a sill and served to hold open a window. Belinda was very fond of steering wheels and had several of them nailed up to these stained walls that lately didn't seem to give him any space.

"You wanna hear what Lizabeth told me about a dead boy?"

"Fat girl," Fiskadoro said. "She bout a quart low."

"A swamp-boy come washed up drownded down over Marathon."

"I know about it. He wash up big as a whale." Fiskadoro started dancing in the kitchen, letting his eyes roll up in his head. "People come on la beach there and go, 'Hi, hello there now—that Lizabeth there? Wake up, Lizabeth!' *Cubaradio!*" He danced, but he knew she saw the big circles under his eyes.

Belinda drifted around the stove in her dirty white shift with a wooden face. Fiskadoro sucked an orange and watched her take the fish he'd left outside and go to the sink to clean them, tossing each one down wearily as if it were her martyred heart. He sat on the porch awhile and watched his brothers playing in the yard and listened to the breeze tick sand against the outhouse and cry along the blades of beach-grass that turned in the wind all day long, drawing perfect circles in the sand around themselves, and then he left for his lesson without saying goodbye.

Mr. Cheung was always aware of his pupil's presence before Fiskadoro could give himself the rare pleasure of knocking on an actual door. Today, as was customary, he ushered the boy in with dignified silence, welcoming him only with his eyes, his Asian face a mask of deference, but not without its impression of good humor, his hair slicked back like someone recently dragged from the sea. He was dressed, as always in the warmest months, in very fine new boxer undershorts and a white tank-top undershirt, with sheer blue dress socks pulled up over his calves, and lustrous, almost smoldering patent-leather dress shoes on his feet. He was a delicate man except for his belly, a big wrinkled thing about the color and texture of a kiwi fruit, which he carried before him as if he prized it highly.

"You're supposed to be a morning lesson," he said.

Fiskadoro was shocked and embarrassed. By what foreign arrangements of time and space had he arrived here after noon?

"I happen to be free anyway," Mr. Cheung said. He stepped back smartly to admit his only pupil, the only other person south of Marathon who had a clarinet.

The front room of the house, which he reserved for the pursuit of the musical arts, was furnished only with a black upright piano and bench, a long church pew of heavy wood, and a red bucket seat—one from a mighty Thunderbird autocar—affixed with wooden rockers and kept for Grandmother's use.

Now Mr. Cheung sat in his church pew, a straight-backed, bowlegged, and potbellied man with his hands on his widely parted knees, and nodded his protégé into the seat beside him. Between them on the pew's dull wood rested the music books, and the music stand all folded up, and his own clarinet in its case, which was a real clarinet case lined with brown velvet, with a depression to hold each piece.

In his teacher's presence Fiskadoro found in himself re- serves of discipline and forbearance of which he had no awareness on the hot beach or in the vegetating Twicetown or the dreaming Army. In this room the cool damp of evening still held its breath. The windows on the west side were covered with tar paper, and those on the east with white sheets that moved slightly in the scarce breezes while the shadows of a poinsettia bush and a small diamond-shaped talisman against radioactivity, cast on the cloth, stayed in one place. It was just barely light enough here in Mr. A. T. Cheung's front parlor to see. The teacher put the music stand in front of them and spread open on it their text of late, *Sidney Bechet's Clarinet Method*. And he seemed to breathe peace and grace into the room just by saying, as he always did—usually it was his first breaking of the silence before the lesson, a greeting, an affirmation, and a formula—a little shyly: "Book Number One."

They assembled their clarinets, and Mr. Cheung picked out a page in the text. In silence the two of them studied the exercise, soaking their reeds in their mouths. They began to play.

In this sparsely furnished space the melody of the two clarinets echoed forcefully, so that even the little mistakes Fiskadoro made in his fingering had a certain authority. Mr. Cheung stopped playing in the midst of the page, motioning for the pupil to keep on while the instructor listened, his head cocked thoughtfully. Then he stopped Fiskadoro's playing, asked for the boy's reed, and gently applied sandpaper to the tender bamboo. When he thought it soft enough, he gave back the reed. They resumed their practice.

Though Fiskadoro had come to recognize them as melodies, the duet exercises in *Sidney Bechet's Clarinet Method* weren't exactly songs—nothing moved inside him when he and Mr. Cheung played them together. When they were no further than halfway through the first one, Fiskadoro was already wondering how many of these exercises Mr. Cheung would insist on mechanically accomplishing today, already impatient to get past them into the later moments, the time of improvisation and song-swapping which constituted, in Fiskadoro's thinking, the actual lesson; but he had to play the *Sidney Bechet* exercises to satisfy the requirements of an education in keeping with his future as a clarinetist for The Miami Symphony Orchestra. He played now alongside his teacher while the afternoon outside grew fiery and the still air began to bake and the sweat dropletted their upper lips and foreheads, trying to mine out of his soul, or out of his sex, or his bowels—wherever it lay—the spilt-buttery tone that Mr. Cheung drew from himself through his own clarinet.

Today was one of those days when Mr. Cheung's grandmother, as she often did, inched painfully into the front room from the kitchen, bringing with her a damp steam of boiling hearts of palm and assorted unrecognizable spices, and settled into the red leatherette rocking chair with the idea, Fiskadoro supposed, of listening to the clarinets, if she didn't happen to be completely deaf. She lowered herself toward the rocker's bucket seat in a gradual and dignified way, but in the end, as always, abandoned herself to gravity and fell the last fifteen centimeters into the chair, one arm outstretched beneath her in a pitiful try at cushioning this descent.

Out of respect for her, Mr. Cheung signaled for silence while she found her comfort, insofar as this was possible, in

her accustomed seat. Then Mr. Cheung and Fiskadoro took
up the piece, the *Sidney Bechet* exercise for two, at the beginning again.

Fiskadoro had nothing against the grandmother except that
the whole time she sat there, every time, she smoked a long
cigarillo backward, with the lit end resting in her mouth and
the spit dripping down to darken the other end, the end she
should have been smoking. Maybe this was how they'd
smoked their cigarets in the old days, but it made Fiskadoro
weak to see her keeping fire so close to her tongue, her
leathery old Chinese monkey face collapsing into her secret
deliberations, her jaw slack, her smoky breath audible in the
silences between *Sidney Bechet* exercises, and her black eyes
so totally opaque he couldn't tell if they were sightless, dead,
or coldly burning. Mr. Cheung sometimes spoke to her softly
and briefly, in Chinese or whatever it was, and Fiskadoro
wondered what her dilapidated brain made out of his words.

She wasn't always the whole of their audience. Sometimes
children came to hear them, never the same ones twice, it
seemed to Fiskadoro. He'd look up from a page of music to
see them standing by the kitchen door, two or three very
small children with black eyes and long straight black hair,
staring at him as if they expected him to do something famous.
There was no telling what sex these children were because
they all wore dirty white shifts that reached their knees: a
sign of status, dressing the children, as befitted the Manager
of The Miami Symphony Orchestra.

But there were no children today, only the grandmother
slowly rocking while they played. She'd hardly had time to
finish her black cheroot and pull the wet stub from her mouth,
holding it in her hand absentmindedly, as if she forgot everything as soon as it happened, when Mr. Cheung called an
end to the clarinet lesson.

The time had been long enough for Fiskadoro. His lower

lip burned from the reed's vibrations and he knew he'd made a lot of mistakes.

"You're tired," Mr. Cheung said. "There's a mark of smoke on your forehead." He unfastened the clamp that held the reed to his clarinet's white plastic mouthpiece, and lifted the reed up to a beam of light that came through the cracked tar paper covering the windows, moving his head into the shaft of illumination and winking an eye against it— examining the flimsy bamboo for splits or fraying. "You were down by the fires last night." Before Fiskadoro could deny this truth, or forge some kind of explanation or trump up an insincere apology, the teacher added, "Like all the young men. But it makes you tired. You need rest before the lessons, Mr. Fiskadoro—because the spirit, the guidance, these are always the first things to fall asleep when you're tired."

Fiskadoro jerked his head from side to side, not knowing how to answer.

"But your Commandant"—Mr. Cheung pointed with half a clarinet at the boy's crotch—"he wakes up all night long." The teacher laughed suddenly and loudly and then immediately his face was the same old mask. "Up all night planning his battles and wars."

Fiskadoro had nothing to say. He kept his glance downcast, and looked at the illustration on a folder of sheet music beside him on the pew. It was a sketchy rendering of a group of musicians, as many as two dozen of them, all seated before their music stands. The folder of music came from the Teaman Music Co., Silver Spring, MD, and this is what the musicians must have looked like at Teaman Music Co., trim youthful gentlemen in the old, very impractical suits they'd worn in those unimaginable times, with hair that appeared to be slicked back in the manner of Mr. Cheung's, but cut much shorter. Everything about them was thin and sensitive-looking —their unreal hands and blank faces and good posture, even the angularity of their many instruments. Except for their clothing and the absence of any paunches, they weren't so very different from Mr. Cheung—not surprisingly, since Mr. Cheung did his best to be counted a part of civilization, with an understanding of civilization based on what had come down to him from the last century—but not by any stretch of thinking, not even in the light of the most exaggerated indulgence, did the men of the Teaman Music Co. resemble anyone else in The Miami Symphony Orchestra.

Fiskadoro's teacher put not just a sound but a whole personality—insinuation, hysteria, denial, laughter, sobbing—through the black clarinet with the ivory-white plastic mouthpiece, and was regarded by the musicians of The Miami Symphony Orchestra as a player with The Spirit, an artist among them, perhaps a great artist among all the clarinetists who had ever lived. But Fiskadoro, in his youth and fire, most admired a man who called himself Hendrix Is, the greasy, completely white-blooded Soundman who managed the orchestra's precious electronic equipment. Hendrix Is owned the generator and batteries that lit up their surroundings and shot the power of life—what he called *juice*, a term he applied in many areas—into the public-address amplifiers for the Israelite singergirl Little Sudan, who, as Mr. Cheung and Fiskadoro entered the orchestra's headquarters, was shimmering onstage in leopardskin among winking automotive lights, smoky and sexy, her long fake-animal dress slit up the middle and fastened at the crotch, her hair braided in accordance with the tenets of her faith, singing:

> *Cutthroat—cutthroat—cutthroat—*
> *You know cain't nobody else . . .*

over the amplified backing of the bass and rhythm guitarists, two dreadlocked Israelite men who generally spoke to nobody but each other and then only during the numbers, their low voices, as now, like rubble under the current of The Miami Symphony Orchestra's musical efforts.

The effort of the moment collapsed around them as William Park-Smith, the Musical Director, catching sight of the Orchestra Manager and his pupil, banged his big stick on the ground. In the relative silence, Hendrix Is's gasoline-fed generator could be heard thrumming outside the headquarters, formerly a hangar for airplanes.

Hendrix Is cut the dreamdemonium stage-lights and put on the floodlamps overhead. He held his box of switches and spidery wires in his broad lap—the proud possessor of light and dark.

All the orchestra members were present. It was an eighteen-piece group, but some of them were only "political" appointees who played simple percussion instruments like the maraca or the tambourine. They relaxed now out of a state of concentration into a daze of heat, while the Musical Director, making haste to greet Mr. Cheung, wrinkled his nose in a polite rejection of everyone else in the room and said apologetically, forlornly, "We must do the blues. We must do the blues, and we must do the Voodoo."

Park-Smith was a small black man who bleached his hair a rusty blond and referred to himself as an Australian. He was dressed in a fresh-looking aviator's flight suit, which must have been very hot for him, and he wore gleaming black combat boots. To demonstrate his goodwill toward the proponents of more popular fare, he began shifting his boots beneath him in a clumsy dance of deferential good humor, the dance of the elderly amusing the young, while Little Sudan, going over part of the song with the two guitarists, sang at half power, demonstrating the rhythm guitarist's downstroke for him with a chopping motion of her right hand:

> *I love you, I love you,*
> *I love you one hunnut dollar fine . . .*

Fiskadoro carried with him his clarinet in the briefcase called Samsonite, but he had no expectation of playing it anytime soon. Mr. Cheung had arranged for him to be along, as he often did, just to give the boy a taste, a sense of the life.

The Musical Director and the Manager spoke quietly and, he was sure, inanely with one another now, accomplishing nothing but their little delays. Fiskadoro breathed the opiate heat, wanting only a place to sleep. He knew their game. Each just wanted to tell the other he wasn't useless.

"I have heard there was a killing," Musical Director Park-Smith announced. A silence as of constraint fell around them.

Little Sudan was no longer singing. One of the musicians began to pick out "By the Rivers of Babylon," an old Israelite hymn, on his bass guitar. The Musical Director turned his hands up and opened his arms, presenting the room to itself in support of some unstated assertion.

"You—your face," Fiskadoro said, "you look . . . a *gorilla*."

"This is your elder," Mr. Cheung warned him, "and your better. He is our Musical Director."

"You were there?" Park-Smith said. "These are your friends? People who can no control themself. Thief—murder—"

Fiskadoro turned away, his head drifting through a vision of those around him—Little Sudan, the Israelite guitarists, the ever-happy and fat and rich Mrs. Castanette, who played the castanets, the serious turbaned cellist David King Rat, all the others in a smear—and he tried to walk slowly from the place, but he had a sense he was probably running, stripping himself of his pride.

"The youngsters don't understand the situation anymore," Mr. Cheung was trying to explain to Park-Smith.

"Do you know where the kerosene comes from?" Park-Smith shouted after Fiskadoro. "It's poison! Live fast! Hah? Die young! Hah?"

Fiskadoro stepped through the doorway into an assault of silver light, where the old airfield lay smothering under a sheet of sunless sky that shed heat like tin. Park-Smith's lecture pursued him: "You breathe your death when you burn those fires!"

Fiskadoro turned away from the field and tried to find some reply. He and his friends burned the kerosene so they could see. It was harmless.

Smiling sightlessly into the glare of daylight, Mrs. Castanette had come to shut the door in his face. Somewhere behind her Little Sudan was singing, without aid of the P.A. but quite audibly, *"He old rule no more rule . . ."*

"Quiet!" Mr. Park-Smith screamed. "The poison is still poison! The poison is for one hundred years!"

"He old rule no more rule," Little Sudan sang, as if there had never been any person from the older generation to scream at her:

> She poison no more poison
> I blinking dread
> I blinking generator light
> I blinking oil light
> He old rule no more rule
> She poison no more poison

. . .

Because it was faster Fiskadoro went back to the Army by the road, the dusty road instead of the sandy beach. His perspiration itched his neck and clouds of gnats besieged his eyes and ears, and he felt the dust sticking to the damp soles of his feet.

Beggars moved along the road ahead of him toward the lowering dusk, people without arms, gangs of pinheads led by their insensate cousins, twisted-up people, the sightless and deaf, and creatures obliged to cover up their faces with rotting burlap, or muslin gone grey, so that nobody would have to see what terrifying portraits the genes could paint. Only the legless immobile ones were put up with in town; all the others had to live in the countryside. He felt like one of them, bent toward the earth and forced by an invisible deformity to walk sideways.

Fiskadoro stumbled suddenly on the road. He went over and lay down under a tree and slept.

When he got back to the compound, the boats were in. The nets had come up empty. The merchants had gone. The men were drinking.

He sat out behind Captain Leon's house with the crew of the *Los Desechados* and when Jimmy wasn't looking, he stole sips of rice brandy from the first mate's bottle; the first mate was a young man, and he didn't mind sharing. After his father went home, Fiskadoro drank too much and felt vague and paralyzed.

In Leon's yard a man from Twicetown did a silly dance, lifting his heels high in the air behind him, almost kicking himself in the rear. Fiskadoro didn't know him and wished the man would get hurt or do something to make himself look completely stupid. Maybe he was off a boat, but he seemed unconnected. This man wouldn't tell anybody his name. Instead he started that stuff they were all doing over in Twicetown these days, putting his face out and saying, "Jake Barnes, private eye!" Fiskadoro wanted to tell this Jake Barnes to leave his father's Captain's house, but the person was red-faced and danced in an almost violent way.

The mate off Jimmy's boat, whose nickname was Skin, felt the same about this intruder Jake Barnes. "Jake Barnes," Skin said loudly to his Captain, Leon Sanchez. "I heard all about Jake Barnes, only es another Jake Barnes who put on a woman's shift and sat on a benches out by la bottle fabrica."

"Oh!" Leon said.

"Could be es the same Jake Barnes," Skin said, "I don't know."

Leon said, "Huh!" But he didn't say anything that might be called a word. "Hm!" he said. "Hah!"—entering no alliances.

"He wearing that blackeye-shadow for the young girls," Skin said.

The intruder had stopped his dancing and stood with his arms crossed over his chest, looking out to sea.

"When he put his feet up on a bench," Skin said, "like I mean wearing a woman shift, this Jake Barnes's old pecker-wood hanging down and the people come outa la bottle fabrica and was laughing and laughing at him. Everybody could see his peckerwood."

Skin squatted down on his heels and looked at Jake Barnes, and then at Captain Leon. But Leon seemed to be looking out somewhere beyond the yard and thinking, suddenly, about something more important. The others scratched themselves, cleared their throats, drank from the bottle.

"Well, that's a long, long time ago now," Skin found it advisable to say. "Not the last time when la fabrica was going. El time before. Pretty long time ago."

"You getting totally personal and insultive against me," Jake Barnes said.

Skin jumped up like a fly when Jake Barnes reached for a gaff thrown down beside the house. "I think you must just didn't understood me there," Skin said. The gaff's hook was almost half a meter long.

"Too late now," Jake Barnes said, hefting the gaff. The flesh around his eyes was shrinking up tight.

Skin looked around at all his crewmates. "Hey. Que pasa?"

None of the others could find an answer to this question. Leon, Leon's son Harvard, Fiskadoro, Beer Wilson—they all awaited Jake Barnes's final opinion on things.

Jake Barnes hefted the gaff.

Skin said hysterically, looking at the hook, "I just ain't connect this up in my mind! Attende, attende there now. Don't make a punto from just *nothing*."

"It *is* a punto," Jake Barnes said. "I don't see any way outa this now." But the meanness was leaving his face in favor of a blank bewilderment.

He took a good swing, and the gaff smacked the ground.

The mate said, "I do! I do! I see a way out, Jake Barnes!"

"What do you mean?" Jake Barnes's momentum had swung him around, and he looked embarrassed to be off-balance. "What way out?"

"I don't know. I don't know. Es gotta be one," the mate insisted.

Jake Barnes came around with the gaff again, but it was more of an experiment this time than an actual assault. Then he held up the gaff's point before his nose and appeared to be inspecting it for flaws.

"I don't think that sticker gone be no good, Jake Barnes," Skin said. "Es inferior."

Jake Barnes was still eyeballing it. "That's right," he said. "I see that if I look right up close here."

"There you go," the mate said. "If es really me getting all personal because for I *wanted* to, don't you guess that stick would fly?"

"You didn't want to?" Jake Barnes said.

"Es what I telling you and *tell*ing you."

Jake Barnes was quiet and pensive.

Skin squatted back down onto his heels, bouncing a little, and wrapped his arms around his shins. The others readjusted themselves, too. Nothing was going to happen. Some of them showed their disappointment by frowning and some by smiling.

Fiskadoro felt weary and ashamed. The men off his father's boat were the weakest and sickest in the Army. It was as if the boat's name, *Los Desechados*, The Rejected, drew that very type.

The parking lot behind Mr. Cheung's house was perhaps the largest region of unbroken blacktop south of Marathon. It was fifty meters wide and at least twice as long, and had to thank for its preservation the restless white sands that blew over this end of the southern-most Key, continually obscuring and revealing things. To-day great patches of asphalt were bare of sand, and the parking lot seemed much larger than usual. Trying to cross the breadth of it in the hard afternoon light, Mr. Cheung experienced himself as a figure of inexplicable motionlessness. There hadn't been any clouds for three days. The rubber soles of his straw shoes, cut from the treads of car tires, stuck to the gooey pavement and made walking even harder. It was interesting. Probably the act of walking had always been like this in the other age, when the entire world had been paved.

The other age came naturally to Mr. Cheung's mind, because he was en route across the asphalt barrens to his history class.

To find the classroom he didn't have to go delicately among treacherous hallways; he had only to walk through a big hole in the cinder-block wall of Key West High and pick his way through a disheveled boiler room. Going past the huge machines of the boiler room he ducked his head—it was an act of cringing prayer and supplication not otherwise necessary to a person barely 160 centimeters tall—and stood up straight again as he entered the classroom next door.

Mr. Cheung greeted Maxwell, who was holding a lighted match to a candle on a wooden shelf by the door. To double its light, Maxwell put a mirror behind the candle. Up high along the opposite wall ran a row of windows through which the bright sky and the cracked green copper lettering on the roofless facade of the Key West Baptist Church of Fire across the road were visible, but the room was gloomy anyway. When they'd reclaimed it from its decay, the Society had washed down its six remaining school-desks and its walls and floor with seawater. It had never quite dried. These days it made a dank breeding ground for all manner of spiders and bugs.

Now that Mr. Cheung had arrived, all five members of the Society for Science were here. Mrs. Calvino was the only woman, in attendance mainly to keep watch on her husband, Bobby Calvino, who sometimes passed his afternoons at the Banks family's distillery-house sampling the rice wine and offering suggestions and advice about the potato brandy.

Bobby sat at the school-desk looking both languid and nerve-wracked, tapping out a funereal rhythm with his fingers. His face seemed swollen and his eyes were bloodshot.

Mrs. Calvino was chattering away at William Park-Smith, the Society's President and also the Chairman of every meeting, and she mopped her face with a terrycloth square cut from a towel and ignored her reeking husband in a way that required all of her concentration.

Mr. Cheung and Maxwell took their seats at the same time. The history class was ready to start. William Park-Smith, at the front of the room, put on a pair of thick glasses that absolutely blinded him, and addressed the class with a shy wave of his hand. He still wore his flight suit, now streaked with dust and spangled with the stains of rice wine, soup, and gasoline. Beside the zipper, above his heart, he sported a radiation-sensitive button, as much as to say, "I am a believer in rationalism and the sciences." Mr. Cheung could see that the badge was counterfeit. Even those who believed in radiation and ardently feared it made no distinction between the real, original badges and the phony imitations. These days the white cardboard and red cellophane served more to identify than to protect. "The Society for Science will now come to attention," Park-Smith announced with a brandishing of his sunshine-yellow teeth.

"Today," he said, "I hope we would begin a simple one. A short book." He held before his breast a greenish book with the faded sketch of some kind of cartoon animal on the front. Mr. Cheung leaned forward, squinting at the lettering across its lower border: *All About Dinosaurs.* "These animals lived in tropical regions like ours. But today they are extinguished and no more."

"Extinct," Mrs. Calvino pronounced with relish.

"Please wait one moment. I want to go forth with *The Sun Also Rises.*" Maxwell sounded wounded and alarmed.

"Ernest Hemingway," Mrs. Calvino recalled.

Park-Smith gave Maxwell a stony smile. "We have finished this book last week. Why didn't you come?"

"But I think it's important for an understanding—"

"Why didn't you come? You didn't come."

"Those dinosaurs are extinct," Maxwell told them all, looking around, "that means dead. But today we have—"

"Extinct! And are you telling to the Society for Science that Paris is *not* extinct?"

"Today we have Jake Barnes all over Twicetown—"

"Okay! Paris is not extinct. Okay," William Park-Smith said, "we'll go to Paris now."

Maxwell laughed despite himself. "It's because of our *culture* has taken this *name* that I—"

"Okay, let's go to Paris now, let's go to Paris now," and Park-Smith made as if to escort Mr. Maxwell to Paris, offering him his arm.

What frustrated Maxwell in this situation was that of the five of them, he was the only one who couldn't read. "If we're done with the book," he humbled himself now to say, "then I never will find out the ending."

Park-Smith smiled and patted his springy orange coiffure like a starlet. "We have done so and finish the Ernest Hemingway."

"Then I won't find out the end." Maxwell threw up his hands. "Obviously."

"Isn't it pretty to think so?" William Park-Smith laughed almost like a bull being beaten. The others were a little embarrassed.

Mr. Cheung intervened. "If you come to my house with the book," he told Maxwell, "we'll read the ending together."

Maxwell saluted him and put his arms across his desk, gripping the far edge, ready to give his complete attention to

William Park-Smith in the hope of enlarging his understanding of the extinct race of dinosaurs.

They passed the book among themselves and read from it aloud, all but Maxwell, who listened carefully.

Under the onslaught of Bobby Calvino's voice—joyless, gritty, and raw with drink—Mr. Cheung started feeling thirsty, completely parched inside, as if he himself were the one hung over. Two hundred million, sixty million, seven thousand—"One hundred and forty million years is a long time, and many changes took place," Bobby strained to recite. With a shock Mr. Cheung saw the truth of his own extinction and it made him dizzy. They were ghosts in a rotten room.

He dropped the book when Bobby handed it to him, and took a minute, as he hunted for his place, to look at some of the pictures. "I believe page thirteen. I believe page thirteen," Park-Smith said. But on page forty-one, Cheung found a drawing of a Chinese man holding a long, sharp cutlass: *"The expedition always had to watch out for bandits."* He turned the page to find three men gathered around two massive bones on the floor of the world. Behind them, the filmy spirits of dinosaurs hovered in the clouds.

"Excuse me. My eyes," he said, handing the book on to Park-Smith.

"The Discovery of Dinosaurs," Mr. Park-Smith read. The certainty and satisfaction in his voice made Mr. Cheung feel that his own brain was turning into sandpaper. "East Windsor, Connecticut . . ." Park-Smith read.

". . . eighteen-eighteen . . .

". . . No one knew to what creature the bones belonged . . ."

Mr. Cheung wiped the sweat away from his upper lip. Today was one of those days when he couldn't concentrate.

How would he get the Hemingway book for Maxwell? All the books came from the Marathon Public Library, which wasn't public. Everything came from Marathon. Their own Society for Science was a breakaway faction of intellectuals, the jealous counterpart of the Marathon Society for Knowledge. There was something darkening his fingertips. *All About Dinosaurs* wasn't green, as he'd thought, but faintly veneered with mold. Mrs. Calvino would read now. When she didn't know a particular word, it was her style to hesitate before the sentence it was a part of, and wait for the others to guess which word she needed help with. Thinking of the personal ghostliness of his friends, how they would all someday be gone, he was surprised to hear her say, "Probably the rocks containing their skeletons lie out to sea."

The dinosaur tracks in England all went from west to east, the book said. By what light was this fact called "knowledge"? Wasn't it just one more inexplicable thing to mystify them, didn't it subtract from what they knew, rather than add to it? The sabotage of knowledge by a wealth of facts—they weren't professors, but guerrillas.

He already knew about these dinosaurs. They were the cousins of alligators and tortoises, and, though monstrous, they were also the relatives of the pale tiny saurios who sunned themselves on the wall of any building. If you held a saurio up to the sun, you could see the light shining through its bones. Hold him by the tail and he ran away, and in your grip the tail stayed behind, whopping mysteriously . . . The room seemed to be expanding all around him, turning yellow and hollow. The time of afternoon had come when the sun would cast its naked-making scrutiny into the room, staring at the five of them for just three or four minutes before dropping behind the Baptist Church to be spelled by relatively cool blue shadows. He recognized the old feeling. The inside of his mouth seemed as large as the room. The voices around him cluck-clucked mechanically, making no sense. It was the feeling again.

Without excusing himself he rose up and waded carefully from the classroom through a sea of molasses and ether.

The long hallway was open to the air at one end but barred by a locked iron gate. He intended to walk toward it and grasp those bars and breathe the air and look out into the day, but a wind whirled him around and he found himself transported through a tunnel of dust that narrowed toward the Tiny White Dot. The current of winds around his feet played with his steps—it was like trying to walk up the curving wall of a barrel. He sat down unexpectedly and softly. The profound familiarity of all this was nauseating. The White Dot rushed in utter silence up against his sight and exploded with unbelievable brilliance, the All White, the Ever White, the Ultimate White of the Nucleus, the Atomic Bomb.

He woke with a band of fire around his eyes and a taste of paraffin on his tongue, looking down at the face of William Park-Smith at rest in a bed of cobwebs.

Blinking, he righted the world. Park-Smith was looking down at him. "I think the back of your head has blood." Mr. Cheung was on the concrete floor of the school's hallway. Park-Smith had put a white candle in his mouth to keep his tongue down. The others were leaving, filing past Mr. Cheung and gazing down at him apologetically, with a bland, disowning fondness.

With Park-Smith's assistance Mr. Cheung found his feet and sat himself at one of the school-desks, holding Mrs. Calvino's terrycloth hanky against the back of his head, his wilted posture bespeaking confusion, defeat, and a guilty conscience. "I think I must be a desechado," he said sadly.

"We are all desechados," his friend said. "There are desechados and there are desechados."

"Still," Mr. Cheung said. But even as he said it, he remembered that a deep personal gloom always succeeded these baffling episodes. It was only to be expected.

"Wax in my teeth," he told Park-Smith.

Mr. Park-Smith brightened. "I hope you aren't chewing too much of your sugar cane," he said with the gusto of someone enjoying a marvelous witticism. "We'll have to melt wax and fill up the holes in your teeth!"

Even alone with him, Mr. Cheung was excruciated by Park-Smith's idea of clever humor. Mr. Cheung let his eyes shut softly on everything.

"You feel bad."

"Yes."

"I feel bad too. You know about the boy washed up at Marathon. Can I tell you it worries me?"

"Why?" Mr. Cheung opened his eyes.

"It's because for these swamp-people—that's not our swamp-people, Tony. Our swamps don't have the—" He made a gesture at his crotch.

"The subincision."

"The subincision. This terrible business, I never heard of it before. But everybody knows all about it from somewhere."

"It's something about magic and power."

"Voodoo? Voodoo? I *told* you the Voodoo is a disease!"

"It's not the same. Not Voodoo . . ." Weariness. He shrugged his brown shoulders in the white undershirt.

"Where did you learn about such things?" Park-Smith asked. "Is it in a book?"

"Do you know who told me about it? Martin, I think—Martin knows about everything. He should write a book, *All About Everything*."

"Martin! Well well, mentioning Martin, mentioning Martin, do you know who's coming this way right now? Down through all the Keys?"

"Who?"

"Our half-brother!"

"Martin? Que pasa?" Unable to focus on things, Mr. Cheung closed his eyes again.

"Fact! Fact! Information from Marathon says he has left the North Deerfield forever!" Park-Smith unzipped one of the pockets of his silver suit. "I haven't seen him, but he left gifts at my house." From the pocket he took a half-pint bottle of Kikkoman Soy Sauce. "Never opened." He set it on the desktop between Cheung's pale hands.

"What name is he using now?"

"Cassius Clay Sugar Ray!" Park-Smith pronounced with delight the new name of his half-brother, who was also Mr. Cheung's half-brother. The Asian-Caucasian half was brother to Mr. Cheung; the Negro part was brother to Park-Smith.

Again with too much enthusiasm for his own intelligence, Park-Smith said, "He has become something of a desechado himself. Some very powerful magic has made him some very powerful trouble."

Mr. Cheung had stopped being fascinated a long time ago by the person now calling himself Cassius Clay Sugar Ray. He shut his eyes again. The White Dot . . . "I saw the Atomic Bomb again."

Such talk made Park-Smith nervous. "Are you able to walk? Come on, come on—I'm ready to help you home."

As the black man helped him across the sandy parking lot, Cheung thought, I'm from the other age—a former life— that's why I remember the Atomic Bomb . . . He had read about the condition called epilepsy and was afraid it came from radiation. Or maybe, he thought, it's a memory belonging to a ghost, which the ghost shoots into my head for viewing, the way a recording plays over *Cubaradio*.

Cheung saw that he was being led toward the street perpendicular to his house. "Why are we going aqui?"

"The dog, Mr. Manager," Park-Smith said. "He wants to bite our legs." At the edge of the parking lot, a starved black dog swept the ground with its nose, unaware of anything but the odor it was reading.

Park-Smith wet the terrycloth with water from the neighborhood well, standing in the middle of the street beside the pump. They were catty-corner across the parking lot from the Cheung family's back yard and its several ragged rows of sugar cane, and Mr. Cheung rested himself, placing a hand on Park-Smith's shoulder, in front of half a building with a sign over the door that read AMERICAN WOOD PRESERVERS' ASSOCIA-TION. "The dog's gone now, Musical Director."

Mr. Cheung squeezed the cloth against his scalp, and the water dripped like strings of fire behind his ears and down his neck—his skin felt highly charged. "American Wood Preservers' Association," he said to Park-Smith. Mr. Cheung had a special fondness for this wooden communication because it was, as a matter of fact, well preserved.

The Musical Director helped Mr. Cheung to his back door and led him along through the high-pitched queries of his children and the fretful conjectures of his wife, leaving him on the church pew in the parlor. Eileen Cheung, a thin woman whose black hair was plastered to her neck by the muggy heat of her kitchen, dabbed at her husband's forehead with the cloth until he made her go away. All his nerve endings were still irritated.

Drifting with his clarinet over the cool floors of his front parlor room, Mr. Cheung exhibited himself before a crowd in his imagination. Voters. I address you. I beseech you. Snakes. I charm you. And he lifted his ivory-white mouthpiece to his lips and muttered a few bars of *Hindustan*. This was the same crowd he'd addressed once, some years before, when running for Mayor of Twicetown.

He thought his grandmother would come to listen, but instead Eileen came out of the kitchen, her manner, although she was sometimes a shrill person, softened out of respect for his condition.

"Grandmother couldn't get out of bed this afternoon."

It was yet one more thing in a day of sadness. "She was in all the big cities of the other age," he said, pleading in Grandmother Wright's defense before her maker. The beauty of sadness overcame him.

"Is the legs again. The gout thing, what you call it."

"Keep them elevated," he said. "What about her appetite? Is she still eating?"

"She still eating and she still laughing. She drinking vegetable soup right now."

"Grandmother lives and lives," he said proudly. "Just by surviving, she's turned into the most important person in the world."

Suddenly he held his head in his hands and said, "The Cubans will be coming to put an end to everything. The Cubans have survived as a Communist entity, a governed state. Nobody seems to understand this, Eileen. Someday the Quarantine will end. We won't be poisonous forever . . ."

This was a variation of the speech he'd composed carefully a few years ago, in seeking the office of Mayor of Twicetown. He'd wanted the people to understand the future that awaited them, and something of the past. They didn't even know, most of them, that Twicetown had been called Key West in the other age. But dud missiles had fallen there not once, but twice, giving the town a new name. The missiles still lay where they'd fallen. Many of his fellow citizens didn't even know what they were.

In his speeches as a candidate he had always begun: "I am a cultural entity. To be a cultural entity is not unique.

What is unique about me is that I know about it." His style had been out of keeping with contemporary passions and beliefs . . .

But the Cubans would probably all die, too, down there in civilization's heart. Pirates—the man now calling himself Cassius Clay Sugar Ray, for instance—traded contamination all up and down the Caribbean chain. Nobody cared. Nobody appreciated anymore how this poison would eventually come to make physical life impossible. "Nobody knows what's happened to us," Mr. Cheung told his wife.

Eileen went back to Grandmother while Mr. Cheung searched under his church pew for a wooden box which he'd made himself and kept filled with marijuana. By the time he'd located it and his beloved Meerschaum pipe, he was too flooded with emotion to bother with anything except his clarinet.

Mr. Cheung began to play the blues, the real blues, the blues from Europe in the eighteenth century, when men knew how to be passionately sad, and not hysterically frustrated and childish—Corelli's *Concerto Grosso*. There was no sheet music for this piece; Mr. Cheung had arranged it as a boy listening to a cassette tape-player when such things still functioned. The people he played this number for were always noncommittal, and he couldn't reasonably expect them all to be touched and moved. They were hearing only one instrument, while he remembered the interweaving of strings and reeds that culminated in a rush of tears, where the violins followed themselves into a forest of pity and were lost.

He wanted to bring back the other age—just to get a look at it, the great civilization of helicopters and speedboats and dance parties atop buildings five hundred meters tall—but there was nothing he could do but to let that epoch pass, as it already in fact had, and to sit here with his clarinet in his lap, smoking marijuana in a cool Meerschaum pipe until the sun fell and sadness overcame him.

The person who brought Mr. Cheung his marijuana was Flying Man, one of the Israelites who lived in their dismantled boats on the Ocean side north of Twicetown. Flying Man never arrived by appointment, but simply appeared at the front door of Mr. Cheung's house in his savage apparel, a belt of feathers and talismans girding his waist, the long thin braids of his dreadlocks parted to reveal his features, over which passed expressions, alternately hilarious and demented, that had no tie to his feelings. Generally he threw down a handful of dry green buds—he came as a patron, a friend of music, and charged Mr. Cheung nothing—walked uncomfortably around Mr. Cheung's parlor, poked his head into the kitchen, sat down stiff-backed on the church pew to smoke some with the clarinetist in the Meerschaum pipe, which he revered, and then relaxed, red-eyed and sometimes delirious, to listen to the Manager of The Miami Symphony Orchestra at practice.

Mr. Cheung always felt obligated to fumble through a few numbers for him with fingers that felt like rubbery bladders, while his legs seemed to get away from his body and go walking across the room, because Flying Man always made him smoke too much.

When Flying Man came today, it was the same, only instead of disappearing after a short visit, by some trick he managed to make himself more visible, leaning forward and folding a large hand over each bare knee. "Oxrago playino, lissenup now mon. Go playino depachu." He licked his lips, and Mr. Cheung expected that he'd now repeat himself a little more distinctly. But Flying Man only scratched his patchy beard.

"Are you trying to say something?" Mr. Cheung asked.

"Didn' I jus'? This ain' I say something right now? I say oxrago playino depachu, Man-*jah*." Flying Man called forth his hidden energies to start putting more marijuana into the bowl of the pipe.

"Mr. Flying Man. Two things, please. Please no more smoking for me, this is very important, because of my floating sensation."

In a few seconds, the Israelite said, "Numb' two?"

"What number two?"

In Mr. Cheung's thought, the conversation was now trailing away into mist and vagueness. I don't wish to discuss these things with you because you seem to be made of porcelain. He was about to put this feeling into words when he was moved by a discovery of Flying Man's breathing presence, the weight of life that filled the room. Suddenly recognizing one another as fellow entities sitting in the same universe, they began to laugh.

"Cosmic laughter," Mr. Cheung said. "A rich experience."

Flying Man looked desolate for a minute, then insulted, pensive, and stunned in rapid sequence. Then sunny, and delighted.

Watching the activities of his face was hard work. Mr. Cheung couldn't help responding with a matching gamut of emotions.

"What I mean, oxra playino depachu, talking later. Jah go come soon soon, late late—Jah go come, that news when res' with Jah."

"You have to speak"—Mr. Cheung demonstrated—"very, very, a lot, a lot, slow."

Flying Man seemed terrified—but then all of a sudden only too happy—to do this. "Okss—rah," he said.

Mr. Cheung shook his head.

"Hey mon you bond, *bond*, mon."

"Band?"

"*Bond*, a *music*, *oxra*."

"Orchestra!" Mr. Cheung said.

"Go—play—in—o—dee—pah—choo."

"The orchestra is going to play," Mr. Cheung said.

"Good good," Flying Man said, plainly satisfied. He stood up, waved goodbye by clasping his two hands above his head, palms together as in prayer, and made ready to leave. "Thank you. Thank to Jah."

Mr. Cheung waved back happily as Flying Man left the house, walking as if his shoulders had no knowledge of his feet. "Of course," he told Flying Man.

In a little while, sitting by himself in the hot parlor with not a drop of sweat anywhere on his body, feeling astral and rarefied, Mr. Cheung blew the breath of life through his clarinet. It wasn't music that mattered, but *sound*. Oh, to have these ears, capturing everything into his head! Which would be more miserable—anxiety tightened his chest—if you had to choose, if you had to choose: being blind, or being deaf? "One minute, please," he said out loud.

"One minute." Was it possible that a misunderstanding had taken place?

Hadn't he just agreed to something? Hadn't he just agreed that the orchestra was going to play? Hadn't he just agreed that soon soon, late late, the orchestra was going to play in a depachu?

THREE

Jimmy's boat had come in with the dawn, with the very first light, which rode the water through the channel from the east, from the horizon, rather than falling through the air from the sun. At that time of day they should have been two or three kilometers out at sea.

Or they should have been coming in late in the day with the sun at their backs, hauling nets of fish. But the nets had been thrown out and then, when the confusion struck, almost immediately brought back into the boat. Now the nets lay empty in wet heaps on the stern while, with nobody there to see it, the *Los Desechados* came in on a sea almost the same grey color as the sky.

Nobody had to carry the news through the village. The men, minus Jimmy, straggled off the boat, and Leon Sanchez went home, taking the mate from Twicetown with him, and Beer Wilson went home, and the others, too, and Harvard

Sanchez, after struggling dramatically with the nets and then giving up his attempt to lay them out on the beach without anybody's help, went home. The sudden appearance of the crew at the doors of their houses frightened their wives, and the lamps were lit and voices raised, and the neighbors were alarmed and asked what was the trouble; in this way, from house to house through the shanty village, traveled the report of Jimmy Hidalgo's death.

As the Captain's wife, it was Towanda Sanchez's job to tell the widow.

Like bits of paper Belinda Hidalgo's cries rode the wash of sea air over the tops of coconut and date palms after Towanda had entered her house; and in a minute her two younger children were screaming.

The oldest son, the one who should have been taking care of his mother, wasn't home.

Fiskadoro was walking along the eastern beach. He'd intended to be back before dawn, but already the sun was up. Its heat came flat-out across the water and warmed him up the left side as he moved parallel to the sea. He met a man on the beach. "Your father is dead."

Near the pit where sand and flies blew around amid the garbage, two old men, naked except for belts of rag, moved upwind toward him with the secret, evil sorrow of old age on their faces. "Your father is dead," they told him.

What had he done? He started to hurry. In the dark shade of the Army, among the immense palms, he began running on the paths between the rows of huts. A fat woman with tremendous drooping breasts and a face drained of all happiness squatted in front of her house. She was wiping her mouth with the bunched hem of her skirt, and as he passed, she called, "Your father is dead," and except for the tiny children who pursued their mindless adventures near the level of the ground, everyone he met had the same news for him. He ran full tilt a long way with no sound but the sobbing of his breath and the smack of his feet on the sand. He saw young girls whose shifts blanched and greyed as they moved in and out of the patches of light among the trees. He saw a trio of young men well known to him; they spoke and then walled him off with their faces. He stopped looking at anyone as he ran in tears beyond the trees toward his house. All of these suddenly unfamiliar people he passed said, "Your father is dead. Your father is dead." With the sun bleeding its colors into the channel before him, the boy carried his fear to the quonset hut. His brother Drake sat out on the step hanging his head down as he did when he was waiting to be punished. When he saw Fiskadoro he jumped up and ran around behind the house. Fiskadoro parted the curtain of beads at the doorway and went in. Three women stood by his weeping mother at the kitchen sink. Surrounded by their feet, his baby brother Mike sat on the floor, tears shining on his cheeks and his soft lips open, staring up at his mother and now at this adolescent brother who'd been out all night.

"Real life now!" Belinda cried as soon as she saw him. "Real life!"

He didn't know what to do but take her in his arms.

"This is it," she sang in misery, "this is it, real life."

As long as she didn't say exactly what it was, he could stand it. He just didn't want her to say it exactly.

"Jimmy got drownded off the boat! She current—" She turned to Towanda Sanchez, squinting at her. "What was it about a current? I don't understand about a current."

"She corriente took him somehow," Towanda Sanchez told Fiskadoro. "Nothing could stop him till he gone."

Fiskadoro sat down at the kitchen table and cried as if something had reached down his throat and were pulling him inside-out.

When he'd calmed down enough to remember that his father was gone, it was like getting the news all over again for the first time.

Drake had come inside and was standing next to him. Fiskadoro felt terrible for him; he was only nine. They embraced awkwardly, Fiskadoro sitting on the stool and Drake standing up. Belinda stooped down to put her arms around both of them.

Towanda Sanchez was still there, and her niece Lizabeth, who'd been widowed herself at the start of the hot season. Another neighbor, Anna Wilson, was there, standing behind Belinda and kneading the muscles of her shoulders. A couple of other neighbor-ladies sat on the dislodged car seats in the living room. Fiskadoro could see that for them it was all a great occasion, because they all knew what to do—it wasn't happening to *them*, it wasn't twisting *their* hearts. He was too exhausted to think about them. But perhaps it was twisting their hearts after all, because the other women were crying now, too.

In the craziness of Belinda's sorrow, a smile blasted out of her face as she wept, and then her face slammed shut. "The tiller knock him overboard," Belinda said. "Did the tiller do it?" she said to Towanda. "Es the tiller, the tiller—"

Lizabeth took hold of both her hands. "Just know this. Know this," she said. "He never go come back. Never!" Wailing filled the house.

Fiskadoro leapt in two strides from the room and onto the broken porch. The village was behind him, and before him was the Gulf, from which he knew—he was certain of it, certain—that his father would somehow return.

Three men off the boat were coming out of the trees

toward the house. They were Towanda's husband Leon, and her son, and probably the mate, Skin; Fiskadoro couldn't see clearly because of tears.

As his father's Captain, Leon was coming to pay his respects to the new man of the house. He brought the mate because the mate lived over in Twicetown and felt uncomfortable hanging around the Army by himself. And Leon's son Harvard was along, too—not that Harvard was anybody, but it was time he experienced some of the bad side of a life on the sea.

Leon Sanchez was wearing a shirt at this special time, a colorful print dulled somewhat because he wore it inside-out to display the label. "Jimmy was a good man. But the tiller come around and kick him over. Come around por nada. No reason. Maybe," he said, "a ghost. I don't know what." His shirt was open, and he kept wiping his hands on the flesh of his belly.

Harvard, a boy a little older than Fiskadoro, was sweaty in the face and looked sick. He nodded and said, "Hm! Hm!" as he'd seen thoughtful men do. "Jimmy was a good man," Harvard said.

The mate, Skin, was quiet. He kept his arms crossed over his chest and looked at the weather above him and the earth beneath, back and forth. He was small and his black curls hung down in his eyes, just as Jimmy's had. At this moment Fiskadoro hated him without cause.

Leon Sanchez asked, "Are the women in with you madre, Fish-man?"

"My name Fiskadoro." He was aware that mucus flowed from his nostrils, but he felt he would demean himself by wiping it away. "My father is dead."

The others nodded. Harvard gouged a depression in the sand with his toes and placed his heel in it.

"My father is dead!" As soon as he'd said it, Fiskadoro saw he'd made it true again—again for the first time. Did it just go around and around? He began to see that his sorrow wasn't simple. It wasn't one thing, but a thousand things carrying him away to the Ocean: the work of a person's life was to drink it.

Empty of any words to make things right, the neighbors helplessly baked breads or cakes, or artfully arranged slices of fruit on precious china platters, and carried these offerings across a pink and blue landscape toward Belinda's house as the sun came up. Even the older women, who generally wore pants or skirts of old burlap and went naked above the waist, this morning donned the white shifts of young women. Most of the men put on shirts, and those who didn't, considering themselves unpresentable, stayed out in Belinda's yard. The sun got higher. Sweat appeared on their mahogany faces. Eating and drinking, the mourners and those who would console them passed through patches of time in which Jimmy was completely forgotten, and then suddenly remembered and mourned again, with wails of fresh disbelief. Fiskadoro felt the feeling leaving him. He was ashamed—he must not care very much for his own father, if he could stand here on the porch and not even remember Jimmy's face.

After a while, the other three boats came in from the Gulf. It was only noon; they were early. Westmoreland Wilson banged and banged the gong before his house at solemn two-second intervals, and the children of the village ran around clacking sticks against coconut shells.

The people of the Army felt ennobled to have to move through their sorrow toward the beach and take up the ropes of the nets. Everyone had to go, even the most miserable.

When they heard the diesel engines, they knew the catch was heavy.

At first a handful of men and women stood waist-deep in the shifting waters and pulled on the rope from the *El Tigre*, two hundred meters out. Then another group waded out into the sea to take the rope-end of the *Generalissimo*'s net, handed them by one of the Delacorte cousins as he jumped off the starboard. The *Business* still lay some leagues out, but before too long the whole population of the Army, even the tiniest children and the very fragile elderly ones, was divided into three groups, each hauling on a rope from one of the boats.

Together they dragged the nets closer when the Gulf poured toward them producing one of its tiny waves, and together they resisted the sea's attempts to take the nets back out in its vague undertow, crying with each straining effort to beach the heavy nets, "*Fish*-a! *Fish*-a! *Fish*-a!" Whenever a couple of meters were won from the tide, the person at the rope's end dropped it on the sand and walked to the head of the line to take up the stretch that had appeared from the sea, wet and shining in the sun, to reward their labor.

Even Belinda was among them, smiling shyly through her tears. Fiskadoro watched her, thinking nothing, as she forgot herself and chased ahead to the rope that emerged from the water, raising the hem of her shift and kicking her feet out sideways as she ran pigeon-toed through the knee-high tide. "*Fish*-a! *Fish*-a! *Fish*-a!" The sweat poured from Fiskadoro's hair; the muscles in his back and down his arms ached at first, and then for a while burned furiously, and then went numb.

Some of the older people weren't really pulling. They stood with their hands resting lightly on the thick ropes, sparing their hearts but lending their presence. Now their frail voices took up a song about sadness and love and the moon, an old one learned from the broadcasts of *Cubaradio*, and other voices aided them:

> *Cuando brille la luna*
> *Yo se que no dormir, ah*
> *Ni me, ni you—*
> *Ah, helgado el triste pasar*
> *Cuando we are always separado,*
> *Separado, separado . . .*

For some who had loved Jimmy, and for others who were just suddenly feeling, on this occasion, what it was like to be alive, the grief kept burning even in the midst of their effort.

As the nets grew visible in the water, coming near, everyone's excitement got the dogs going, and they bounded into the surf, nearly a dozen little mongrels, and snapped at the fish struggling in the mesh.

The *Business* and *Generalissimo* and *El Tigre* had brought in hundreds and hundreds of twenty-centimeter silvery fish whose multitudinous flip-flopping, when the nets were beached and opened, made a rainbow of mist in the air and a sound like the variable hiss of rain. In the face of this miracle the villagers behaved as if they'd never seen any fish before, exclaiming at the fact of them, prodding them with their toes, picking them up and peering closely at them. Fiskadoro watched his neighbors jealously and hated them for forgetting Jimmy's death.

The men off the three boats moved in a group toward the grove of trees, leaving the nets on the beach to the possibilities of the tide, weeping openly about Jimmy Hidalgo. Fiskadoro walked with them amid a death-stench of seagoing things. He was glad that the new force of their mourning would start his father's funeral going again.

Billy Chicago, a roadside merchant who lived on the other side of the village, dug up jugs of sweet and nauseating potato wine his family had kept fermenting under the dirt.

At first the gathering had no focus, because there wasn't a dead body to be dressed and cried over and buried at sunset. But the wine caused them to sing more of the sad songs, first raised up in the voices of the men squatting out by the porch, and then in the voices of the women, thickened by wine and full of a sentimental love for the sorrows that made life real.

Fiskadoro felt as if he were deserting his mother, lurking outside in the company of the older men. But now, under the circumstances, he didn't know how to be with her. It seemed he had never known. He drank too much wine and everything looked flat in his sight. He clung with one hand to the post by the door, but even that kept moving. The other men out front were the same.

He took a step off the porch, and suddenly he wanted to keep going. "I gotta get outa here," he said.

"You mother inside," Leon said. "Don't desert her."

Fiskadoro felt these words like hooks in his heart. But he insisted, "I going now."

"You deserting you madre," Leon said.

Maybe he was saying it for the ears of Towanda, who was standing on the porch now. "What's he talking about going, Leon?" she said. "His mother inside here dying of the hurt."

"I going to Mr. Cheung," Fiskadoro said.

The name of Fiskadoro's clarinet teacher should have stopped their mouths. But Towanda was confused and completely unimpressed. "You gone desert you own mother," she said blackly.

"Big organizer!" Fiskadoro shouted. "Es ain't you home. Es *Jimmy's* home," he shouted, and suddenly aware that he could say anything, because his father was dead: "big fat-lady organizer!"

In walking the several miles to Mr. Cheung's house he was safest on the beach, away from the road and any people not of his village, but he was already walking through the Army toward the road, and he didn't know how to turn left or how to turn right on this afternoon of tragedy.

As he passed from under the trees and out of the compound, its vaguely choking musk of dampness and rotten fruit changed to dust in his mouth. The road was hot out past the shadow of the village palms. A thousand years ago, it seemed, he'd been dancing on West Beach, and he hadn't slept since then. Purple triangles raced from the borders of his vision toward the center, splashing into invisibility.

The sun seemed stuck in one place above the glaring road. Fiskadoro sensed with panic that he, too, was staying in one place. He started to run, and once he'd started he couldn't stop, faster and faster, until he was choking.

Now he could hardly lift his legs. He felt sick, his hands and feet tingling unpleasantly. When in a few minutes he'd caught his breath, he wept for Jimmy again.

There were others on the road, shirtless men toting straw baskets full of wrought plastic jewelry or wooden tools or scavenged items to be traded in the afternoon market at Twicetown, and women lugging bundles of vegetables, and the naked children who spent their days going up and down the roads looking for excitement. Here and there he saw hopeful families with straw mats laid out and some of their vegetables or handiwork displayed in ragged piles: potatoes, sugar cane, cucumbers, tomatoes; sandals of woven straw; rolling pins and large spoons and other such kitchen utensils; eye-catching pieces of mirror cut into letters, symbols, or talismans. They ignored Fiskadoro as they ignored all the others who passed them by. But he was on fire with feelings. He couldn't understand why these people weren't blinded by him.

As the road closed on Twicetown the ragged edges of more permanent enterprise began to show, palm-thatched kiosks where women held out bite-size chunks of spiced meat on pointed sticks, and roadside gambling games set up on wooden tables, where a young man like himself might pay a coin to send a marble bouncing down through a maze of nails into one of five slots, but never the winning slot, Fiskadoro had learned painfully, because the nails were rigged to prevent it, and one day he'd lost all his coins. And who had been alive then? He wept, and these things his father would never see again dragged across his sight like scarves.

Less than half a kilometer from Twicetown, a copse of banyan trees marked where the swamps put out a long thin tentacle of marsh from the mainland all the way down the Keys and as far as this road. Here, in the shadow of a tree, from one of its branches, hung the corpse of an alligator nearly three meters long or even longer—it was hard to say because its tail curled in the dirt—with its pale grey belly slit from neck to crotch. It was suspended by a short stretch of cable tied to either end of a rusty metal spike driven through its skull and coming out the soft throat. The people of the villages on the lower Keys, walking their careful barefoot walk, crossed the asphalt rubble of the thoroughfare to come near and look at it and see the former contents of its abdomen—a heap of entrails and a stump of wood the size of a person's arm and a hefty swamp-tortoise in three only slightly masticated pieces—lying on the ground before it. But nobody stopped for any very close examination of the alligator because its slayer, a chanting Black wearing pants that were only khaki rags, stood next to it drooling through dust-covered lips and bleeding from wounds he'd dug in his own bare chest.

Fiskadoro looked at the tortoise and at the stump of wood, evidently a piece of cypress root. He made himself stay within the radius of the dead reptile's stench, in the arena of the swamp-man's crazy gaze, feeling a giddy nausea and the hope that maybe here in the alligator-killer's rotten breath there was the power to change everything. They fermented things back there in the swamps. They drank the fermented potions and danced inside the fires and were never burned. They had eaten all the white people back there. They had drunk up all the blood.

He moved on, into the noontime funeral-carnival breath of Twicetown, the stalls and tables crowding either side so that now to leave the road was impossible. The asphalt here was in better shape, pieces of it flat enough to catch the sun and give up an odor of baking tar. He wished he'd left the road before the town had him. There was nothing he wanted here. The atmosphere was one in which something was being smothered in sleep before it could happen. Scavenged bits of cloth, trinkets made of nuts and bolts and pieces broken off of unidentifiable machinery, colorful pens without ink, parts of old cigaret lighters incapable of making any fire—these things were proudly and yet somewhat wearily displayed on the tables by the roadside merchants, most of them old women who fanned themselves with their hands, looking off to the east or west without curiosity.

Not far from Mr. Cheung's house, Fiskadoro had to stop and get his strength. Where a wall had fallen in, he sat on a heap of stone with his head down on his knees and let the sobs shake him until he thought his ribs would crack.

This afternoon Mr. Cheung was alone in the kitchen of his house, polishing wood from which he made jewelry, one of his numerous sidelines. His half-brother, the great merchant, something of a pirate—a famous, almost legendary figure on the Keys, one of the founders of the Alliance for Trading— sometimes trafficked Mr. Cheung's carved charms and talismans up the Coast. Mr. Cheung had developed his woodworking skill out of his attempts to manufacture such wind instruments as clarinets and oboes, attempts which had generally been said to come to nothing.

His tools and wood cluttered the family dining table next to the enormous black stove. There were pots going on the stove, and the air was unpleasantly hot and damp and dizzying with spices. Mr. Cheung wore white Jockey shorts and a scarlet bandana wrapped around his head to keep the sweat out of his eyes.

The door banged repeatedly out front, and a young voice bawled, "Manager, Manager, Manager!" The grief in it alarmed him. He left the kitchen and hurried through the dark empty front parlor.

When he opened the door he found his pupil Fiskadoro standing on the step. But for an instant he didn't know who it was, because the boy's face seemed to be falling to pieces. "Mr. Cheung, my father," Fiskadoro sobbed, "my father, my father, my father!" Mr. Cheung knew right away, as a person knows whether it's day or night, that another marinero had been paid to the sea.

He stepped aside to let Fiskadoro in, and as he did so he held out his hand to the boy, who suddenly grasped it with both his own and bent over to put his forehead in its palm, a gesture neither of them understood. Mr. Cheung removed his red bandana; he wiped the dust and sweat from Fiskadoro's face. "Manager Cheung, my father Jimmy Hidalgo is dead!"

Standing in the parlor, Fiskadoro threw back his head and screamed like a blown conch, emptying his lungs with a seamless cry of despair, filling them again, and then reiterating his misery.

The door to the kitchen struggled weakly in its frame and then opened. Mr. Cheung's grandmother moved as if under the weight of a great stone into their company. Her hearing wasn't very sharp, and Mr. Cheung guessed she'd probably mistaken the boy's howling for the music of clarinets, for which she had a fondness. "Grandmother Wright," her grandson said to her.

The sight of her interrupted Fiskadoro's weeping. He stood still with respect for her unbelievably advanced age, taking ragged breaths, as she happened to be doing also.

"Grandmother Wright," Mr. Cheung said to her again, and this time she appeared to hear him, "we aren't having any lessons today."

Grandmother Wright looked at him now, and with a shuddering movement hitched her black shawl more snugly around her shoulders. The long dress she wore was so old that at its hem it was decaying into dust. Although her face looked as if it might belong on one of the heads that some of the black people were believed to shrink down to the size of a fist back in the swamps, Mr. Cheung loved his grandmother more than anyone else alive, and loved her face most of all. From it issued a tone of voice as brittle and fragile as the ancient permanent-press fabric of her dress. "Bremerton, Seattle, Tacoma . . . are blown to shit," she said.

When she talked like this, it broke his heart.

"Is Denver left?" she said.

"We'll go into the kitchen," Mr. Cheung said. He put his arm around Fiskadoro's shoulders and guided him, slowly so as not to startle Grandmother, toward the kitchen. "We'll go in the kitchen now, Grandmother Wright." She turned around with some effort, seeking the door and yet surprised to find it there in back of her, and they all three entered the kitchen. Inside he sat the young boy and the old woman at the table, clearing away bits and shavings of wood to make a space for Grandmother's hands, because she liked to keep a tight grip on the table's edge.

Fiskadoro sat hunched over the table and cried softly, every now and then a sob shaking him like a hand. "They said I desert my mother," he told his teacher.

Patiently Mr. Cheung stood beside the stove. When Fiskadoro chose not to keep talking, he opened the gate and threw in a couple of chunks of cypress root. He took the water pot off the woodpile in the corner, stepped to the back door, and called "Fidelia!" into the yard. His young daughter appeared there and he handed her the pot. "Get the deep, good water for us, please," he asked her.

"He wash, wash away. He wash away!" Fiskadoro said.

"He was on the boat?" Mr. Cheung said.

Fiskadoro nodded. The kitchen was really just a shed attached to the house, and its floor was dirt. When he nodded, his tears fell between his legs and beaded the dust at his feet.

Mr. Cheung felt terrible for the boy, but everybody had to die. "Do you know that I have some tea?"

"Tea?"

"It's a beverage from long before. From China," Mr. Cheung said.

"I know about tea what it is," Fiskadoro said politely.

"Fidelia is coming with some of the good, deep water from the well," Mr. Cheung said. "Then I'll show you how I make my tea."

Grandmother Wright inhaled the odor of strong black tea that sweetened the kitchen's climate of soy sauce and curry. It wasn't anything like the tea she remembered, but more like the rotten tea leaves that had filled the garbage pails in the kitchens of her childhood—kitchens where the stoves had spiral-shaped electric burners on them that grew so hot their metal glowed orange. Stoves like that boiled a pot of water in only a few minutes.

Now she watched the pot for half an eternity, it seemed, while the young boy grew so weary with waiting he started to cry and cry and could hardly stop himself. He called her grandson Anthony Cheung, "Father, Father."

Grandmother Wright was half Chinese and by now more than a hundred years old. She had the power to see through walls. It was a quite usual thing for her to bore with the smoldering chill of her vision through the center of the earth and the layered decades and to see clearly the face of Arnold Wright. Arnold Wright was her father. He had been a British importer of some kind. In honor of his memory she'd kept her maiden name all of her life.

On the day of his death, father and daughter had been living with her mother, Hua-ling Kaung Wright; and the little girl, now a sucked-out old woman with the face of a monkey and the skin of someone who had drowned, had been beautiful and hadn't been called Grandmother, but Marie. The three of them had lived in Saigon, an Asian city that later took the name of a great Communist leader and then became a cipher in the cataclysm.

Whenever she imagined, against her will, that triumph of death over the world, the hordes of skeletons dragging the sacks of their skins behind them through the flaming streets, the buildings made out of skulls, the empty uniforms coming inexorably through the fields, the bodies of children stuck full of blast-blown knives and forks—the bottom of everything, the end of the world, a grey blank with nobody to remember it, the vision described, passed on, preserved by *no one*—it was in that city that she saw it, in the city of her father's death.

And it was on the day when her father took his life—shot himself with a shiny automatic pistol no bigger than his hand —that she marked the end of the world as having begun. As a matter of fact, however, only that small war, between the Americans and the Vietnamese Communists, was turning toward its end on the day of her father's death. Their downstairs neighbor, Mme. Troix, a frail, sleepless Frenchwoman who lived alone, came to their door wearing only a sheer black slip and fanning herself violently against the heat with a little round fan, to drip with sweat and say out of a strained face that more awful rumors, too unthinkable not to be true, were swarming around the American Embassy. This, she insisted, was the finish. They must all get out of the city, take themselves back to Europe, to China, to Britain—to any place that wasn't falling apart.

Marie and her mother, Hua-ling, stood half out in the hallway listening to her complaints. Mme. Troix wore her hair in a bun pulled back tightly from her forehead, and it was there at the borders of her scalp that the perspiration seemed to start, collecting in tiny beads that grew pendulous and then plunged down—it was damp and hot everywhere; you had to move slowly on any errand. Having made herself into a collection of nervous disorders by worrying, Mme. Troix now hoped Hua-ling would assure her that things were fine. But Marie's mother was far too polite to contradict her. Mme. Troix exclaimed something briefly in French, in the manner of someone dealing with an uncomprehending street vendor, and raced in tears down the stairs. No detail of this was unavailable to Grandmother Marie now, nine-tenths of a century later, even down to the three dull patches of sweat in the hollow of Mme. Troix's back, along the spine of her nylon slip.

And next, within a few more minutes, Mme. Troix was back again, ushering up the stairs two policemen in khaki. They moved too quickly for normal people—they were part of this hallucinatory city, driven beyond all limits by the Americans, who ate up the time from under everything. The policeman in the lead held a shiny Baretta pistol on the flat palm of his hand, and he shoved it repeatedly toward her mother as if trying to get her to take it.

Hua-ling raised her hands above her head. So did Marie. Mme. Troix stopped fanning herself and stood still.

The policeman spoke in Vietnamese; the mother shook her head, because she couldn't speak it; he insisted; she grew even more frightened.

And then he said in English, "This you hesbunt gun?" When she nodded, unable to find reason to deny it, he said, "Why he kill himself? Shot himself?"

"Who did?" Hua-ling Wright said. "Who shot?"

The second policeman abruptly turned on Mme. Troix with an intention of inspiring fear, and the fear on his own face was more intimidating than any trumped-up malevolence he might have managed to show her. She dropped her fan as if it were a weapon.

The first officer put the Baretta in his belt and said to Hua-ling Wright, "You come right away. Now. We get it taking care of, baby."

"He's *work*ing," Hua-ling said. "He's at *work*."

When Hua-ling came back from identifying her husband's body she seemed to have acquired the tight-faced, berserk efficiency of the two starched officials. The same darkness of trouble stained her eyes.

A cremation and funeral were arranged; today, however, in her life in the room off the damp kitchen and the rocking chair in the parlor, Grandmother remembered no cremation or funeral and wasn't sure she'd attended any kind of ceremony for her father at all. What she remembered, instead, was a vision of him standing in their cramped living room next to the air-conditioning unit with a tumbler of Scotch whiskey and ice in his hand, letting the refrigeration spray over his face, ducking his head and reaching back to lift his collar and let the cool air spill under it onto the pale English flesh of his neck, while simultaneously, not three meters across the room, Hua-ling talked to herself angrily with a swollen and terrified face, ticking off the factors that kept them from joining her brother's family in Seattle. Clearly Marie's father was already dead in this picture. It was his ghost standing there in the room.

"Perhaps you're saying that a squall took him off the boat," her grandson Anthony said. There was a cup of tea before her, as motionless as a stump or a rock. If they were on a boat, the sea was calm today.

The boy was crying as if his own cup of tea were the origin of all the world's torment. "It was the tiller," the boy said.

Captain Minh nodded—he'd grown so old.

How long had they been on this boat? Hang on! Everything else is nothing. Remember that, remember that.

But she wasn't on the boat yet. She was still in Saigon. She was trying to get to America.

Because Hua-ling's brother was an American citizen, mother and daughter not unreasonably hoped to be granted visas by that country. Hua-ling managed to reach him in Seattle by telephone, an accomplishment demanding rare energies and a tremendous will; but the sense of dishonor surrounding the world, the troubled nature of anything to do with America, the people and things that wouldn't behave, the official machinery that was out of synch, the frayed hearts, the broken faces, the ugly rules, all of these things kept them in Saigon when they should have been able to leave for Seattle right away.

The dry season ended and the rains began, driving the grease up out of the streets and tearing up the surface of any road that wasn't concrete, and eventually eroding great potholes over which the taxis and personal sedans slammed obliviously. The drivers of mo-peds and Hondas careened among the chasms bearing a relentless faith in their immunity, while the bicyclists shrank themselves against the margin of whatever street and forged straight ahead. The traffic ate up the precious time and the pointless distance, the rain grated and sighed over everything, and in spite of her grief, to Marie Saigon was music.

Months later Marie saw the policeman again, the one who had pushed her father's gun on her mother, looking almost the same. He stood in the midst of police barricades around some kind of accident, pointing his finger and shouting orders to a straining crowd of citizens who lurched forward dangerously against the wooden sawhorses, unbalanced by the weight of their curiosity. In a manner intended to startle them and keep them back, the policeman stamped his foot and gestured flagrantly toward the butt of his holstered pistol. It had rained, but it was clearing now, and one of the spectators poked his umbrella out of the group at the barricade like a rifle, and some people laughed hate-filled laughter at the policeman. Behind him an ambulance waited while a stretcher was being loaded through its open rear doors.

A mo-ped in perfect condition lay on its side near the ambulance. A street boy in khaki shorts, squatting like a monkey, wrestled with one of its saddlebags until another policeman, backing off from the ambulance, noticed and shouted something that drove him away.

Marie turned to see her father, tall and pale and caressed by a white shirt. He was sipping a cocktail among onlookers in a streetside bar, all of them mildly diverted from their own troubles by this anonymous street tragedy.

"Daddy!" Remembering the moment these many decades since, she couldn't tell it from a dream.

"Daddy!"

Perhaps it had been only a dream.

He saw her but pretended not to. Rather than drinking his drink, his drink appeared to be drinking him. Rapidly he was consumed by it until the glass hung in the air and then exploded. A woman in a blue dress sat there instead of her father.

"Daddy?" she called. The khakied policeman looked up, the man who had held her father's gun in his hands. He searched for the one who had called to him from the crowd.

Her mother went to sleep in her face, as a Chinese expression went, at about this time. Marie was surprised and confused to find one day that Hua-ling had produced an armor of lifelessness around herself. She'd transmitted to Marie the faith that to suffer over generations was unremarkable, and now because her husband had killed himself, one man in all this panorama of endlessly masticated hope, she collapsed inward like a dry toadstool and spoke neither yes nor no. She couldn't think of going to Hong Kong, or even England, but only to her brother in America. Marie had to learn to care for herself and her mother, bargain with merchants, avoid traps, and navigate bureaucracies, while they all invented new ways of delaying her and she passed her sixteenth birthday.

Much of Hua-ling's correspondence and many of her trans-
actions regarding their visas, it turned out, had been only
imagined or dreamed. While Marie came to appreciate how
bad off her mother had been immediately following the
suicide, Hua-ling got even worse. She starved herself, took
too many pills, passed out, swelled up—kidney problems
were evidently killing her, and she could hardly drag her
fattened legs beneath herself from one room in the apartment
to another. Something happened to her sweat glands and she
ceased perspiring, even on the muggiest days when the air
conditioner was worthless. The hot weather drove her tem-
perature up to nearly fatal levels, from which she shouted
down at imaginary goblins in a fever-world, sometimes finding the crazed strength to move things around the living
room, barricading the door or building herself small shelters
from private, terrible eventualities. She couldn't be left alone
for more than a few minutes, and even so, one day Marie
came back from shopping to find her mother stretched out
and looking dead on the sidewalk in front of their building.
She was alive, but from that day forward her English, formerly
perfect, was so elementary she hardly ever spoke it. All day
she smoked Peace, a Japanese brand of cigaret, and coughed
with a tearing sound and beslimed hundreds of Kleenex
tissues with the congestion from her nameless disease, scattering them like white blossoms over the tabletops. Often she
had to take her breaths from a yellow compressed-air tank
labeled "O_2."

As the people of Saigon came to appreciate, against all
belief, that they'd be abandoned by the Americans and eaten
by the Communists, the city's atmosphere grew much more
crazed and scary. Marie dragged herself among government
offices where the Vietnamese employees, some made rabid,
others lobotomized by betrayal, failed to help her in the

matter of visas. Everything that happened around the American Embassy was taken as a sign of hope or of disaster—a change in gate personnel, the early or late arrival of the gardener—and everyone had a theory or a rumor, but there was never any official news except what everyone knew just couldn't be true: that nothing of significance had been decided; that things would go on as they had.

But the machines moved paper to the extent that such movement was possible, and on a day when the news was official, and Danang was falling and Saigon would certainly fall, and sources said there were no spaces on the flights, no flights, no way to get to the airport, no airport, no pilots left in the country, no planes, the papers arrived for Hua-ling and Marie. Marie raced back down Tu Do Street with the manila envelope soaking sweat under her blouse, restraining herself to a pace befitting business rather than panic, more terrified to have these precious papers, even, than she had been of the chance of never getting them.

She crossed Tu Do in the hope of skirting a group of six or seven ARVN officers who moved along the sidewalk with a shopping cart full of what seemed to be gold bullion. When they came to the broken curb of a cross street, four of them had to take hold of the heavy cart and ease it down, and then up over the next curb. The group stopped in front of a closed goldsmith's, and one of the officers, who carried his sidearm unholstered, banged on the door with his free hand.

Marie turned left and got off Tu Do. The side street she entered was empty. Dressed in the anachronistic white suit of the tropic colonial, a man who made no sound of footsteps strolled toward her from its far end. Her father.

The heat of their surroundings smelled of fear, a humming, ozone fragrance. She stopped still and waited, stroked by its sickly fingers until she felt weak. He kept walking but got no closer.

When she moved back onto the larger street, the ARVN officers were out of sight inside the shop, and except for a patrol of their subordinates passing in a jeep, white-faced, weeping boys manning a high-caliber machine gun and draped with belts of its ammunition on the day of their defeat, the traffic seemed suddenly usual.

Mme. Troix bid Marie and her mother goodbye. She'd been on the phone, and was crying and dancing jerkily through the hallways in fear. "The big helicopter have seen leaving the roof of the U.S. Embassy. You see everything is finish! I have predicted it! I have predicted it!"

There were barricades up, she said, along all the roads between the city proper and Tonsonhut Airport. People from the countryside were crowding into Saigon. The American Embassy was being mobbed. She herself had made secret arrangements for Hong Kong. The black mascara streaked down her face as she cried and kissed them goodbye, because they'd all grown very close in Hua-ling's illness, and Mme. Troix had been nursemaid, friend, and, finally, hysterically loyal family member, refusing to take herself out of the doomed city until she knew that Hua-ling's and Marie's papers had gone through.

Wiping her neighbor's tears from her neck, Hua-ling seemed to grasp the situation for a moment. She wished Mme. Troix a passage without hazard, and gave her a black lace shawl for a gift of parting. But a stealthy satisfaction firmed the lines of her mouth, as if the end of things in Saigon was something she'd arranged single-handedly, to get back at everyone.

Were they on the boat yet? Where was Captain Minh? Grandmother went to take a sip of her tea, and it smelled amazingly like curry. Stuff was floating in it . . . it had turned into soup. A thin white hand set down a cup of rice next to it. Now arrives the metal spoon with the wooden handle. Now you're going to put a napkin under my chin. "Let me put the napkin, Grandmother," her grandson's wife said. It had been like this for as long as Marie could remember.

But what had she been remembering? She couldn't remember. The boat, the helicopter, the airport, the apartment—her mother, Hua-ling, standing next to her yellow oxygen tank with a cigaret lighter, threatening to blow up the world. "Where are you taking me?" she said in Chinese. She hardly ever spoke English anymore.

"America. America. Look—see? The apartment is empty. We don't live here anymore," Marie told her.

When she appreciated that they were leaving the city, Hua-ling dropped her cigaret lighter and found strength to gather up a nylon robe and put it on, moving with pale force, swimming through fuzz. She took from the black walnut table by the door a cigaret she'd been dealing with and abandoning for half an hour, while Marie hefted a suitcase holding a few essential items. "Do you have a match?" Hua-ling said. The power went off at that instant and the air conditioner ceased humming. Hua-ling looked around herself curiously, as if just getting there.

When they got outside, they found their neighborhood completely changed. The afternoon had surrendered any pretense of control. Marie choked on the smell of sweat, exhaust, and smoldering rubber—they were burning piles of garbage on Tu Do Street. In the movements of the people all up and down the thoroughfare—khaki or black or white movements, everyone seemed to wear khaki or black or white—everything was being done for the last time: people who for years had been the walking dead were now awake; eyes that had been filmed and cynical were glittering and blind with adrenaline.

Hua-ling, wearing a nylon robe the color of cream and spattered with coffee and whiskey, appeared alert and walked slowly on her own power. Marie wore her most businesslike dress and carried only one small suitcase, which she held in her lap in the crumbling taxi, sitting next to her mother in the back seat.

The taxi's driver was afraid of the airport. When Marie told him to go there, he looked out his side window for other passengers, his nostrils widening and his wooden lips clamping shut. She offered him a wad of piasters without counting it, but he refused, talking in Vietnamese to this Eurasian girl, as everyone did.

"I'm British! I'm American!" Marie said, waving her British passport with the American visa.

These documents were more persuasive to him than money. "Police blocking barricade on a highway now," he said, but he drove along Tu Do, steering around humps of debris—belongings grown too heavy for the people walking into or out of the city, three or four of whom now stepped aboard the taxi's rear bumper and rode on the back. Marie ignored them, but her mother turned around and tried banishing them with an irritated gesture. "Excuse me! Lice of rodents," she said in Chinese.

Marie, as they got closer to the airport, felt powerful enough to pass through any kind of trial if she and Hua-ling would ultimately be lifted out of the war. Her mother, too, had drawn some energy from the prospect of getting away, but the air seemed to go out of her as the cab shook her back and forth, until her head was rolling from side to side and thumping against the window whenever they had to swerve. She looked dead, but she was still half-conscious, suddenly rousing herself to demand a light for her cigaret.

The young men in charge of the advance barricade—two

ARVN and two policemen—were willing to let whoever manned the later obstacles take care of the actual work. They turned back every second vehicle automatically and let all the others through. Marie waved her papers, but the guard wasn't even looking as they passed. He was already busy turning back the car behind them. Hua-ling said, "Thank you, thank you, thank you," to him, intoning the Chinese words expressionlessly, and belched up a stench of brandy. "Do you have a match," she said to him long after he'd disappeared from her window, "do you have a match, do you have a match?" Her head drooped. "Gimme a light," she said in English.

As they approached the last highway barricade, not quite a mile from Tonsonhut Airport, the men riding on the trunk jumped off and left the road. The bulk of the traffic moved against their progress slowly like volcanic rubble, while a swifter current of pedestrians ridden by huge bundles overflowed the roadside ditches. Twenty meters out in front of the makeshift thatched kiosk and oil-drum and sawhorse roadblock, a policeman stood waving one hand with a shooing motion and resting the other on the rifle slung across his chest. All passenger vehicles were being turned back automatically.

Now the taxi driver behaved like someone trapped under water. Over Marie's threats and despite her offers of money, he started yanking at the wheel and raising up halfway in his seat to look behind them and begin a U-turn, broadcasting relief with his body heat.

"I just want a cigaret. You're denying me this small thing," Hua-ling said.

"Don't turn around!" Marie told the driver. "I'm trying to get us out of this," she said to her mother. The driver was successfully herding his cab into the flow of cars going back into Saigon.

In English her mother said, "A facking cigaret. Give—me
—a facking—*light*." Her eyes were curtained with hatred.

Marie and the driver couldn't heed her. The driver ignored
Marie as well, until she slapped the back of his head finally,
weeping. Now that he found himself able to inch along in the
crosscurrent, he wouldn't give up his tiny momentum to let
them out. "You greasy bastard—stupid, stupid, monkey!" she
screamed, wrenching open her door and stepping out dizzily
from the moving cab. Within a few feet the taxi was jammed
up in the stalled warfare of cars and small trucks. Marie
reached in through the open door and tried to assist her
mother in getting out, but Hua-ling pulled her hand away.
"Where are you taking me!" Her face was slack, her vision
unfocused, but she had a firmness to her voice born of angry
fear. "Don't pull me," she said.

"We have to get on the plane now." Marie put her knees on
the seat and tried to haul her mother out by gripping her
under the arms; but her mother was limp. "It's time!" Marie
cried out.

"Stop pulling," her mother said. "Fack you," she said in
English. "I'm not go *nowhere* until I have a *rest*, and smoke
a *cigaret*."

The cab was in motion again in a lane of vehicles that had
somehow found space to move. Marie backed herself out of
the cab and nearly fell in the road beside it, exhausted of pleas
and strength, holding her papers and their only suitcase. The
suitcase eluded her grip and spilled open on the road, and she
knelt to stuff the contents back into it, but then understood
that there was nothing in it valuable enough to stop for. She
stood surrounded by machines that honked, gunned, roared,
screeched their brakes, and she watched an airplane take to the
air over Tonsonhut Airport, realizing, as she yearned after it
to the point she believed her vital organs would tear them-

selves free, that in order to save her life she had to do what she'd actually been in the process of doing for some time. She had to abandon everything and escape. She had to let go of the suitcase. She had to leave her mother behind.

The forward patrolman ignored her as she passed him hugging the edge of the roadside ditch, at one point stepping onto the bumper of a car and clambering across its hood to bridge the mess of vehicles. But at the barricade proper, the guards stopped her cold, not at all impressed by her papers. "Gimp me your ticket!" the man insisted. "Show me!"

"It's—my ticket is *waiting* for me," she said.

"Show me one ticket!" the guard said.

Marie moved her mouth, about to tell another lie, but instead said, "I have money. I have money, no ticket."

The guard laughed and turned from her. He was brown and Polynesian-looking. She wanted to throw herself at him, and she saw herself crushing his Adam's apple. The other guard was pounding bitterly with the butt of his rifle on the hood of the only vehicle to have floundered all the way to this last barricade, a black Mercedes that had evidently been mistaken for some kind of official transport, but which now turned out to be filled with a Saigon businessman, his wife and children, and several white-uniformed servants. As he pounded, the rifle discharged with a single loud crack by no means overwhelming in this cauldron of noise, and the guard, who couldn't have appeared more startled if he'd shot himself, gingerly changed the weapon from hand to hand, and wiggled the safety. The Mercedes leapt into reverse, banging into the edge of the kiosk, and then instantly forward again, the driver making haste, after this gesture on the guard's part, to turn around and leave. Everyone in the dust-streaked automobile was crying except for the owner, who sat in the front and managed to look only mildly set back by the sundering of his household and the destruction of his way of life. Between the business-

man and a white-garbed maidservant, Marie saw her father's
ghost.

He looked at his daughter in some confusion, and then took
off his glasses and wiped his eyes with his hand, for he too was
crying.

She turned away from him. "I will fuck you," Marie said to
the guard. "My mother is dead," she added. The guard looked
at her in genuine amusement and also seemed a little shocked.
"I can *get* a ticket," she said. "Just tell me—what do you
want?"

"Go!" the guard said, waving her on. "Go airport! You'll
die tonight." He pointed to the area of the airport beyond
them, the sunburned fields and the control tower diminished
by open space. His expression showed real concern about the
whole situation and possibly for Marie herself. "Nobody—"
He just stopped there, weary of seeking foreign words for
unprecedented things, and dropped his hand and turned away.
Behind them, people were abandoning their cars and taking
to the fields, avoiding the barricades entirely.

Marie moved past the guard and made for the tower in the
distance. She picked up her pace, losing one of her high-heeled
shoes and kicking the other from her foot. When she stepped
on a sharp rock she knew about the pain but did not actually
feel it. In the same way she knew that she was looking around
inside the moment when her father had thrown it all away—
Marie his daughter, her mother his wife, and the war in
Vietnam—the instant in time when escape rises, rippling trans-
lucently, out of a stifling landscape. Already the noise behind
her was drowned in itself. What she could hear was the wind
through the chest-high blades of coarse grass, and faintly a jet
engine, like chalk across slate. A plane that seemed unconnected with this sound lifted into the film of heat. Ahead of
her, people who'd made their way through the field's sharp
teeth were coming out of them and taking to the road.

It was clear from the scene at the end of the paved service street that nobody was getting into the terminal today. At the entrance, under a modern awning whose aluminum gave a sting to the echoes of terrified and angry voices, the plate-glass windows and electric-eye doors were shattered and covered with boards. Dozens of purple-bereted Vietnamese Special Forces soldiers and Saigon Police guards held back a mass of city people at bayonet-point. Marie took in a picture of men who'd forgotten their purpose here and wanted only to be heard for once, their faces the color of bruises, the veins in their necks like ropes, and the black shocks of hair leaping from their heads as they let themselves be pushed from behind, oblivious of the bayonets, their eyes fixed on the faces of the guards. When a small man vaulted between two riflemen and tried to clamber through a space in the boards across a window, one of the guards turned and smashed the butt of his rifle into the man's kidneys. He doubled up and fell to the pavement and crawled backward, driven before a bayonet, until he was consumed and trampled by the others.

Marie orbited the crowd's periphery as if caged, checking through a route that touched panic, dull hope, and nauseated surrender. Lingering on the airport's centerpiece—a broad disk of lawn, now trampled bare, and a flagpole still exposing the colors of South Vietnam to the wind—she found she'd drifted among the ranks of those who'd given up. Enclosed with their flag in a circle bounded by the asphalt drive, old men and women squatted on their heels, making pillows of their arms across their knees, and slept. Women sat on wide bundles of their belongings tied up in sheets, with children on their laps and other children standing around them, and here and there a husband waited with his arms wrapped around himself and his head bowed, exhausted and pensive, trying to find a way. Not even the children moved here.

The only thing to catch her eye was a figure in light khaki, and she followed his progress along the rear of the crowd. He moved deliberately but not slowly, looking at everybody and acknowledging no one. As he neared, peering right through her, she recognized his outfit as distinctly military. On the flap of his blouse pocket he wore an insignia of wings—Air Force flight personnel. His eyes scintillated as if he were drugged or dreaming. He was just a skinny boy who looked no older than Marie.

Marie was instantly sure he'd stolen this uniform. She grabbed him by the back of his shirt as he passed, and he turned around, smiling and dazed. "Where can I get?" She jerked the cloth of his blouse. "Where? I want a uniform. Uniform!" she repeated in anger, seeing he made nothing of the word.

As if they'd been together all day, he took hold of her wrist and pulled her along toward the rearward fringes of the mob before the terminal's entrance.

"Merican money," he said.

"Yes!" Marie said. "I have! I have it!"

With blows of his fists, like a figure come alive off one of Saigon's theater posters for karate and t'ai-chi fantasies, he advanced them through the crowd and lunged at the first guard he reached, brandishing identification. The guard stepped back, and the boy dragged Marie between barricades. The guard shouted at the boy now, the two spoke heatedly in Vietnamese, the guard pausing to threaten the forward ranks of the crowd with his bayonet. "Vietnam money," the boy said to Marie.

"Yes!" Marie said. "I have! Have Biet-nam mohnee," she said.

There was no way through the boarded-up doorway. The guard led them behind the line of soldiers and police for some fifty meters to the terminal building's east corner, where the windows ceased and only cinder block presented itself, past more sawhorse barricades, and then through a metal door. When they were inside with a few soldiers and two desks—where an odor of boiled coffee overwhelmed her and gave a fearsome homey ordinariness to things—all the men raised their voices. Talking fast and with great confidence, keeping her upper arm in his grip, the boy shook her at the soldiers as if she were compelling evidence, complete proof, that nothing was what they thought it was. Marie nodded emphatically, reaching for the money in her blouse and saying, "Yes, yes, yes," to the Special Forces officer, a lieutenant she guessed, who was soon doing all the talking. What she might be bartering for was unimportant. The language of Saigon trans-actions was being spoken, the push and pull, the forefinger repeatedly jabbing the open palm. This man had something which he believed she could be made to want. She wanted it.

The sound of propeller engines was loud through the rear door of the office. There were bursts of small-weapons fire of a type familiar to Marie, the submachine guns of the Saigon police. At this time the Special Forces Lieutenant drew his sidearm and put the barrel of it in the socket of her left eye, against the fluttering eyelid.

This was nothing to her. It was no more alarming than the over-familiar grip of the strange boy's hand on her biceps. She kept her other eye wide open and watched the cylinder turn as the Lieutenant drew back the hammer with his thumb. A peace and clarity seized the room. She thought she might fall asleep. "I wanna have all your local money," the man said. "Captain Minh is gonna take your dollars. Care to make some trouble about it?"

"Thank you, sir," she said. Her life was all around her. She could not, in any sense that mattered, be killed.

The man had an excellent American-style accent. "Cap'n Minh-baby," he said.

The boy in the Air Force uniform let go her arm and re-moved the bundle from her blouse, reaching with surgical detachment between her breasts. When he took her packet of seven one-hundred-dollar bills for himself, she gathered that this was Captain Minh, his middle name become his last, as often happened these days. Captain Minh gave Marie's packet of Vietnamese money, tens of thousands of piasters, to the Lieutenant, who put it inside his purple beret and replaced the beret on his head. The three other soldiers in the office looked on without any interest.

Real light broke into the room as the boy Captain pushed through the back door. He invited her with a toss of his head to follow him onto the asphalt of runways.

The sun was low—the afternoon was half gone. Heat came up miserably from the black tarmac and blew into their faces off the whirling blades of a helicopter skimming the grass between runways a couple of hundred meters west. Backed by the sun, the helicopter looked flat as a shadow in the air, converged on by the tiny figures of desperate people turned bright green by the glare in her eyes. A 707 taxiing out made sound waves and heat waves that blended into a single force she had to turn away from.

The Special Forces Lieutenant was with them. He drew ahead and led them to a hangar in which a U.S. helicopter the size of a house sat on the flatbed of a six-wheeled transport vehicle that must have been some kind of truck, she imagined, but looked more closely related to a golf cart. The Lieutenant jumped into the truck's seat—there was only room for one, just a seat, a dashboard, and steering wheel—and began trying to get it started, pushing a button so that the engine yowled and died. For ten seconds he waited with a face of stone, then tormented it again, getting nowhere.

Standing with Marie in the parallelogram of light that fell

through the hangar's entrance and turned the greasy asphalt so intensely silver that their legs were invisible below the knees, Captain Minh pointed to a DC-3 that was landing. "Danang plane," he said.

She didn't quite grasp what she was seeing; it seemed that shredded humans—arms and legs and half-torsos, the torn-off parts of citizens and even, as the plane landed across their line of sight, even the uniformed parts of dismembered military people—were stuck to the landing gear and dangled from under the wings. Then it was way down the runway, moving far past the terminal building to stop near a group of minuscule figures at the runway's other end. Jeeps and a luggage cart and people who seemed to come from nowhere, running at top speed, left the terminal area and raced in pursuit of the plane.

And as soon as the Lieutenant had the helicopter out of the hangar and Captain Minh had positioned himself at the controls, a swarm of weeping, shouting people, most of them wearing military or airport-personnel uniforms, began clambering all over it. The Lieutenant gave Marie a hand on board, making way for her by kicking one man in the chest and then suddenly, when he was unable to dislodge another from the doorway, unholstering his sidearm and shooting him in the face, an incident that would return to her over and over, both waking and dreaming. Yet once the blades began turning and the three of them were on board, neither the pilot nor the Lieutenant paid any heed to the people crushing themselves through the doors. The Lieutenant busied himself replacing the spent bullet in his revolver. Captain Minh concentrated on the levers and dials before him as if closeted alone with certain problems of aviation. Panting and whimpering strangers crammed against their backs, and Marie felt what might have been someone's mouth on her neck. Complaints of discomfort became screams of terror barely audible in the roar of the blades as the helicopter moved along only half a meter above the runway, pursued by faces, and after a long time rose up trailing strings of humans who clutched one another by the pants, the shirts, the ankles, dragging each other down and falling to the asphalt beneath. Still there must have been more than a dozen people in the helicopter with them, those by the doors still helping aboard the ones who clung by their fingertips to whatever might be clung to—the edges of the open ports, the skis of the landing gear, even the barrels of the machine guns protruding from either port. The load was so great that the helicopter hardly cleared the shacks beyond the airport, but as it gained speed and lurched once, then twice, finally unburdened of people who couldn't hang on any longer to the skis, it took to the upper air. Captain Minh was a savior shining in his own drugged eyes as he lifted them all above the war, and they left that world behind.

Whoever was saved that day was saved, though many of them were lost again only a little while later, and all of them were lost now but Marie.

It seemed to her that she very often had to endure more now, as an old woman, than she'd had to endure then. She dragged herself from bed into the kitchen and toward her grandson's music through crowds of voices and long streamers of pain. Whatever room she escaped was always a war in itself, a harried landscape that could at any second be blasted out from under her, revealing a world made of memories, most of them more real than these shifting walls.

And now she was being led out of the hospital at Sangley Point—no, no, toward the red rocking chair in the parlor where she'd been all her life. The Officer's Club smelled of spilt liquor and re-run smoke. The Rolling Stones made one layer in the layers of voices: *"This coat—is torn—and frayed/ It's seen—much bed—der days . . ."* Outside the gates of the Sangley Point Naval Base she looked down the road of whorehouses and cheap shops of Cavete City, P.I. Somebody said, "Sige!" and a carabao nearly ran her down in the street, pulling a wooden-wheeled cart at a rate slow as its glazed eyes. In the country of her father's death they called them water buffalo, giant living barges with dark elephant tusks set on their heads sideways and curved back, and the same impenetrable hide as an elephant . . .

She was standing here in the road to the Saigon Airport. She had never seen these things before, the deformed offspring of the Rolling Thunder: Napalm's stumps and Napalm's obliterated eyes, at least a dozen of them, several so extensively cauterized they had to be pulled along in this cart by this water buffalo walking in its sleep. Others, those who could walk, trailed the cart. A white missionary woman herded them along, very red in her cheeks, huffing and puffing, unbalanced and hopeless. Marie backed out of the way. From a faceless face one black pupil of an eye, like a marble in a puddle of fat, took her measure.

Captain Minh was screwing together a carbine; he checked its sights, placed the barrel in his mouth—Jagger goes, "*Thang you—for your wine—California/Thang you—for your sweed an—bitter fruit*"—placed the barrel in his mouth . . . her grandson began to play the oboe. He'd made it himself from bamboo. Even in the simplest melodies, the notes cracked into falsetto like the voice of a sobbing teenage boy.

Fiskadoro had to stay the night because in darkness the roads were unsafe. Mr. Cheung kept his children out of the parlor and made a place for him. He brought Fiskadoro a folded curtain to use as a pillow or a blanket in the hammock of fishing net. He walked around the room with a leafy twig of oleander, slapping at mosquitoes. "Everybody dies," he told Fiskadoro.

"But es wrong for Jimmy," Fiskadoro said with bald conviction.

"I know. I know," Mr. Cheung said. It was true. The boy's father had been too young.

"Do you know about my Grandmother Wright?" Mr. Cheung asked him now, pointing at her across the parlor as if she were far away. Evidently without regret for the past or concern for the coming night, she rocked in her red rocking chair, loudly breathing.

Fiskadoro shook his head. He was beginning to weep again. His throat would be sore tomorrow.

"Nobody really knows about Grandmother Wright," Mr. Cheung said. "It's not really for us to know. But she was in a war, I know, and she lost her mother and father, my own mother told me that. My mother, Carol Cheung, was her daughter. Carol Cheung told me this: When Grandmother Wright was running away from the war, she was in a helicopter, this is a flying machine with a propeller on the top, not like an airplane. And the helicopter machine fell into the ocean—not our Ocean, and not the Gulf, but the Pacific, the biggest ocean de todos—and the people had to swim, and swim, and swim, and one by one nine people sank down forever. The others went on a small boat that finally came."

"Grandmother was on the boat?"

"She was saved from the Pacific Ocean. She and two others swam for more than two days."

Fiskadoro was astonished to think of the old woman floundering indefinitely among the waves, stronger even than Jimmy—and then was more taken aback to realize she must have been young then; once she must have been a girl.

Mr. Cheung said, "My grandmother went to different countries. First to the Philippines, this is where she met some people in my grandfather's family, and then eventualmente to America, this is where my grandfather lived."

"Aqui," Fiskadoro said.

"Aqui, in America, but far away. America is huge," Mr. Cheung said. "I am an American. You, too. Jimmy was an American." He was casting about now, trying to remember what it was he'd been wanting to say. "My grandmother went through different wars and different countries. Everything that she lost—it's really gone, all of it, that's true. At the same time, look at her! Think about her! She's more than a century!"

Fiskadoro nodded and tried to look soothed. He knew that Mr. Cheung was trying to make him feel better, even if Mr. Cheung was failing. But Mr. Cheung had left the room.

He was back almost instantly. "From my yard, Fiskadoro." His teacher handed him a stick of sugar cane longer than his hand. "It helps you to have sweet dreams."

Her grandson Anthony Cheung helped her from the rocking chair and toward her bedroom off the kitchen.

Grandmother was sorry to have the concert end. Her grandson's aimless tootling comforted her by bringing back the vision she'd experienced when surrounded by Muzak only minutes after coming to Seattle from Manila. The first thing her uncle had accomplished when they'd arrived in China-town on the bus was to take Marie out of the rain into an American quick-stop store, where the few bedraggled shoppers, most of them also Chinese, looked less actual and permanent than the blinding rows of goods. Her Uncle Kin-lau Kaung was a fine citizen of the Chinese-American community, a round-faced man always wearing a white dress shirt, grey pleated pants, and aqua-blue plastic loafers with tapered toes. He bought her a tube of toothpaste, two bars of bath soap, and some roll-on underarm deodorant, handing her each item to carry as he took it from its place on the shelves. At that moment Marie had no idea she would pass through much more

—including a happy marriage, a long widowhood, and even the end of the world—before she reached the afternoon of her death many decades later in Key West, Florida. Here with her uncle in the quick-stop store she felt she'd reached an end, and she experienced a zeroing-in, a hallucination of purposiveness to her suffering, as if she'd lost her father and abandoned her mother, been raked across life after life, in order to stand here in the enamelling brilliance and receive these things.

Fiskadoro took his sugar cane out in front of the house, where Mr. Cheung's little children would be less likely to spy it and set up a campaign of outrage. He chewed it, and it made the salt taste of tears in his throat go away. It was unbelievably sweet and delicious. His heart raced with love. As night fell, he stood in the street and watched the light leave the dust. The mosquitoes that came at early twilight raged whining all over the air, but up and down the dirt thoroughfare there was a silence coming. The voices of the neighbors died away. He sucked the sugar cane, letting the sweet syrup comfort his throat. As soon as the dark was thick enough that he couldn't see the old school building in the neighborhood behind Mr. Cheung's house, the bugs thinned out. Then the dogs started barking, far and wide. All over the world they barked, numerous as stars. His head rang and his sight whirled. He felt sleepy. The first day of his father's death was over.

FOUR

I no eat! I no sleep!" Darkness and sweat. "I no brain!
Rapto!" Fiskadoro danced in a perimeter of orange light
that flashed off the thunderheads of smoke above the
fires. He could hardly see the band of Israelite musicians
playing their steel drums outside the jerking illumination of
the dance-ground, but their banging and clanging rhythm
took up all the room available in his head for sound. The
sweat-shiny figures around him, crossed out continually by
the shadows of smoke and the silhouettes of other dancers
against the light of driftwood bonfires and the blazing kettles
of radioactive fuel-oil, cried, "Rapto!" and so did Fiskadoro.
"Rapto! Rapto!"

Though he could make out nobody really, Fiskadoro con-
trived in his heart to believe that everybody—all the others
who seemed so oblivious—had an eye on him. He was nearly
fourteen. He was changing, but the world stayed the same.

He was growing, but it wouldn't make room. And yet in the sight of some people, it seemed, he wasn't growing fast enough. The young woman known as Loosiana had said that she was too tall for Fiskadoro, or that he was too short— whichever it was, the news of her opinion had come his way as soon as he'd appeared on West Beach tonight. One of the steel-drummers, an Israelite boy who smoked marijuana leaves in a clay pipe and stiffened his hair with salt water so that it shot from his head like the fur of a scared animal, had made a point of mentioning it right away, as Fiskadoro stood apart from the others and waited for the sun to drown in the Gulf before the darkness and the dancing: "Hey, you know the gel Loosiana, mon, she say, 'Fish-man too small on me!'" The young drummer held up his bottle of beer and measured off two centimeters of its neck with thumb and forefinger. He was drinking Silent Man Beer, each green bottle of which bore the hand-painted insignia of a winking human skull.

Fiskadoro felt the blood shoot into his face and hands. Had Loosiana really called him Fish-man? For weeks he'd been putting it about that his name might also mean Harpooner— and this was the truth, almost. That she'd called him Fish-man was insulting. He burned to know if this Israelite had Loosiana's words *exact*, but he was afraid he'd make himself a fool if he asked any more about it or even if he spoke to this Israelite ever in his life again. It was still light yet, and he put his hands on the rim of a kettle of oil and looked at himself in the liquid, finding that he appeared there exactly as he felt—rubbery, dark, his face twisted. One of the bonfires was already burning; he grabbed a flaming brand and tossed it into the kettle, screaming, "Yaaah!" Nothing happened except that the brand was doused in the oleo. He pretended to himself that he'd been joking, hadn't really wanted a startling explosion, it was too early for a lot of looney toons.

A good joke. People had probably been frightened. The sun fell, the sea went black, and the fires stood up amid the gaiety of people who would never be his friends.

Now, an hour later, he was psychotically dancing; and then suddenly he was tired of being Fiskadoro. He was finished. He was standing inside all this revelry with what he was convinced was a soul that had just died. It happened to him whenever he found himself in a crowd of people. He didn't know anymore why he came here to West Beach.

He ran off down the shoreline, out of earshot of all the others, a collection of people his age or a little older, most of them from the Army, but many from as far away as Twice-town or even Marathon and, on the edges of the dancing that was just getting wild now after all the Silent Man Beer and Punto Beer, a few black boys and girls from the neighbor-hood of swamps and lowlands over the dunes—shy, curious, and dazzlingly aloof, the girls dancing with the girls, and the boys dancing with the boys.

Fiskadoro took a blow to the heart each time he caught sight of Loosiana, who was easily picked out even across this distance because of her tall figure and her unique personal decoration, a sky-blue plastic tube like the inner tubes for autocar tires, only this inner tube buckled around the front of her waist over her white shift, resting on her hips and making her look deformed. It was a scavenged device, a thing once intended to bring about weight loss in flabby people. The owner was supposed to fill it up with hot water. Loosiana was aware that it set her apart, and her willingness to be set apart was one of the things that drew everybody to her. She was so wonderful that he'd never spoken to her. He couldn't guess how she'd found out about his yearning. There were a half dozen others who had the same effect on him.

The tide was going out, and the beach stank and lay there like a shield of smoked glass, upholding rank lengths of sea-

had to count himself among, the boys without girls, and the older men who did in fact have women but who now, at an advanced stage of domesticated wisdom, usually tried to keep away from them.

Fiskadoro was shocked to see a new person holding forth before his friends. Everything went away from him except the face of this famous man, the wide flat nose with monstrous nostrils, the African hair and bushy eyebrows made twice as thick by their shadows in the firelight.

". . . go out there and catch fish," the man was saying, "or you can go out there on the sea and catch Allah. Catch the destiny."

Allah, destiny—it was just what Fiskadoro might have hoped this man would say: something that was real and true and not stupid and not small.

Fiskadoro sat at the circle's edge, up on his knees to get a clear view of the man over the heads of the others. There were almost a dozen young men here, all listening quietly and pretending not to be totally unnerved.

It was incredible that this personage should appear on West Beach. He was known to be a rich man, somebody connected with the gamblers, a dealer in goods and substances. But he had a crazy side to his nature that made him fail, because of completely irresponsible actions, just as often as he succeeded. Failure made his legend more appealing. He was supposed to be related to A. T. Cheung, but he looked nothing like Fiskadoro's clarinet teacher.

Dropping his talk, the man stared at Fiskadoro. The others made room, and the boy joined the circle of listeners as if commanded. The man was speaking of the great things he'd done. He was telling them how he'd become a legend.

"Bob Wilson brother, Michael Wilson, he had the power of moving dice, and so the gambling men they kept him in chains. They kept him incognito on the North Deerfield, way

weed, empty shells, worn stones, dead urchins, skulls of fish, the bits and pieces deposited here for a while by the ocean in its endless rumination over these things it had collected. Under the half-moon's cold light each object was mated to its blurry reflection. He was half a kilometer upwind of the others, but still he could hear them. He imagined himself going back. He imagined himself taking over the entire situation, riveting everything to himself: striding forth; maybe he was a different color; maybe he'd turned to gold, and was twice as tall, and held balls of fire in his hands and sang his song—"*Oh Loosiana/your lose-weight heat-thing/your special eyes glance/we make our friends dance*"—he knew it was a silly song. In the real situation, better words expressing greater thoughts and the largeness of his special feeling would come to him. But *this* was the real situation, wasn't it? There was nothing here for him tonight. The swamp-girls hadn't come alone tonight, there would be no chasing them, and Loosiana scorned him.

He saw himself pitied tenderly by future admirers. How Fiskadoro had suffered in the hard time of his youth! Eventually, in the real situation, all the people dancing there across the sand would be remembered as fools.

And his sentiments were so out of control, he felt so sorry for those who would someday feel sorry for him, and so keenly grateful for their future understanding, that even walking around by himself on the dark beach he was embarrassed. He was afraid he might bring his thoughts into a ghost-life right now, and people would have a laugh to see his private dreams parading through the air around his head.

He had nothing to do but wander over to the gathering of other outcasts, the men circled around a wood-fire, absent-mindedly combing sticks out of the sand with their fingers and talking about nothing much. These were the people he

up past the contamination. That's why we had to go. That's why we lost two men. They were good men. Their business for them that day, it was to die.

"Remember this that if you are a human man, when you scratch your nose you ass gone start itching. Same thing, same way, what Allah say: 'Every hardship is followed by ease. Every hardship is followed by ease.' Say it twice that way.

"Something else it say that I thinking about right now, for the women who commit adultery. You know que dice adultery?" He passed his hand undulating over invisible waves in the fire. "Somebody all night long with your wife. Or even in the morning, or the afternoon. It say about a woman like that—" He closed his eyes and sang, with deep feeling and a tense throat, "*Confine-them-to-their-houses-till-death-over-takes-them-or-till-Allah-finds-another-way-for-them.*"

The mouths dropped open. It was all Fiskadoro could do to contain himself. He crossed his arms tightly to keep his chest from exploding.

"Confine them to the houses," the great man said. "Maybe I did and maybe I didn't. Well well, I don't remember now.

"I am not blind. My wife laying down with James Melroy from the Twelve Shacks below Marathon. Gone all night and all morning. You think I don't know that so hard right here in my heart? You think I don't know that until ten-thousand-dollar fine? Fugdat shit." He looked directly at Fiskadoro. "I am Cheung's half-brother. Got the Negro blood inside me. My newest name Cassius Clay Sugar Ray," he said. "The First." His black kinky hair was so long it was beginning to lie down, and he wore several necklaces. He could easily have been taken for somebody from over the swamps. "But the secret of my being is just that I leave alone the most personal thing," he said to all of them in general. "I do the thing that's for my business.

"The boats put out after the fish. It been their business. But my boat stayed behind. My business never in no Gulf that day. My business never up by Marathon. My business with the Atlantic Ocean. Bob Wilson brother. Gamblers.

"My business told me: Go out in the fog. Keep walking. Walk through fear. Fear is a door! On the other side"—he pointed—"Fiskadoro meets Fiskadoro." He swiveled his arm, pointing his finger at another: "Glen gonna meet Glen."

The boys and young men were more and more astonished by every one of his words. Some of them trembled visibly, and their teeth clacked with fear.

"I don't need fifty rules. I don't need *twenty* rules. I don't need *ten* rules. Every day have one, two, three problems. Every day have one, two, three rules. That day my rule come to me like, Do your business, fool. Leave alone the most personal thing today!

"When my head gotten clanging because of my personal wife laying around naked and tangle up with James Melroy in the Twelve Shacks, my rule come to me like, Do not kill a wife, do not kill a man who you can call him by his name, James Melroy. Personal is crazy! Go do your business!

"But I was afraid of my business. I was afraid of to be seen. Everybody would question to me, Where the wife now, my pal? Is she visit up to those shacks below Marathon? You know James Melroy live up those shacks, isn't it now? Maybe somebody was ask me like this: Brother, you gonna 'bout to visit up there and shoot that man? I was afraid of them see me go in my boat and say, That man, he is not going up toward Marathon. That man, he is a frighten coward.

"But I telling you, Allah is there. His words are 'Courage' and 'Obey.' I was afraid of to be seen?—in the blinding sun nobody wasn't see me. I was afraid of questions?—questions never draw no blood, but yes except inside the stomach of a frighten coward. I went out. I walked through fear. I meeted myself. I did my business. I obeyed the rules for the problems of one day. Now I got business in every place on the Keys. I don't worry about who was my wife then. I don't know her name.

"But she know my name now. Every day. Every day she call on me. Every day she come crying and beating her face. And I say, If I knowed your name, stranger-woman, I surely be go speak to you. But I don't speak to you because of I don't know your name."

They waited in silence. He picked up sand and let it drift away between his fingers. The shapes of the young men, flattened out by the firelight, seemed to shift when the wind plagued the flames. Whenever the drift of smoke turned around and came at a man, he ducked his face thoughtfully into the crook of thumb and finger, covering his eyes and nose with his hand.

It began to seem they might not be permitted to hear about Cassius Clay Sugar Ray's business of that day, which had made him famous everywhere. The boys and young men got anxious. One tossed a smooth rock into the fire. Others said, "Hm! Hm!" but couldn't fathom how to prod him into going on. Finally one said, "Tell it to us 'bout the words of Allah." A couple of others said, "Right!" "That's right!"

As if he'd never spoken the words in his life before, Cassius Clay Sugar Ray repeated, "Bob Wilson brother, Michael Wilson, he had the power of moving dice, and so the gambling men they kept him in chains. They kept him incognito on the North Deerfield, way up past the contamination. That's why we had to go.

"I took four men. Bob Wilson. The person called Holy Apples. Michael Torres. And a sailor name Smith, that's all anybody know now, Smith. We went in my fisher, the *Guerrilla*.

"After one half morning we come around the Twicetown

Key to the Ocean. The Ocean side ain't put there for our boats—they tell you that, but we never said it that day. We took the Ocean, brother. We took the Ocean, my pal. We sailed the fog full of ghosts. We was hear them talking but we wasn't understand the words, because of they were the Ocean ghosts who we never knew them, not any ghosts from around here, who one time they used to be our friends. Then when the fog let loose of us, we have the wind and rain.

"A storm been our mother all the way. She pick us up—sometime the boat she flying. The hands of the Ocean come out and took Smith. There wasn't nothing we could do, we wasn't see it coming. But we see it coming for Holy Apples because of Holy Apples started to glow as loud as this"—he picked up a coal, holding it with complete serenity in the palm of his hand, and blew on it to make it flare. "We knew he gone be next, Holy Apples, and we clutch onto him, Bob Wilson and me, while Michael Torres kept up screaming at the wind.

"The person called Holy Apples was glowing so loud Bob Wilson and me was look at the bones glowing inside of our hands where we holding him. Then the mighty wind yelled words like, 'Rock an' Rooooll! Bop-a-loooola!' and it turned the boat around three times, and the tail of the sea come up and stole Holy Apples out of our little arms. We knew that was all. She agua won't take a crew, or even half a crew, without she taking the whole boat. We knew she wasn't reach up for no more others of us.

"The storm cracked open right in the middle and fell down the sides of the sky. Way out at the edges of the east, now, we watch the water boiling. On the west we saw the city Miami. Just like the Ocean been boiling on the east, the storm been making the city Miami remember the old war again. The air stand black and boiling all around it, but the towers they come on fire from the sun. Some buildings in the south they still there. Some buildings they high as fifty fish-boats put together, some buildings they look like made out of a thousand mirrors, some buildings they black and shiny as a person's eye. I try to remember but I really ain't can't, because of that day everything I watch been bigger than my mind. The city goes from all the way in the north to all the way in the south. The North Deerfield, that's a part of it. You know when you get to the North Deerfield because of after that you ain't can't never go north no more. The Ocean take you in and beach you. The biggest sail we got over in Twicetown ain't can't fight the struggle against that corriente.

"Me and Bob Wilson talking while the boat move in, and Michael Torres cried a little bit, until when we told him what we talked about. We said, Fugdat shit, now, that's all. We said, Whatever happen go happen.

"I didn't know the name of Allah then, but I said, 'I think I hear one word from God's mouth, and that word is Courage.'

"Bob Wilson said, 'I think I hear a word, too, and it's a different word and that word is Obey.'

"When we telling that to Michael Torres, he say, Fugdat shit, too. He say, Whatever happen go happen, too.

"The *Guerrilla*, you understand me now, the *Guerrilla* she beach there, right up against the North Deerfield face, and we go sleep right in her. Let them come! All night we heard whispering all around us that we wasn't figure it out— water-ghosts whispering another language. And rain-ghosts came. Let them come! Fugdat shit! But I never slept for one breath, though, I admit it, it's true.

"And then a strange morning. Rain all night disappeared with the dawn, like dreams, and the sun soft on the North Deerfield two hours. We hiding in the boat and watch the North Deerfield fish-men. Next thing, cool arms been in the air touching us. By the time the North Deerfield fish-men ropes toss on the boats and them put out, such a *cold* fog come unrolling like a prayer mat, off the Ocean side. The fish-men they just only let that fog chase the boats out to the Ocean. Didn't let it stop their journeys.

"I never did felt a town so cold. Almost of everybody in the North Deerfield stayed in by the stoves. If you walked about, ghosts going in and lick the juice of your lungs. Their tongues they rough like a cat's, but cold. They hide in the fog. You cough up pink fog and die. We got off the boat and march around—*cold* water in that harbor! We shook like baby canes and had a stupid thought—we thought we gone walk around, no problem. We thought nobody never gone go out but a thief or a vagabond from far away, on a cold day like that, which we never saw before in our life. Rubbage, rubbage—hey, watch me now—in the North Deerfield, they ain't can't *feel* the cold. They walk around *inside* it, and say, Oh, what a *hot* day it is!

"And when they find a vagabond like us, *they throw him down in chains before the big gamblers.*

"Cold town," he said. Sweat ran down his face. He was out of breath. "Cold town. In deep."

Abruptly Cassius Clay Sugar Ray produced a pipe. He took a minute to fill it from a pouch on a string around his waist, and tamp it down and find a good brand in the fire and light it. "Cold town. In deep. Last chance coming down!" They smelled the smoke of Israelite marijuana moving across the fire. They all knew how he'd escaped. Fiskadoro knew, but he waited, like the others, to hear how it would turn out.

"Mostly," Cassius Clay Sugar Ray said, "the mercy of Allah cleans out my brain of those terrible time. And it don't make no sense telling you what those gambling men of the North Deerfield look like," he said, "I tell you why. Because of those big gamblers have change their faces and their bodies when I be go back the second time, and ever since from that time until now, they have never did return to the way they looked the first time I looked my eyes across them. Just this much: they show long teeth coming out here, like big mean dogs: show claws on the end of their fingers. They push breath coming out in my face like a dead animal shit on their tongue. The mercy of Allah cleans out my brain of those terrible time, so I ain't can't remember did I weep and beg like a coward, but I know this, which I say without no shame, when I dream about it, I wake up and I weeping and begging like a coward, all right, well well, yes Cap'n.

"Our arms and legs lock up in chains. Bob Wilson crying, too. Michael Torres just curl up on the floor all stiff in front of the North Deerfield gamblers and try go die. I been breathing so hard I might make myself faint unconscious. I try go look at those big gamblers, and they turn blue, with yellow sparks. I wasn't know who was Allah then, but I prayed to God, God, without knowing nothing.

"The biggest big gambler come walking right up to me. He choosing me for the leader. Bob Wilson he bawling like a seagull. Then to remind Bob Wilson what we say, I say, 'Whatever happen go happen. Fugdat shit!' Bob Wilson hear me, but he keep bawling out.

"Gambler say, 'I am the Hootchy Kootchy Man!'

"I say, 'Shit!'

"He say, 'I control all the games down unto the shores of Cue-bar!'

"I say, 'What games? What games?'

"He say, '*All* the games.'

"I say, 'You control the Twicetown games? I see those Twicetown gambler-boys yesterday. They spending every coin at the still-house.'

"He got mad and he say, 'End—of—discussion!'"

"I say, 'Every coin at the still-house. They don't save out no coins for you.'

"His teeth grew.

" 'Old women run half those games,' I say.

"Blood spilled outa his eyes.

" 'Those old women, they never hearda you,' I say.

"He scream like I hammering on his feet. I felt sick to die, I been so chicken in my guts to hear a man make that type noise. Bob Wilson he got faint unconscious on the floor in his clattering chains and locks.

"But the biggest big gambler, he *knew* I go be reporting out the facts. He got calm inside his face. And I tell to them all, 'You gone kill us. You gone turn us into ghosts right now.'

"They say, 'That's right.'

" 'You gone keep Bob Wilson brother in chains.'

"They say, 'That's right.'

" 'You gone talk about that hootchy and that kootchy down to Cuba. And everything I say, gone stay be true forever: Twicetown games just belong to everyone, no percent out of it for you big North Deerfield gamblers.'

"They didn't say a sound.

"I say, 'If you deliver us three back down to Twicetown, we gone take your message that you control all the games. We gone bring your percent, and we gone have Bob Wilson magic brother controlling some dice sometime once in a while for *you*.' "

Cassius Clay Sugar Ray looked around him at the faces in the flames, going green and blue in his sight, possibly, as had the faces of the gamblers from North Deerfield. "When Bob Wilson wake up and found out he ain't dead yet, I told him, 'The Mainland-Keys Alliance for Trading, we now in session!'

"I laughing and crying both at once, but those gamblers say, 'You gone go back alone by yourself, nigger-person. We keep these two white boys till you come on back to here with a new report.'

"I say, 'All right.' I repeated to them, 'Fugdat shit!'

"They took off my chains and locks and put me back on the *Guerrilla*. I be sure go die, they all knew about it, plain and obvious. But the biggest big gambler say, 'My name is Ernest Bodine. Would you like a Bible?'

"I say, 'Yes Cap'n,' but he say, 'I haven't ain't got one. But I give you the Koran of Mohammed.' Then he made a sinful sound, "Moooooo-hammed! Ha ha!' like a cow.

"I said, 'Fugdat shit!' But I took the book and I readed part of the page one to him, so he can see me as a schooled aficionado of words.

"They set my sail and push me out into the corriente on the Ocean.

"If ever I need to come about only once, I not never gone make it. I need the luck of Allah with the wind, to sail one person alone to Twicetown in the *Guerrilla*. But I didn't know Allah then, I didn't have no information about who was Allah. The corriente took me out till the land she been far away on the edge of the world. And next thing, before I knew what, this land we live on and walk on she be *gone*, gone from outa my eyes, and I there on the Ocean of agua y nothing but agua.

"Five days and four nights I sailing on, and I ain't can't never come about without no mates to help me. I make my best way to go south and west, but time I make east with the corriente, time dead west, sometime the forces turn me around and head me dead up to the Pole Star. Half-liter of water in a bucket disappeared. It rain and I catch a few drops in my hands. A few more drops in the bucket. I going fast.

Thirst dry me up flat like a rag. North. South. East. West. A simple person, a little coward, on the Ocean.

"I tell to the Pole Star, 'Who making you take me there?'

"When the boat gone west and the sundown look at me like a big eye, I say, 'Who are you?'

"And I go down on my knees on the deck to pray: 'You there up high! Heavenly Eye watching this trouble! Put your secret message in this book!' "

In the light of flames, Cassius Clay Sugar Ray held out his two hands together, the palms up, like the open pages of the sacred Koran.

"The line my finger pointed say, *Would you deny these blessings of the Lord?*

"I say, 'Scuse me what? *What* blessings?'

"One more line down the page, it said me again, *Would you deny these blessings of the Lord?*

"I say, 'Look at the sea all around! This is me I go drowning! Who talking about any blessings?'

"But one line, two lines, three lines—all over the page I see been Allah's one message for me: *Would you deny these blessings of the Lord?* It say that on those pages of the Koran *thirty-two times*. When Allah make a message, you don't get *no question.*

"Now I gone ask to you this," he said: "What that message mean?"

The men and boys around him knew he'd been carried on uncharted currents over the Ocean and washed up against the rotted pier at Plantation, above Key Marathon, and they knew the story of how he'd been carried in a hammock by the Plantation people into Marathon, a completely transformed individual bearing a book about Allah and news of an Alliance for Trading that would make a storm of business over the following decade, until boredom, laziness, and the easy life among laden fruit trees beside a generous sea made work seem too much trouble for the citizens of the Keys. Only the Gambling Alliance remained in effect—also the legend, always larger—and they knew these things by heart, but they didn't know what the message meant, *Would you deny these blessings of the Lord?*

"It mean, Give thanks," Cassius Clay Sugar Ray explained. "It mean even in the middle of the Ocean, give thanks to Allah. It mean, *Dance with your partner. Get it while you can.*"

Cassius Clay Sugar Ray sensed they didn't need to hear the end. "Live in total faith!" he insisted. "Would you deny these blessings of the Lord?" he asked. His own excitement seemed to confuse him to the point that he didn't know anymore what he was saying. "Every minute of my great deeds I felt the *fear*. I was tasted *puke* in the back of my mouth."

The men and boys were a little embarrassed now, because this last statement had the ring of a thoughtless departure from the usual text. In a moment, however, as everything he'd told them took its shape in their minds, their embarrassment left them. They considered his submission to fate, to what he called Allah; they admired his dangerous flaring honesty in talking about his wife and her lover and about personal fear in the middle of brave deeds; and they felt that he hadn't lowered himself, exactly, so much as raised them up.

Still, the events of this night, so different from the usual boredom, cheap talk, and staring into flames, were upsetting every stomach, and the men and boys were already trying to forget this encounter even as it came to an end. They'd always been confident that the sea would bring home a warrior, that the sand would whirl into the shape of a President, and that from time to time in their lives people would be met with who would show them the way. But they'd expected to meet these figures only in dreams.

. . .

Cassius Clay Sugar Ray's two bodyguards—Uncle and Sammy, both small men, neither of them very fearsome, almost as well-known on the Keys as their employer—had been watching the dancers, and now they came to get him. Cassius Clay Sugar Ray shook hands all around and got ready to go back, under their protection, to his new home in Marathon.

One of the bodyguards, Sammy, was a white man who wore long pants and even rope sandals, like a big business-owner, and he said to Cassius Clay Sugar Ray, "Shake it, Boss." Cassius Clay Sugar Ray smiled as if he didn't understand, and kept on giving out pieces of dried fruit to the others from a bag he carried around his waist. Sammy said, "We got moves to make." It irritated Fiskadoro that Sammy's tone of voice seemed tainted with some faint failure of respect.

By the time the visitors had gone it was already three hours past dark—those still on the beach would have to stay together now and pass the night here sleeping or dancing or having adventures with the other sex. Fiskadoro stayed away from them. To have met this great man, to have touched his hand, heard his story, his legend, made Fiskadoro feel crazy. He wandered the shore. The Ocean, so perilous simply because of its size to any who might be faring out onto it tonight, was unagitated. A roll of surf fell at his feet with the hollow exhaustion of a drum calling from far away. Fiskadoro came no closer to it than a couple of meters. He didn't want to let the Ocean touch him. I am not for you, he insisted in fear. I am not my father Jimmy. Things took him away from his father, stories and dancing carried him off, but every time, he seemed to land at the border of this black country where his father lived. He was afraid he'd find something here at the Ocean's edge one day, a lump of something he couldn't make out. He'd go closer and see that it was a man, closer and see that the man was dead, closer and see that the dead man was Jimmy, his father. He didn't like to think about it. He was frightened even of his own name, Fish-man, Harpooner, because it suggested some prior arrangement with the hungry sea.

Every day he imagined the moment when his father, thinking of nobody, totally cut off from everyone he knew, totally, as if he'd been born swimming for his life and never known anything else, gave up and drew the first breath of water.

The several Blacks from over the swamps—and yet they looked a bit different, their heads caked with mud or he didn't know what, not like most of the swamp-folks—were heading back over the dunes toward home; he could see them detach from the party-time in a group and straggle off.

Fiskadoro moved along the shore, keeping abreast of them as they made toward the shallowest rise of earth. His neck felt constricted by a rush of desire, and his groin ached. The only two women he'd ever made love to were young girls from over the swamps.

One of the swamp-people lagged farther and farther behind. Fiskadoro moved with a heavy and guilty heart but with quick, light strides to catch her. He could make out the backs of her thighs. She turned when she heard him, and he saw her face, a shadow in which he might read whatever he wanted.

She watched him, half-reclining against the rising slope of the sand dune. Her eyes were wide and white. Fiskadoro took hold of her by the ankle—it was gritty with sand. She slid down toward him with a silky sound. She held him by the thighs and bit his breast softly and licked his belly. But then she got up and began climbing the dune again. They were both out of breath—he could hear her panting with a slight catch of her voice, a whimper, a small cry in every breath.

Fiskadoro felt he was tearing himself away from his life to pursue her into the swamps where he'd never been. But even across this distance some of the firelight caught her, and he saw the tendons of her ankles, the start of her buttocks below her ragged denim skirt, and he chased her. She stayed ahead of him.

As soon as he'd topped the round of the dune and looked over into the darkness where she was disappearing, her skin no longer touched by orange highlights but as empty of them as the hide of an animal in a cave, he had to hesitate. Where was he taking himself? The patchwork of marsh and tangled vegetation down there was covered up with night, but it exuded a thick presence like the sea's. Two steps into it he felt as if some kind of laughing-gas were licking his shins. She was gone into nothing, but he knew how to follow her steps as certainly as if he carried a map—there wasn't any way to go but down. Below the level of the dune the wind was stuck. It was like being swallowed alive. The air choked him, and he recognized the odor—it was hers; she smelled like the swamps, like her birthplace and her home. To follow her over the dunes and out of earshot and eyesight of his people, his head spinning and his throat blocked with the honey of tears, was not to know whether he would live or die. Don't look what I'm doing! he begged the dark sea.

FIVE

There was so much vibration up where the Israelites stayed on the Ocean side north of Twicetown, so many people loitering there, such a big crowd of hangers-out and self-elected interpreters, everybody with a secret opinion or a loud explanation concerning the white boat the Israelites were ceremoniously building, that vendors started dropping around, too, and Bill Banks made it the place for one or two sound-shows.

The vendors quarreled with one another about the positions of their stalls, drumming up excellent reasons, each one, with threatening gestures and a wild face, for having the place nearest the shade, which was the gift of only a few trees here in a region mostly scrub and tall grass. When Bill Banks put up his sound-shows, yesterday's recording stars roared words in voices that sounded as if they should clear their throats about things nobody understood, while the big rhythm that needed no explanation, crackly and fogged with use and buzzing in Bill Banks's old speakers, got some people dancing.

But the white boat was what it was all about. It was just like a little ship, with small hand-carved dinghies on it for escape in case of a disaster, and tiny portholes strung along its sides, and numerous decks and two smokestacks, every piece whitewashed, and every piece blessed by Flying Man before it was attached to the vessel. Just the same, it would never float. Everyone could see that. But they all understood that floating wasn't the point. This wasn't about sailing anywhere on a ship three meters long: it was about magic, about religion, about Jah. The Israelites were happy to explain the ship and what it was supposed to do, but nobody could make out what they said.

Mr. Cheung went up with Eileen to take a look at the white boat. He was uncomfortable when Flying Man made a big show of welcoming them, because it was all too clear that he hadn't let go of his idea that The Miami Symphony Orchestra was going to do something or other for the Israelites, probably, Mr. Cheung guessed, something totally embarrassing, and possibly something he would regret forever. But a person wanted to please these immigrants. They were bizarre and unrestrained. So he smiled with a lump in his throat and gave his every attention to Flying Man's indecipherable speech about this white boat. Once in a while, with the effect of reaching out and touching Mr. Cheung with a bare electric wire, Flying Man said the word "oxra." Eye contact, Mr. Cheung noted, was also painful. Flying Man occasionally focused his bleary pupils like targets, without mercy. Spittle flecked his lips and beard.

Eileen seemed to take some light from the relentless sun and the glaring water. Her face appeared smoother than usual to Mr. Cheung, her eyes larger and younger, and her features more relaxed. "No Mr. Banks today? No sound-show?" she asked. It wasn't a secret between them that Eileen liked the sound-shows better than The Miami Symphony Orchestra's ridiculous efforts.

"He's left the scaffolds up," Mr. Cheung said. "He'll have another soon, and we'll come."

Flying Man cupped his hands together and shoved them right and left, as if bailing water. "One day someday Babylon go sink down deadndrownd-oh." His beard jumped when he talked, moved when he showed his foul teeth. "Dat news when res' with Jah. Dis—dis—dis—dis—"

Eileen turned her back on him and smiled with blank eyes at the air above the vendors' stalls. "You don't make sense so don't talk wild at me now. What they gonna catch in that boat?" she asked Mr. Cheung. "Little tiny fish?"

"There's something spiritual going on here," Mr. Cheung said, "a symbolic thing. But I don't want to learn what it is. I'm certain of this."

She laughed. It hit him hard—she almost never laughed these days. "What's to be afraid of about a little boat that's just only pretty?"

"I don't wish to be caught up inside these forces," he said. "They aren't my forces."

But what were his forces, after all? Now, on a pleasant morning that was fairly cool, relatively dry, somewhat brightened by the hope of these lunatic aliens and Eileen's uncustomary good cheer, he grew concerned about his philosophical stance, and wanted to stop in a patch of shade and consider it. Eileen was saying something about coins—she wanted melon from a vendor. Mr. Cheung held up a finger to request her patience while he asked himself these questions: What are my forces? With what am I aligned? I am not aligned with anything real, only the past. I am against everything.

It was an excellent thought. Against everything! What a

beautiful day to be alive, to walk with one's wife, to see the lonely truth!

Shyly he took Eileen by the hand. "No forces are my forces. I am against everything that is happening," he said. "I will this. I will this from my heart and mind."

"Thank you, thank you, Señor Mister Mayor, I already heard this speech until a thousand times." She picked a slice of melon out of a row of them on a vendor's collapsible table and backed away, sucking on it loudly and pointing at Mr. Cheung, to whom the young vendor held out his flat palm and said, "What you go give me on that melon now? She already eating it till es gone. I want hunnut dollar now. Es my *best* one I ever have of a melon since I *born*."

Mr. Cheung gave the man a copper penny from his coin-purse. "I see you as a decayed person," he said as he watched the man's face. "Electronic machines once managed all the money, did you hear about it? In those electronic times, nobody made a drama from one small piece of melon."

The vendor's flat face went cold. He popped the copper coin into his mouth and swallowed it. "Penny ain't nothing." He shooed them away with a fluttering hand. "Go, go, you steal my melon, happy days, you welcome, bye-bye, keep touch, I don't care." He turned his back on Mr. Cheung, and Eileen made as if to throw the rind at a spot between the vendor's shoulder blades, laughing.

Mr. Cheung reached out to take another slice of melon. "Two for a penny!"

His hand was shaking. He was astonished at his own anger.

"Look who coming now!" Eileen said.

She took her husband by the elbow and pulled him toward the road that emptied onto the beach, where a mist of dust boiled toward them from a crowd of racing urchins—dozens, and most of them too little to wear clothes—followed by ranks of other people in order of advancing age: adolescents, parents and uncles and aunts, weary but smiling old people, and then Bill Banks, distiller and proprietor of the great sound-shows, leading a party of his employees, who happened also to be his family, and a gang of burros pulling two carts full of his sound equipment. The slowest bunch, stumbling behind the carts and breathing all the dust, were the sad old drunks and the wild young drunks, harassed by dogs, confused by rice brandy, paired up to support one another at the finish of this long march from Twicetown. Wherever Bill Banks appeared, these people seemed to hover, not just because he made wine and brandy, but because his appearances meant excitement and dancing—yet Bill Banks himself was a small, skinny person with a face that said he didn't understand and a posture that claimed he was sorry for everything.

Mr. Cheung was happy for Eileen. "I told you a show would come."

"Sí, and I told you Bill Banks converted now," Eileen said. "Look, look there at Mother, she right there by the second cart."

It was true. He hadn't picked her out—Mother always dressed in ragged pants like a fisherman, and from a distance she might have been anyone. Mother was nobody's mother; she was the leader of the Church of Fire, a group without a building since their roof had fallen in. She ruffled Bill Banks's hair, kissed his hand, gave him a hug, and climbed, quite nimbly for a silver-haired old white lady, onto one of the scaffolds for the sound equipment. "They gonna have a microphone up here for me in two minutes," she shouted. "But I never have done my talking out of a microphone before so I'll get a start on things right here and now—shoo! Shoo!" she said to the children climbing onto the scaffold. "You're turning into monkeys. Little monkeys."

"Hurry up, Larry Wilson," Eileen muttered, recognizing one of the boys setting up the electric boxes and loudspeakers. "Music time."

They got the generators going, and the red-and-white police lights on the scaffolds began to whirl behind Mother's grey head.

"It was predicted in the Bible," Mother said in a rich, clear voice that carried out to the shore toward the Israelites at work on their tiny white ship, "that the scientists would look down through a telescope of a kind to see the prehistoric beginnings and they'd say, *We see monkeys a-crawling at the start of time and turning into humans.* And do you know what?" She bent over with a hand on her knee, pointing to the people on her right, "Do you know what?"—pointing to those in front of her, "Do you know what?"—now pointing at the left—"It happened just like the Bible did predict it. Gimme that microphone. I never used one," she said in a suddenly amplified voice whose ringing blurred into a piercing yowl. She shouted at the black microphone and the yowling got worse until she dropped it onto the scaffold and clapped her hands over her ears and stomped on the instrument with her bare foot. It jumped off the stage and burrowed into the sand. The crowd cheered and clapped and whistled while she screamed, "Wait a minute! Wait a minute! I got something to *tell* you-all—we're turning into monkeys! Monkeys is the point of it, backsliding out to the deep-down primitive state where Bob Marley can't never find us!" She could hardly be heard because the crowd went on applauding, without hostility, but clearly preferring their own noise to hers. Soon the music started, and it caught them by the throats —loud guitars that sounded to Mr. Cheung like someone rhythmically beating the life out of a frog until the singers rasped, "*I'm er-reddeh f'love!—Ooh baby I'm er-reddeh f'love*." Mr. Cheung enjoyed trying to make out the words. Feeling a little stupid, he danced with Eileen, merely standing in one spot and bobbing his head. He was delighted to see his wife having such a good time.

When he caught sight of Mother standing, somewhat dazed, beside a loudspeaker, he held up a finger to Eileen and then went over to help the old woman get away from the noise. "Don't stand beside the speaker," he told her. "Sometimes it makes vibrations to confuse your thoughts."

"You're dead right about that one," she said, letting him help her across the sand.

Mr. Cheung considered her a part of his neighborhood—though where she lived, he had no idea—because the old Church of Fire stood close to his house and he laid eyes on it every day. "Can I get you a slice of melon, or some yellow fruit?" he asked her.

"No way. My stomach feels all backward." Clutching his wrist, she settled herself to sit on the beach. "Wild business. I thought they blew all those electric things up," she said. "They're just a nuisance—did you *hear* that thing *screech*?"

Mr. Cheung hoped she was finished talking, so that he could go away. "I'll leave you now," he said.

"Do you know the goodness of Bob Marley?" she asked him.

"I am against the forces that took the machines away," Mr. Cheung said.

"So is Bob Marley! I mean, not that he gives two shits for all that electric juice—but it's the forces of destruction and the ways of backsliding down to primitive cave-people, that's what our father Bob Marley is against."

"I have to go to my wife," Mr. Cheung said.

"You are one of those persons," she said, "who got away with our pews when the Devil sabotaged our roof."

"Excuse me?"

"Keep it for now. But don't you own it, you just sit on it. We'll get us a roof one day—or a whole spang-new church!"

Her enthusiasm made Mr. Cheung uncomfortable. "I treat your pew with kindness," he assured her.

"I'll be up on that stage preaching soon as I find my feet. Don't think I'm daunted. Don't think it for a second."

"I'll leave you now. My wife—" He knew he was being rude. His neck burned with embarrassment as he walked away.

She called after him, "Don't think I'm daunted! I'll be up there hollering through that electric snake before too much longer!"

Closer to the sound-show, he collided again with its blathering fusillade as it rocketed out over the sea and disappeared there, like everything else. He stood beside Eileen, who'd stopped dancing and now only swayed in one place as did the others, letting the music pierce her through. This music was good now, this was Dylan, the great poet of the times of hard rain:

> *You know sometimes*
> *Satan*
> *Comes as a man of peace . . .*

Mr. Cheung tried to fix himself somewhere at the edge of the crowd, to the left, to the right, back ten steps toward the sea, where he might be able to hear the words. But he stopped listening and only wandered over the sand stupidly, like a puppy who'd been smacked on the ear. I suppose, he spoke inside himself, that I'm very much like Mother. But he could hardly make out the tone of his own ruminations inside all this head-hammering rhythm. History, the force of time—he was aware he was obsessed in an unhealthy way with these thoughts—are washing over us like this rocknroll. Some of us are aligned with a slight force, a frail resistance that shapes things for the better—I really believe this: I stand against the forces of destruction, against the forces that took the machines away.

Against the forces that had taken Fiskadoro away, the forces that would also keep hold, forever, of the boy's clarinet.

"Our father Bob Marley a-coming to take us home!" True to her promise, Mother was back on the scaffold with the microphone, and the music had ceased. She held the instrument carefully and kept her head away from it so it wouldn't whistle. "But I was a-talking back there about monkeys, which is going to be us, like the science said." She was still winded; the breath from her nostrils pulsed heavily through the speakers and made it seem she was crying out in the middle of a hurricane. "My cousin was a scientist, and for what I know, my cousin still *is* a scientist, my cousin's hiding away down in a hole somewheres still inventing the dynamics to get to the moon. I mean to talk about faith! I'm so full of the Spirit— wait now, let me get the thread of this that I want to tell you." The crowd of Twicetowners, drunks and dogs excluded, all watched her with the same curious goodwill with which they'd attended Mr. Cheung's speeches the time he'd run for Mayor. They felt, Mr. Cheung believed, that the person on the stump was watching them: that they were on display, and not the other way around.

He'd lost his place in this sermon; now Mother was calling out, "The scientists said we had a billion stars, and we believed, and we had a billion stars—"

The way Mr. Cheung looked at it, everything that counted was being moved out from under them by these forces. Even, also, the boy Fiskadoro's clarinet. Fiskadoro had been gone long enough, now, that he would obviously never come back; but Mr. Cheung hadn't been able to get the mother, and the cousins, and the myriad other relatives, to give up the dead boy's clarinet. Little by little all the coins, and the books, and the musical instruments, and also the musicians, were sucked down into the rocknroll of destruction. Goodbye!

"—and if we *believe*, only *believe*, that we are *people*, and that Bob *Marley* a-coming to take us *home*—" The woman's eyes were rolling up in her head. The microphone trailed from her hand and dragged, creating thunder, on the wooden planks of the scaffold.

Mr. Cheung hoped that the deranged Israelite boat-builders, to whom his back was resolutely turned, these people who thought they had an agreement with him, were as basically muddled as this old Baptist sorceress. Under the pretext of scratching his shoulder, he threw in the Israelites' direction a quick glance that gave him no comfort at all. The tide was creeping toward them and the air was full of words, but the dozen or so Israelites at the water's edge applied themselves to their drill as busily and as certainly as insects.

Fire had come into Grandmother's life. For the big stove in the kitchen Mr. Cheung had acquired a new door, one with a glass window in it, so that as the cooler season came on she had something to look at from her station nearest the heat.

The moments turned back and forth patched with blank spaces, people appeared and disappeared right while she watched them, visits with old friends suddenly became interviews with these mystifying figures who might be her relatives and might be her captors, and her breakfast could easily turn into a pillow of burlap she was supposed to lay her head on for a night's sleep to be accomplished, by her reckoning, fifteen minutes after daybreak; but in the deep red event behind the stove's glass window the filament of time was never tangled, nothing had a name or a reason, everything was itself, and the things she would always know, even if you took her head away, even if you killed her, were confirmed: It catches, then burns, then blazes; it rages and sings, it wanes, it shifts and flares, it burns a little longer and then weakens, whatever it is, and goes out. But if you lay the small wood across it in the morning, it all begins again. The little girl came often to sit on Grandmother's lap, and went away, and then came back grown larger and louder. It was the same thing. Whatever it was, it was happening now, today, all of it, this very moment. This very moment—*now*, changing and staying the same— was the fire.

This morning she'd put on her white dress to go to Mass with her father. Pulling on her grey knee-socks, part of the uniform of Ste. Bernadette's, her French girls' school, she'd caressed her own thighs and spread her legs, feeling guilty but laughing, and then on these same legs she'd walked six blocks down Dien Tin Street, holding her father's hand, to the Church of Ste. Thérèse. They'd entered the cathedral, nodding to old Père Georges, who stood by the doors recognizing nobody and greeting each one with a glazed friendliness, and suddenly Marie had found herself traveling all alone toward a huge aquarium filled with fire. Now she sat before the kitchen stove and drowned in the wet cement of old age, hardly able to lift her hands to her face. Grief tightened her chest and she expected the tears to flow, but none came. The holes for tears were pinched shut, and her eyes were always as dry as two corks.

A man and a woman came into the room and tumbled yellow and green fruit onto the table.

After dropping the melons and yellow fruit onto the table, Mr. Cheung flexed his fingers and then rubbed the back of his neck, "I'm not the one to carry so many melons on such a long hike."

"How are you today, Grandmother?" Eileen said.

The old woman turned her head toward Eileen, seemed not to recall why she'd turned her head, and said nothing.

It had been fun to go out, hear a sound-show, watch the weird doings of the Israelites, but now Eileen was weary. The day still held too much time to get through and too many things to bother her. "Tony, we can just eat the fruit, okay? My back is too tired and weak to make supper. I figure out the hot sun ate all my strength."

Her husband wasn't listening. He stood by the kitchen door and studied the dirt yard as if it were a book of words. She could see he was deep into his thinking. To bring him back she said, "Tell me the Constitution. Tell me the Declaration Indepension."

He took his mind out of the yard and looked at her. "Independence," he said.

"Go 'head, say to me."

"When in the course of human events it becomes necessary for one people to dissolve the political bands which have connected them with another, and to assume among the powers of the earth, the separate and equal station to which the laws of nature and of nature's God entitle them, a decent respect to the opinions of mankind requires that they should declare the causes which impel them to the separation," he told her.

Eileen felt better as he settled into all these words. Whenever he told someone the Declaration of Independence or the Constitution it took the lines out of his forehead. Eileen often asked him for one or the other, because he was always thinking too hard. It frightened her, his habit of trying to keep the world in his mind, the whole world, to keep it turning in the space of his brain, from the start of time to the last day—that's what brought on the terrifying fits—

". . . the establishment of an absolute Tyranny, with a

capital T, over these States, with a capital S. To prove this, let facts be submitted to a candid world. Period. Dash . . ."

—explaining and explaining, working it all out in his head, coloring his attitude black, that's what started the tiny cells in the brain popping and bursting—

". . . swarms of Officers, capital O," he said, ". . . and eat out their substance . . ."

—four times she'd seen her husband go down, his eyeballs switched off, only the whites shimmering in the sockets, and it had crushed her heart, it had twisted the very life in her, to see his body with the soul gone out of it, jerking like a decked shark. I'm gonna slice some fruit, she thought, and that's all the supper there is.

He went on and on without once having to stop and think. ". . . He has plundered our seas, ravaged our capital-C Coasts, burnt our towns . . ." He was coming to her favorite part, the part about the capital-I, capital-S Indian Savages. ". . . and has endeavored to bring on the inhabitants of our frontiers, the merciless capital-I, capital-S Indian Savages, whose known rule of warfare, is an undistinguished destruction of all ages, sexes and conditions . . ." These Indian Savages had eventually warred-out almost everybody.

". . . in the most humble terms . . ."

Pretty soon he would get to the names. Eileen bit into the melon and only then realized how thirsty she was. She'd gotten too much sun. She dropped her slice of melon and covered her ears.

". . . FREE AND INDEPENDENT," he shouted, "STATES."

Eileen wished he wouldn't yell that part. She liked to hear him pull it out of his memory like a long necklace, every pearl the same. The Declaration of Independence was warm in her ears, and it soothed her to listen, just as it seemed a comfort to

Grandmother that she could sit in this kitchen and look at the fire, chewing on something when there was nothing in her mouth, not even a tooth.

"Hancock," Tony was saying, "Button Gwinnet, Lyman Hall, Geo period Walton, Wum period Hooper . . ."

But this afternoon the Declaration only seemed to rouse his feeling, and now he wasn't telling them the Declaration any-more—he was complaining about the names again. "You know Mrs. Castanette in our orchestra? She only calls herself that because she plays the castanets. It is a fact that her name is Margaret Swanson. But her husband now calls himself Swanson-Johnson. They don't see how they themselves are the ones who—who mangle the way of things." He moved his hands as if gnarling up a bunch of string. "In the time when it was cold, we, my family, we burned our copy of the Constitution to get the fire going one day. Everybody was in despair, the children were coming out crooked, every tide left dead poison fish, nobody put out the boats, nobody could get together and say, Let's keep the fires going in our stoves—I remember this, my father told me and I remember a little bit. Our family burned a copy of the Constitution and all the books to stay alive, but first they memorized the Constitution, everyone took two paragraphs, they clung to the ways they knew—they did this, Eileen, because it would keep them going on, step by step. It isn't good, calling yourself Swanson-Johnson, as if a name is a joke. Next a word will be a joke, and then comes a time when even a thought is a joke." Worry swelled the tiny veins around his eyes. He sucked short gulps of air.

Eileen saw she hadn't helped by bringing up the Constitu-tion. "Tony, those veins around your eyes are getting big again. Please. Please, you finish worrying now, and get a happy face."

"Grandmother knows," he said. He sat down at the table and looked at Grandmother. "Not in her mind any longer, but still she knows inside her heart. But the people don't think, even the people with minds."

"I have to take a siesta," Eileen told him.

Later, when she woke up and came from the bedroom, Eileen smelled something bad in the kitchen and found that Grandmother had fallen asleep in her chair and wet herself.

She went to tell Tony, because she always felt sick when something went wrong with Grandmother. It made her feel better, it made her feel less worried, to tell him about it and let him be the one to worry.

Mr. Park-Smith was in the parlor with Tony, and they were both excited, sitting together on the church pew and talking low.

"Grandmother wet herself," Eileen told them.

But Tony just said, "Yes, yes, I know," and then said to Mr. Park-Smith, "Let's walk," and together the two men left to go walking through the dusty neighborhood.

Fidelia came back from the neighbors' and helped Eileen clean Grandmother with a cloth, lifting the black dress and trying not to look.

They ate. Eileen sliced out tiny pieces of melon, and Fidelia pushed them gently between Grandmother's lips.

"Father coming," Fidelia said—she always heard people coming when nobody else could hear.

He was without Mr. Park-Smith. Eileen didn't like the way he looked.

He was pale and shaken, and she felt his fear and tasted something sour in her throat. "Did you go down? Tony? Tony, Tony, did you get a fit?"

He was all balled up in his thoughts again, thoughts that were making him tremble and turning the blood white under the skin of his face.

"Tony?"

"I have to make a trip to Marathon," he said. "There's been some news from the Marathon Society for Knowledge. The Twicetown Society is going to have a journey."

On the same day that Mr. Cheung learned he was going to make a journey—on that morning—as Belinda ate coconut meat off the shell, one of her dog-teeth fell out.

She held the hem of her shift to her gums and cried about it as if this tooth were everything. In her mind she saw the tooth as gigantic, the last tooth in the mouth of an old, old whale who was eating her.

She buried the tooth in the yard and said, "Mwe pa geñe para sak pale pu mwe," although she kept no shrine in her house and had no friends among the gods.

Afterward she found that automatically, when she said something to the baby Mike, she covered her mouth with her right hand to hide the black space. In this life crimes had come against her one by one, as fast as days, and now her husband was dead, her first-born was—not dead, you can't call a boy *dead* like they were calling him till you had the dead shell!—but in any case Fiskadoro was gone, and Drake, her second-eldest, had left home, even if he lived only ninety meters away; and where she'd been daubing at her gums with the hem of her shift the cloth was all bloody.

She left the baby crawling around the yard and saying, "Wuf! Wuf!" while she went inside to change her shift. Already it was after noon—where did the moments get away to? In the dark she hefted the shift above her hips and sat on the tick mattress and looked at her knees. Even flexed they showed wrinkles like gouges in a dry wood stump, one more thing to cry about. The wind and the Gulf were dead and there weren't any sounds on earth but her breathing, and the coals clinking in the stove, and the wet heat pressing in against her mind. She drew the shift over her head and wiped away the sweat from her face, shoulders, armpits, and ran the bunched linen up between her legs and then between her breasts. Pillowing her head with it, she lay back on the bed and felt her nipples. They were as dry and distended as figs now, and sought after and used by nobody. Next to the left nipple she felt, in the meat of her flesh, a hard thing like a pearl that moved around under the probe of her finger. Her breath seized up, and she stared unblinking at the crosshatched palm leaves of the ceiling without a word in her head while the sweat leaked out of her hair and down behind her ears. I got to make a move, she thought, and then, as if somebody were doing it for her, she was raised up, and her legs took her to the doorway. "Mikey," she said.

Mike was talking in a game and didn't hear her. His legs weren't chunky anymore, his belly was smaller, his face was a boy's, not a baby's.

Belinda went back inside and found a pair of Jimmy's old olive Army pants, and with a fish-knife she cut open the crotch and made a skirt. She punched holes in the waist, on either side of the zipper, so that she could tie it around herself with twine. When she'd put the skirt on she said out loud, as if talking to some invisible person who'd wounded her unaccountably, "Now I gone hang my tits and be old."

Bare-breasted, she stepped into the yard and sat down to watch Mike playing games.

The tide was in. She heard wood knocking and men calling

from a place out of sight, downshore. The *Los Desechados* was making ready to put out, which meant that Towanda Sanchez would be open for a visit soon. Drake sometimes put out with them now, and Belinda's brother Pressy was one of the permanent crew. No other boat on the Keys would have had him because he was bent left, right, and sideways in the head, but he was the handiest replacement for Harvard Sanchez, who'd been next in line for Captain and who—much to everybody's surprise, a good boy like Harvard Sanchez— now slept out by the still-house in Twicetown and never let out a breath that didn't stink of liquor. And these days Drake lived over at his Uncle Pressy's with Pressy's cousin, Alfo, who was also Belinda's cousin. They were three bachelors with big holes in their roof and crinkled aluminum cans lying all over the floor dribbling wine.

I got to eat something, she told herself, and went inside, took three butter-clams from the bucket, and laid them on the stove. But when the shells opened and the leathery black feet came out they looked just like her own nipples. She left them there to fry.

"I gonna go see Towanda. Not too long," she told Mike. She scraped a circle around him with her heel. "Es you perimeter," she told him. "Shark gone bite you legs off when you go outa you perimeter. You stay inside you perimeter."

Mike patted smooth a small mound of sand and put a blade of beach-grass in its center for a flag.

"I can't fetch you 'long through this compound like a mess of fish. I too old, I too sick. You have kill me."

As soon as she said it, she heard it: the pearl in her breast was a tumor of the kill-me. Her finger on her breast had already sent this news to her heart, but now her mouth had told it to her brain, and there was nothing left to do but go crazy.

With a metal spoon Belinda dug her last penny out of its hiding-spot among the ashes inside her stove, and then to cool it off she dropped it in the clam bucket. She ran to Towanda's, past the falling-down shack that Pressy and Alfo and Drake called home, clutching the wet coin in her fist.

The *Los Desechados* wasn't half a kilometer out yet, but Towanda was already in the bedroom, a lean-to attached to their quonset hut, rifling her husband's pants-pockets and hunting in all his hiding places for coins.

"Es a heavy day!" Belinda said.

"You hanging your tits now like you know your age," Towanda said.

"My age? My age es dead." Belinda was crying. "I feel how I got a little dureza of the kill-me in my left one here."

"When?"

"Today."

Towanda closed her eyes. "Es a heavy day," she said. "Nothing to do behind this trouble but drink and cry."

"I got a penny," Belinda said, opening her fist.

"Leon got seven penny in this room," Towanda said. "Help me. Help me."

Glad to be doing something, Belinda helped her turn over the mattress, felt in the slats of the palm walls, and poked at the thatched ceiling with a broken gaff. Towanda got angry when nothing came of it and turned on Belinda with a burning tongue, as if it were all Belinda's fault. "From *today until forever*," Towanda said, making her eyes tiny with hatred, "I got to have *one penny* every Sunday. That man es a *Cap'n*, and I a *Cap'n woman*, and don't you know I shame to walk on the world have never no more coin than a little children have? He gone on the sea! What happen if emergency? *Leon!*" she hollered, "*you don't trust with me! You don't faith with me!*" Suddenly she seemed very calm. "That mean I got to take it outa his souvenir," she said. "That's all. Leon, you gone on the sea and left me only one chance."

Belinda waited, feeling the breeze across her breasts, while Towanda went into their hut and stole Leon's souvenir penny. "He come off the first day of when Leon Cap'n on that boat," she said, "number-one penny of his command. I *sorry*, Belinda, but es a heavy day and I *got* to take it."

"Es true," Belinda agreed. "You got to, es necessario." But such a grim feeling was all around her that her voice sounded far away.

They went to Billy Chicago's place across the compound, near the road. Billy was off somewhere, but his old mother was always home, sitting in her big cane chair just inside the door and looking for somebody's ear to eat, waving at bugs and neighbors with a big dirty rag. "Morning!"—"Afternoon!"— "Evening!"—Ms. Chicago always called out of the darkness. But people never stopped unless they wanted liquor, or had a medical problem.

"Afternoon!" she said to Belinda and Towanda.

"Como esta?" Towanda said.

"Oh," Ms. Chicago said, "just yer basic. You hanging you tits now," she said to Belinda.

Ms. Chicago's radio said, "Un programa bilingue de *Cubaradio* empezara dentro de cuarenta y cinco minutos. A bilingual broadcast of *Cubaradio* will begin in forty-five minutes. Por favor invite a sus camaradas a escucharlo. Please invite your comrades to listen."

"Be a radio time soon," Ms. Chicago said with satisfaction.

"We got two penny for wine," Belinda said.

"Miz Chicago," Towanda said, very worried, "Belinda got a dureza in she left tit. Look like a dureza of the kill-me."

Ms. Chicago was delighted. She knew all about medicine. "Dureza de vientre, dureza de teta," she reminded them—a way of saying that if you were a constipated kind of person and hard in the guts, you were bound to find a tumor of the kill-me in your breast one day.

"Who say I dureza de vientre? My reputation all strangle up around here," Belinda said.

"Reputation ain't fix the kill-me, girl. You better throw your misery down on your shrine, es the only thing to help it."

"I never have make a shrine. Es just a lot of foam, that religion."

Ms. Chicago looked at Belinda out of a face too squashed by the weight of years to show what she was thinking. "Ain't gone be foam when you lay down all cover up with tumors burning loud as the sun, girl. You gone holler, *Kill me! Kill me!*"

"Not today," Belinda said, but she had to sit down in the doorway.

"Tell me the last thing you lost," Ms. Chicago said, "or the last thing you found."

"I lost a dog-tooth here," Belinda said, pointing at the gap in her mouth.

"That's it. What you see?"

"Nada. Didn't see nada."

Ms. Chicago wiped the sweat from between her breasts with her grey rag. "Think now, girl. Don't you thought some kind of thought when you lost that tooth?"

"Only just a small one," Belinda said.

"Tell me," Ms. Chicago insisted.

"I thought about a big whale eat me up, like my dog-tooth es the last tooth in his mouth."

"Oh!" Ms. Chicago said with a tone of great respect. "That's good!"

"That's good, Belinda!" Towanda said.

"How you know es good?" Belinda said. "You just wanna talk like Miz Chicago talk."

"Gimme that tooth," Ms. Chicago said.

"Es gone," Belinda told her.

"Es gone? Who gone it? Devil gone it?"

"No, Señora, the Devil didn't gone it—es me. I dig it down in the yard."

"What you said when you dig it down?"

"Nada."

"Tell me. What you said?"

"What you said?" Towanda asked her. "You said something?"

Belinda closed her eyes, tipped her head back, breathed deeply. "I say, 'Mwe pa geñe para sak pale pu mwe,'" she admitted.

"Oh, yeah!" Ms. Chicago was overjoyed in her crackly, invisible way.

"Que dice—mwe pa hen-yeh—what es?" Towanda said. She looked scared. She wrung her hands. "Don't *say* those thing like that, Belinda."

"Mean, 'I got no family to speak for me,'" Ms. Chicago said. "Es exact proper wording de la Voodoo. Go find me that tooth, Belinda. Maybe go be a loa para tu."

"I don't want no loa," Belinda said.

"Then why," Towanda asked her, "you go round say magic on a tooth you lost? Oh sweet Saint Mary—Belinda, you have start it now."

"Girl, that's right—you have start it now," Ms. Chicago agreed. "Go bring me that tooth. Then we drink a little potato-buzz."

Belinda saw there was no way to stop it. "I be back," she told Towanda and Ms. Chicago.

As she rounded the corner of Towanda and Leon's, she found Mike wandering sideways on the path with an open mouth and a faraway look, dribbling urine out from between his legs. She hooked an arm around his belly and lugged him home. "What happen if a puppy bite you face?" she said, trying to remember where she'd buried the tooth. "Then you crawl under a leaf and bleed and nobody gone find you. I gotta dig out that tooth now."

The place where she'd worked the dirt was damp and easy to spot. She sifted the sand through her fingers and found her dog-tooth. The tooth was dry now, nothing more than a pebble that seemed never to have had anything to do with the gap in her mouth.

"Now I gone leave you by the well." She dragged Mike along by the hand so that his feet hardly scuffed the dirt. "You have make me be see by alla them skags," she told him angrily.

The crones at the well all had an exclamation to make or some smug thing to say about her new appearance, and they sounded like a mess of shells being beaten with a spoon, but Belinda was just too tired to let it all loose. She dropped Mike down among three or four other children and left without a word. The muscles in her neck and shoulders were so tight they felt cold by the time she got back across the compound to Ms. Chicago and Towanda with the tooth.

"Radio time come in fifteen minute," Towanda told her.

"Don't say nothing," Ms. Chicago said instantly. "I feel you got the tooth. I taste the power of that tooth—es a loa."

Towanda said, "Go-head find out who es that loa. Please, Miz Chicago, Belinda got to know."

"I need two penny," Ms. Chicago told them.

Towanda dropped the two pennies into the lap of Ms. Chicago's skirt.

"I told you we go get *wine* from those penny," Belinda said.

"*Psss, psss,*" Towanda said, shushing her.

Ms. Chicago grabbed the pennies in one hand and the tooth in the other. She held them so tightly the veins in her arms puffed up.

In no time at all, Ms. Chicago entered a trance and said, "Es a bomb-pilot Major Colonel Overdoze got the power of Atomic Bomb to work for you, get rid of the kill-me and bring everything back but not the dead. If Fish-man not dead he coming back. Major Colonel fix it. If he dead he not come back. Both way you gone know." She left the trance, and sat with her arms crossed in front of her chest. "Truth go set you fire make you well."

"Overdoze?" Belinda said.

"Major Colonel Overdoze," Ms. Chicago said. "Atomic Bomb pilot."

"Oh—oh—oh," Towanda said. "That's the most power of all."

"You got a power loa," Ms. Chicago said. "Most power of all."

Belinda looked at her feet. "We bringed those penny for wine," she told Ms. Chicago.

"Now ain't you glad you dug after this tooth?" Ms. Chicago said. "Truth go set you fire make you well."

"Why you don't send Major Colonel for a expedition to Fiskadoro?" Towanda said.

"That's all turn backward," Ms. Chicago corrected her. "Loa don't make no expedition on a dead—Saint Expedit send a *dead* on the expedition to a *living*."

"Fiskadoro ain't dead," Belinda interrupted, "plus also we bringed those two penny for wine, Miz Chicago. Es a mistake about those two penny. Towanda, why you go buy shit with my penny when I didn't say you go-head buy shit with my penny? Es a mistake. *My* mouth gone talk about my penny," she explained to Ms. Chicago. "Es *Towanda* mouth talking before."

"You very turbado," Ms. Chicago said. "I gone give you two penny of wine because of you upset and I too scared of your loa. That's a power loa."

"Deal. I gone live with that," Belinda said.

Ms. Chicago opened the cabinet with a key she kept belted around her belly on a little chain, and took out a two-penny jug of potato wine.

The three of them stood out front where the air might help keep their heads clear. Belinda watched their shadows, made crooked on the corrugated wall of the quonset hut, hanging their tits and passing the jug.

Before long, Belinda said, "My head just ain't clear. Potato-buzz ain't make me happy today."

The radio inside said, "Un programa bilingue de *Cubaradio* empezara dentro de un minuto. A bilingual broadcast of *Cubaradio* will begin in just one minute. Por favor invite a sus camaradas a escucharlo. Please invite your comrades to listen."

They passed the green jug. "This potato-buzz burning up inside my stomach," Belinda told Ms. Chicago and Towanda. "I don't want no more."

"Entre menos burros, mas elotes," Ms. Chicago said, taking a big swallow—among fewer mules, more corn.

Suddenly she gripped Belinda's hand, and Belinda thought the old woman had gone weak and needed help to stand, but Ms. Chicago said, "Feel me aqui, girl," and shoved Belinda's fingers up tight against one of her shrunken breasts. "You feel that dureza?" Ms. Chicago's breast felt hotter than Belinda's hand. In the meat was a tiny pebble. "I felt her time when Billy's first son come. Now Billy's son about tall as me, but my loa keep on controlling la dureza."

The radio inside said, "Es *Cubaradio* bilingue. This is bilin-gual *Cubaradio*. En la proxima hora, le deleitaremos con la popular e inspiridora musica Cubana. For the following hour, we will entertain you with some of Cuba's popular and inspira-tional music. Ustedes, los radioescuchas, viven bajo la protec-cion del Gobierno de la Habana. You who are listening live under the protection of the Havana government. Las guerras terminaron, el pueblo es libre y la vida sigue adelante," the radio said. "The wars are over, the people are free, and life goes on."

Above the sink in the kitchen Belinda kept a photograph of snow, a very old postcard showing the naked tangles of a bush which, for all she knew, never had any foliage except this white stuff daubing the tips of the twigs like blossoms. Next to the bush stood a black pedestal holding up the black stone figure of a bird. In the picture's foreground, one icicle dangled from a dark branch.

Belinda had no reason for keeping the photo. It was just there, above the sink, in front of her face, that was how that story went. She spent no small amount of every day in its presence. She'd heard about snow but had no clear understanding of who made snow or what snow was supposed to do.

Tilting slightly and banging her elbow against the sink, she took the picture down from its nail and rested it on a cypress stump in the dank closet where precious or useless things were kept: boxes of her trinkets and some clothes she never wore, a rifle that wouldn't fire, some bullets that probably wouldn't explode, some books full of crumbling pages that had somehow escaped being burned in the cold time; and Fiskadoro's clarinet in the briefcase called Samsonite. She propped the scene of winter upright against the wall and laid before it the supercharged loa, formerly just one of her dog-teeth.

When she opened the briefcase called Samsonite, she found the clarinet in pieces—who made it broken? She stood the pieces in a circle, around the yellow tooth, before the picture of snow. One piece wouldn't stay upright, and so she laid it out in a position she hoped was pleasing to the loa.

Maybe she didn't completely believe in these things, but she saw how the loa Major Colonel Overdoze was gracious and kind, putting in her head, whether she believed in him or didn't, one comforting thought: not today. If she grew the tumors of pain until they held her down to the bed, a hundred kilos of tumors of fire, and she begged in a tiny voice to be killed, it wouldn't happen today. And today was a big place that held everything inside of it—the Keys, the sea, the sky, and the outer space of stars. Today didn't close around her throat like all the other days.

I seen three shadows on the dirt, she prayed, shadows out of three us old womens hanging our tits and passing the potato-buzz like they all do, me too. Now I getting bit by religion, she prayed, putting in a shrine and praying on a loa like they all do, me too. Atomic Bomber Major Colonel Overdoze, take out this tumor of kill-me and bring my first-born back.

You'll be better before we get there," William Park-Smith promised Mr. Cheung, but Mr. Cheung, himself, guessed that he would expire of this bottomless nausea sometime in the next few minutes, and felt certain that at the very least he'd still be quite seasick when the boat reached Marathon. He hardly ever traveled by water. He hardly ever traveled at all. What he liked to do was to stay in his house, whose chief attraction in his mind at this moment was that it never moved. The *Catch*, the diesel-engine fisher on whose deck he was trying to keep his balance among several other members of Twicetown's Society for Science, demonstrated a bewildering repertoire of motions: side-to-side, up-and-down, and horizontal—east by northeast, and now dead north—along the Keys toward Marathon. Generally the vessel hugged the shore because a storm threatened and the sea, as Mr. Cheung felt compelled to testify, was rough. They passed along the gap between Summerland Key and Ramrod Key, where two frayed sections of the highway called US 1 had given up reaching across the distance to one another and fallen down asleep in the water. People riding on the ferry-raft between the two islands shouted at the *Catch* and gestured happily, and one man took off his shirt and waved it around above his head, but their cries of greeting were lost in the wind.

Mr. Cheung estimated abysmally that it would be another two hours to Marathon. Everything he'd been feeling at the start of this journey—excitement, curiosity, an undirected gratitude, great fear—had been emptied out of him with repeated vomiting. His throat ached, and he trembled with weakness. The salt spray and diesel smoke thickened in his lungs as he gripped the rail without strength, looking forward to his death impatiently.

"Try some salty biscuit. Please, one bite," Park-Smith yelled out amid the wind. A gust jerked the boat's prow to port—this move was a new one, a kind of half-spin that left Mr. Cheung astonished at the world's inexhaustible evil. The biscuit Park-Smith was threatening him with like a poisonous nugget was one more thing. Mr. Cheung didn't want the biscuit and in fact hated the biscuit, but he indicated nothing. He'd found this discomfort to be an incredible teacher, one that had practiced him, right at the start of this trip, not to nod his head or shake it.

The young mate, a white boy, stayed at the bow and peered ahead for uncharted obstacles in this shallow water, while the Captain, also a youthful white, one from the famous Wilson family, responded to his signals with unexpected and excruciating shifts in their course. Mr. Cheung was the only seasick passenger. Other members of the Twicetown Society for Science—lumpy Maxwell, Park-Smith, Bobby Calvino, who would be dangerous without his wife and was already drunk —had been having a good time, and now looked bored. They'd been nearly three hours on the water, and the overcast heavens were getting even darker as night approached.

Below Key Marathon, Captain Wilson took the *Catch* through a channel and came at the largest town on the Keys from the Ocean side. The water was calmer here today. Mr. Cheung felt his nausea dissipating even before they docked behind the local slaughterhouse. The slaughterhouse had once been a hotel. The stripped, headless carcasses of several dogs and goats were hung from poles laid across the width of the swimming pool. A small man, apparently the only one working at this hour, tightroped across the poles with a bucket, casting spicy salt over the meat. As Park-Smith helped the Orchestra Manager along the pier and toward the streets, Mr. Cheung saw, through the glassless window behind the swimming pool, a dead goat laid out on the bar in the cocktail lounge. "Hold shut your nose, Tony," Park-Smith warned him, but Mr. Cheung had already stopped breathing. The stink of the slaughterhouse kept everybody away. The buildings on this street housed only drifts of sand and the barnacled supplies of fishing boats.

By the time the four Society members had walked through several shanty collections, where families sat outside their doorways eating suppers of fish and rice and worrying about the weather, and then through a flat neighborhood where old houses had been torn apart and stacked into lumber, Mr. Cheung was completely revived.

"I can't remember where the library is," he told the others. "How far?" Now he was excited again. He tried to expect nothing, but they wouldn't have had the Twicetown Society travel so far, wouldn't even have condescended to invite them here, if the book weren't important.

"Two more streets, I think," said Maxwell, and Park-Smith said, "Two streets."

According to Park-Smith, the Marathon Society for Knowledge had traded a boat for the book. It must be the one—the history they'd all been looking for long enough that they'd given up hope of finding it—the text that would explain the End of the World.

Thinking about the book put Mr. Cheung into a panic. "It's dark, they might be starting already." He picked up his pace. He was willing to leave the others behind if necessary.

The library was a stone building left upright where all the wooden ones had been torn down, and now it stood by itself at the edge of a field. Great steps marched up to its entrance, on either side of which a flagpole jutted from the walls, one dripping a ragged Florida state flag that hopped up fitfully in the wind to broadcast its crimson X, and the other one naked. Even before they reached the steps and passed between these flagpoles, they heard the buzz of voices from inside.

This was an occasion. As they entered, Mr. Cheung could see immediately that a lot more people than the Marathon Society's thirty members were gathered here. Their bodies stifled the room with heat and breath and everybody was talking at once, at least fifty citizens in various postures on the cool floor of the main room. Most of them were white people from the merchant families, but there were fishermen and layabouts present, too, wearing shirts as at a wedding or a funeral, and there were even some desechados among them: Mr. Cheung saw a young blind man with a humped back, who held himself sideways in a corner and turned a grotesquely large ear toward the speaker at the front. Precious kerosene was being offered up in lanterns to give them light.

The generalized chatter trailed away and then resumed quickly after the Twicetown Society members had made themselves evident, hesitating in the doorway.

Roderick Chambers stood behind the only piece of furniture in the room, a wrecked Xerox device the size of two goats; behind him loomed the metal shelves holding the Marathon Public Library's several hundred volumes. Backed up against this wall of words, he welcomed the Twicetown Society for Science with a lonely gesture of embrace, which he altered by bringing his hands together as in prayer and pointing at some vacant spots in the front row almost at his feet. People moved their legs for the new arrivals as Park-Smith led the way through those assembled. The ones by the wall made room without squabbling. It was the kind of courtesy Mr. Cheung would have expected during a disaster. He was pressed against a tiny dark woman with scraggly Negro hair who looked evil-tempered, but she smiled at him and wrapped her arms around her knees, giving him as much space as she could, and continued waiting quietly.

Roderick Chambers was responding to some kind of dissatisfaction among the Society members. "And then again," he was saying, "running through all the possibilities, finding pretty much nothing. We've been a long time after a book like this book. We cut the only deal we could."

"Sounds like no deal at all," a voice called from the rear.

"We cut the only deal we could."

"They got a damn boat. And we still don't know *what* we got."

"We got a straight guarantee about the pages—any missing pages, the deal is canceled. But aside from that, what we received is what we received. No more and no less."

"We need an all-time policy laid down," somebody said. "We usually look at the Table of Contents, and we better say from now on, *always* see the Contents."

"Most of the time we buy by the kilo," Roderick Chambers said. "We don't even look—"

"When it's a *regular* book, you mean to say. We see Contents on a high-price type, and *this*—"

"We cut the only deal we could," Chambers repeated against a volley of comments, shaking his head and closing his eyes, "we cut the only deal we could, we cut the only deal we could—"

"How do you know it ain't contaminated, if you didn't even get to *see* it?"

"We know because it didn't come from Miami. It came from here. It was originally the property of this library."

Many were outraged.

Chambers seemed to enjoy shocking everybody with the news that they'd traded so steeply for their own book. "It got stolen a long, long time back," he said. "Now it's been returned."

"What was the source?" several people shouted. "What was the source?"

"It came from a usual type of source," Roderick Chambers assured them.

What's the point of all this talk? Mr. Cheung thought. By now he was speechless with tension. He looked neither right nor left, took nothing in, and tried to calm himself by thinking that it had been bound to happen someday. Someday was today. It had to be the kind of book they'd been hoping for.

"I can't believe," Chambers said above the noise, "that you-all just mean to sit here slinging this dead issue around when we have the book right here." He stepped back and pointed dramatically at a book, just lying among the other books, on one of the shelves behind him.

. . .

Pressy was bored and sipping at potato brandy as the windy dark came along. The *Los Desechados*, of whose crew he was the newest and least respected member, hadn't gone out today because all the gulls had been flying east toward the Ocean side, a good sign there was a storm somewhere out on the Gulf.

Pressy's cousin Alfo was staying across the compound with his sister, whose roof didn't leak. Drake was napping inside, but Drake would run home to his mother when the thunder started. Pressy intended to stay here, where he lived, even if he drowned, which was a possibility because the hut's front section was falling down. Generally this little building wasn't lived in. Coconut shells, wood to be split, and miscellaneous unwanted things found their way here.

Pressy clicked his tongue at a grey kitten hiding under the house. "Come on, Señor." Wearing a worried, intelligent expression, the kitten stepped out from under what was left of the steps and uttered a cry.

Pressy took another pull of his brandy. He stuck his finger in the bottle's mouth and offered the wet finger to the kitten, but the kitten only sniffed the air and turned its back.

When Drake woke up from his siesta among the stacks of kindling in the house and wandered, rubbing his face, out front to sit with him, Pressy felt happier. "Rain gone come down in the roof," he promised Drake. "Thunder gone smash thisyer casa. Lightning gone burn us alive. Sarge know all about it." Pressy's dog Sarge was hiding in a dark corner of the quonset hut, his mind already in pieces, listening to thunder nobody else could hear yet. Drake didn't say anything. He shivered in the wind and put his arms around himself.

Pressy went inside, came back with half a coconut shell, and poured some potato brandy into it for the kitten. When he set the shell down, the kitten gave it a little sniff, but got no closer than the length of a hand to the source of this aroma. "Ain't you thirsty?" Pressy said. He got a whole coconut from the house and whacked it with his bolo knife, shaking milk from the cracked brown fruit into the improvised bowl. "Scientifig esperiment," he explained to Drake. This time the kitten didn't even come near it.

Drake went inside, and Pressy said, "Where you going?" just to have something to say. Presently Drake came back out wearing a shawl of burlap draped over his head and shoulders.

"In order for this kind of esperiment," Pressy said, "you go find some milk."

"Es your esperiment," Drake said.

Solemnly Pressy told him, "Fiskadoro help me many times, Drake."

"I not Fiskadoro," Drake said.

"Oh"—Pressy put his face in his hands—"when you say that it make my heart go dark, talking I ain't Fiskadoro, talking I ain't my own brother, talking I don't believe you scientifig esperiment, Pressy, talking I ain't you cousin, don't wanna put out on *Los Desechados* no more—"

"Sí! I *wanna* put out on *Los Desechados*!"

"Well why you don't get me some milk? Make my heart go dark till I don't never wanna see you face around my boat." Pressy dumped the shell of its contents and handed it to Drake. "You say Towanda Sanchez, mi madre need it because of her stomach burning up."

Holding the burlap shawl shut tightly under his chin with one hand, Drake carried the bowl to Leon Sanchez's and soon came back, walking carefully and watching the milk inside it. Now the evening was dark. The edges of the burlap flapped around his shoulders in the wind.

"She doesn't like to give me," he told Pressy. "She goat not making much today."

"Es important," Pressy said. He poured some brandy into the milk and clucked for the kitten. The kitten came out from under the house and smelled of the offered mixture, jerked back, approached again, put a paw into the bowl and scratched at the liquid as if trying to scrape aside whatever smelled improper, sniffed the paw, touched it with the tip of its tongue, sneezed, turned away in disgust, walked around awhile, repeated all these moves, and at last took one sip from the bowl and sat back, licking its lips and turning this experience over in its mind. "She gone drink it," Pressy predicted. He drank some himself, from the bottle, and then marched back and forth with his hands clasped behind his head and his elbows jutting out.

Less and less reluctantly, the kitten sipped the reinforced goat's milk until the bowl was empty. Drake and Pressy watched without comment. There was a little thunder, faint and low, from far out over the Gulf.

The kitten hopped about at their feet and struck at imaginary small prey, but for the most part behaved as if perfectly sober. Pressy was disappointed. "Why she don't fall down?" he asked Drake. "Always every time I drink it, I gone fall down." A louder clap of thunder drove the kitten back under the little house.

"Kitten don't fall down when she drink brandy," Drake said.

"That's right," Pressy said. "We know that because of we have make a scientifig esperiment."

They sat on the broken steps, side by side, waiting for the next thing to happen.

"Now que pasa?" Drake asked.

"Now a storm," Pressy said.

. . .

"*Nagasaki.*" Roderick Chambers took a step backward and then a step to the right, getting closer to the lamp on the wall. "*The Forgotten Bomb.*"

Ah, God, Mr. Cheung thought.

He would have been able to hear the people breathing around him, if not for the gusts throwing the first raindrops at the boarded-up windows. His own breath was coming too rapidly. A vibration of the storm shook the room's shadows. This wasn't a particularly bad squall, certainly not a cataclysmic one. This early in the wet season came rough weather; hurricanes arrived late. By the compelling power of reason, he tried to drive away the fear that merely by reading about this bomb they might wipe themselves off the earth tonight.

Drake helped his mother drag the window-boards out from under the house as the rain came down and Mike howled inside. Belinda said nothing, but managed to convey, by flattening the look of her face and moving with a certain weary, triumphant pomp, that Drake should have accomplished this chore many days ago, that he shouldn't be out on the Ocean after fish because he was only ten, that he shouldn't be living with Pressy and Alfo, that he was a demon and a criminal. The boards were slightly mushy and eaten away by salty dampness around the edges. In places their borders were too flimsy to give good purchase to the wooden latches that were supposed to hold them, and by puckering and unpuckering her lips repeatedly as she twisted one of the latches Belinda made it plain that Drake was also somehow responsible for this. Blinded by his sins, he ran a toe painfully against the battery she'd moved from the windowsill to the floor.

The wind was letting up a little as the rain fell harder, but the curtain of beads over the door still chattered against the door-board as they latched it in place, and then the beads scraped back and forth across the wood like something clawing its way in. Now they were reasonably snug against the storm. Mike stopped crying, the candle flames stopped dancing in the glass jars, and the rain stopped sounding like death. "What you want aqui?" Belinda asked Drake, as if just discovering him here.

"I got a sick stomach," Drake said.

She made motions of unplugging a bottle and tipping it back. "Party on down."

"Es ain't a party. Come from I ate until almost ten green coconuts."

Belinda grabbed Mike and violently washed his face with salt water from the clam bucket, and then wiped her hands back and forth on her new denim skirt while Mike let out with fresh cries.

"I sick. I got to stay here. Es raining," Drake said.

"Oh!" Belinda said. "Ha! Hm!"

Somebody pounded hard on the door-board.

"You gone break my door, Pressy!" Belinda shouted. She unlatched the door-board and moved it aside.

Pressy was holding his dog Sarge by the scruff of the neck and peering through the bead curtain.

"Ain't no party aqui," Belinda said.

"Sarge got those looney toons," he explained, "that's why we gone stay here tonight." The dog pushed his way through to the stove where he tried to hide under his own flattened ears. Pressy hurried in after him.

Within a couple of hours, it looked as if nobody wanted Roderick Chambers to go on. They interrupted his hoarse reading with questions they knew he couldn't answer: Was this the first bomb? Was this the last bomb? "Why is it talking about Japan?" a fisherman asked, standing up in the back and pounding on the window-board for attention. Thunder answered him. Meanwhile the listeners argued among themselves. Some claimed that the book wasn't true, that it was only a storybook. While they fidgeted and bickered, Roderick Chambers read silently to himself, until people shouted, "Read! Read!" He picked up at the place he'd reached alone. *"Mrs. Yoshiyama was peeling potatoes in her kitchen, and she watched in disbelief as the potato skins flew out the window a second before she was hurled to the floor."* Immediately there were new interruptions as the disbelievers tried to point out that nobody could have known whether this woman, Mrs. Yoshiyama, had been peeling potatoes or oranges: it must be a story. "We traded a *boat* for this!" someone yelled.

But the talk ceased, only the strokes of rain on the field outside and the occasional thunder competed with Roderick Chambers when he read an account of three men who'd flown an airplane over the city soon after it was bombed:

"Lieutenant Komatsu had never seen anything like it . . . A huge volcanic eruption with many layers of smoke rising from it. The black cloud ring was churning like a thing alive . . . The sun coming from behind gave the illusion that the cloud was undergoing instantaneous changes of colors—from red to blue to yellow . . ."

Mr. Cheung believed he was dreaming of a previous birth-and-death existence as he visualized what Roderick Chambers recited. Which one was I? he asked himself.

". . . he opened the cabin window and stretched his hand out. Quickly, he pulled it back in. Even with a glove on, it was as if he had plunged his hand into live steam . . ."

I was there, Mr. Cheung told himself. The locks were

blown from the doors. As the bombs fell, already we were forgotten. The bomb said, I will not remember.

"*All Nagasaki surely had been destroyed. And he was about to fly into that ominous cloud. Cold perspiration . . .*"

I was there. My eyes burned up. It was the only thing I felt. I remember.

"I can't stand it!" someone shouted suddenly.

My eyes burst into flames. I died.

"That's just what it says in the book!" Roderick Chambers said. "Look here—you read it: '*I can't stand it!' someone shouted suddenly, and when Lieutenant Komatsu turned he saw Chief Petty Officer Umeda vomiting.*"

A man in the front turned around to address everyone. "The book is telling us what to say."

Thunder clapped and a window-board fell in, dangling by a couple of nails. There were screams. "Shut that back up," Roderick called over the noise.

"But that's what it says in the book!" the man he'd handed the volume to said. " '*Close . . . the . . . window,' he gasped. 'Close it! Quickly!'* " The man waved the volume around above his head, and Roderick Chambers snatched it back.

By now Mr. Cheung was so convinced that he was only dreaming that he felt let down and disappointed in the whole experience. It wasn't real, it was only a dream. His seasickness seemed to be coming back. He had a terrible headache and he felt nauseous.

"*. . . either the fumes or the heat,*" Roderick Chambers read above the protests of the hysterical listeners, "*had given him a terrible headache and he felt nauseous.*"

Because they were all in the house now—her two youngest sons, her baby brother—Belinda felt large and strong: older, but older in a way she liked. She sat on the bed beside Drake and Mike, both of them curled up against the chill. Pressy took it on himself to throw more wood into the stove, trying to show the world that he'd come around here to be a help. The noise of rain grew smaller, then louder. The storm's eye was passing. "Only one who walk out in a lightning gone be Bruce Lee," she said, stroking Drake's hair.

"Es who?" Drake asked, lying on his side and turned away from her, staring slack-mouthed at the sleep that was coming over him.

"Bruce Lee. He was all over letric, with letricity for eyes. He could hear letricity inside you and tell you if you lying or not."

"Where Bruce Lee come from?" Drake asked.

"Come from China. Down deep in a hole in the world."

"Mama, you telling me bullshit?"

"Es a story," she said.

"Es letric inside the batteries," Pressy told them. He was sitting against the wall, with a view of Sarge in the kitchen, trying not to flinch when the thunder rolled over the Army. The lightning was far away now as the storm's whipping tail passed east by northeast, up toward Marathon. He listened to Belinda's stories and kept watch on his dog, willing to wait all night, if it had to be that way, for Sarge to get back his courage.

Mr. Cheung wasn't alone in thinking that reading about the bomb had brought on a totally destructive storm. The others wept and shouted that the reading must be stopped. "We need a discussion time!" "We're bombing the Keys!" "That doesn't make *sense*," Roderick Chambers insisted, but he was obviously nervous himself, probably, Mr. Cheung thought, because he faced a wall of panic. "Make sense?" people cried. "Make sense?"

When lightning struck the field outside, its glare through the gaps in window-boards lit up a room full of people whipping their heads down between their knees in unison. "There's nothing to be afraid of! We're in the best building! The lowest stone building, the strongest!" Roderick Chambers shouted.

Ah, God, Mr. Cheung thought.

On the trip home the next day, Mr. Cheung didn't get seasick. He enjoyed the ride, though it went on a little too long, and he had a good time leaning on the rail and sighting at the shoreline so that it seemed to be going by too swiftly to keep track of. The beaches were hard as slate and almost yellow after the heavy rain, imbedded with boards and branches and lacquered with black leaves and red and white oleander petals. The sea was bottle-green. Everything was invisible below its cloudy surface, and so the *Catch* stayed out in the deeper water.

The reading of the Nagasaki book, the attempt at understanding, the reconciliation of the Twicetown and Marathon Societies, the whole experience had been a failure. Now the confusion was only deeper and more troubling. It would have been easier, Mr. Cheung believed, to have accepted their ignorance about the destruction if only they all hadn't been aware that sixty years ago, any little child could have told them all about it. "I'm giving up on that kind of history," he told Maxwell, who had done his turn comforting Bobby Calvino, today's victim of seasickness.

"I know," Maxwell said. "I think maybe it just keeps us away from the practical things."

As they passed Big Pine Key, a tall island given over mostly to rice paddies, they saw naked boys above the water on a low cliff, jumping on the lip of it until the soil that had been undermined by the waves gave out beneath them and they tumbled into the Gulf, laughing at life while their families thought they were at work in the fields. "Is Maxwell," Mr. Cheung asked, "your first name or your second name?"

"It's one name." Apologetically Maxwell added, "It's very simple that way." He went down in Mr. Cheung's esteem for having thrown away part of his name. Later he surprised Mr. Cheung by saying, "I think there's an alien life-form inhabiting inside my body," and finally he disgusted the Orchestra Manager completely by telling him in confidence, as they were docking, "Our Society rejects too much. Some of that Voodoo may be a helpful thing, I think so."

SIX

Because he was thinking deeply, Mr. Cheung moved without appreciation of his feet along a route that wasn't the shortest one. By the time he took a minute to look around, he was over on the east side of town, ten minutes' walk from the road to the Army, where he'd been headed.

Hardly anyone lived on Twicetown's eastern edge. Fishermen toured the area in groups to keep the desechados from putting up shelters here, and within a few minutes Mr. Cheung passed one of these informal patrols. They eyed him closely and greeted him—"Buenas!" and "Hey there!"— and he wondered if any of them knew Fiskadoro. The seagoing people, from here to Marathon, all took an interest in one another. Maybe he should have told them the boy had returned.

He came out of an alley and walked alongside One.

The rubble of brick and concrete buildings One had plowed through had been moved back, over the years, to create a kind of stone arena in which it rested impressively, and this clear space of sand and chewed asphalt with an Atomic Bomb laid out in it had become a gathering place for political and religious functions. When a great man died he was brought here. The missile itself was almost as big around as a house. A person could count to six before the fastest runner in Twicetown raced from end to end. Its skin was scorched and welted, in some spots still olive drab, in others stripped of all paint and shiny as glass. The other one, the one called Two, was just a black warhead over-grown with grass in a field north of town. But One was intact, from head to tail. People said it was an American bomb that had gone off course.

Keeping left, Mr. Cheung entered a pocket of industry, passing the bottle factory and the candle factory, both of them closed now and awaiting the time when some flurry of demand would call forth a great man to pry the boards from their windows and take them through the cycle of confused life and premature death generally enjoyed by businesses along the Keys. There were other buildings in the neighbor-hood that had never hosted any such resurrections and inside of which the machines hulked inscrutably, scaring away the people who might have lived in them. Even Mr. Cheung walked past these places with a dread of something that lurked here hoping to churn people into grease.

William Park-Smith was waiting for him on the road out of Twicetown, resting in the shadow of a brick wall behind which grass grew up through an old foundation. He had one of his combat boots off and his face down in its mouth, apparently inhaling the odor of leather.

He hopped up to join Mr. Cheung, walking along lopsidedly with one bare foot. "Do you think we'll get the clarinet?" he asked.

"It isn't about the clarinet," Mr. Cheung said. "It's about my pupil Fiskadoro, who's returned now."

"Yes, yes. But I thought of the clarinet."

With nothing to talk about, Park-Smith developed an ear for the enticements of vendors, delaying the whole trip several times only to buy nothing in the end, until the two musicians passed beyond the fringes of town, beyond the vendors and then into the region where the asphalt gave out and the dirt thoroughfare, heavily trafficked with nomads and beggars, cut through a kind of beach jungle interrupted by the rubble of buildings. Park-Smith stopped and took off his other combat boot, then walked along barefoot beside the Orchestra Manager carrying a shoe in either hand.

He wished that Mr. Cheung would chat about a few matters. The walk seemed longer without any conversation to relieve its sameness. The Manager was very preoccupied. He lived too much inside his head. "We'll require, you know, to spend the night there," Park-Smith concluded, acknowledging the lateness of the hour—the sun was low in the west. "Won't tomorrow be soon enough?"

"It's urgent. The young brother Drake came to me this morning."

"Yes, yes—you sent him to me." Immediately Park-Smith was worried. "Don't you remember?"

In another hour they reached the Army. The fences that once had separated the compound from civilian Florida had long since disappeared, and the coconut and date palms that seemed to gush from every square meter of unpopulated earth overcame the dwellings, so that the habitation blended into the countryside around it. Now it was sunset. Among the trees the shade was no longer shade, but darkness.

Behind Fiskadoro's house, just offshore, an old fishing boat hovered in a violent, rusty light, attracting villagers. And there was Martin, known lately as Cassius Clay Sugar Ray, standing in water up to his bare knees and resting a hand on the anchor line. The late hour gave to the beach an ineffable wanness. The boat and the people seemed small and far away.

"He has a boat now?" Park-Smith said when he recognized their half-brother.

Mr. Cheung stopped and looked. "We should have guessed," he said. "They traded a boat for the book."

"The Nagasaki book!"

"We should have guessed."

They were only a few meters from Fiskadoro's door, but they waited to greet Martin—who was waving to them as he marched through the water hefting a sun-bleached canvas duffel bag—because in any situation it was always best to find out, first of all, what Martin's presence might signify.

"The white bodyguard," Park-Smith said, seeing that Martin was accompanied.

"Ha! Ha! Ha!" Martin shouted as he and the white man approached. He dropped his duffel bag on the sand and patted Park-Smith's shoulder and said, "How is our father?" He shook Mr. Cheung's hand and said, "How is our mother?" It was an old joke; both of these people were dead.

Martin indicated the white man, who rested a rifle across his shoulder. "Sammy Goodman. Tony and Billy are my brothers, good men. Sammy Goodman is a good man. I am called Cassius Clay Sugar Ray. I am a good man."

Mr. Cheung said, "Your new name has reached me."

"You traded a boat with the Marathon Society?" Park-Smith asked. Martin only smiled as if he didn't understand the question, and Park-Smith said, "Perhaps?" But Martin only smiled.

"Why did you come today?" Mr. Cheung asked.

"A lot is interest me," Martin said, "about the boy Fisk-adoro, your once pupil."

"What?" Park-Smith said. "He was kidnapped. He was returned."

"A person have told me Fiskadoro is not the same."

"Of course not," Mr. Cheung said. "An ordeal, he's had an ordeal."

"A person have told me very, very not the same." Martin picked up his burden and they all went in.

Inside, the quonset hut suffocated under layers of odors—smoke, mildew, mackerel both fresh and putrefied, fruit rinds dwindled to a state of fermentation—and at first Mr. Cheung stayed close to the door and the fresh air. Villagers waited outside in the dusk, keeping their voices low.

Martin lit a candle by the bed and moved around the place lighting others, making a big show out of each match.

Fiskadoro, the cause of all the trouble, lay in bed in the next room with a grey sheet full of holes pulled up to his chin, and the mother sat on an old car seat with her hands straight-armed onto her knees and her shoulders curled, hiding her breasts. She was in shock. So was the boy. Fiskadoro's hair was caked with a thick even layer of mud that made him look large-browed and bald. He wore a headband of tiny shells. He had holes in each ear, top and bottom, with strings tied around through each hole. Mr. Cheung had seen such insignia among the swamp-people. He came close to the bed and peered down. "Fiskadoro. We want to lift up the sheet and have an examination." Fiskadoro looked right at him, but didn't acknowledge. As soon as Mr. Cheung drew the sheet back and saw the massive scab like a barnacle on the boy's crotch, he realized what had happened.

He'd been half-expecting it and remained unblinking, but Martin and Park-Smith started dragging the breath down their throats.

"Can you remember an accident, Fiskadoro?" Mr. Cheung asked his pupil.

The boy didn't answer.

The white bodyguard Sammy spoke up. "I promise you he don't remember." He glanced at the mother, as if perhaps he didn't like talking about it in front of her. "They fix it up so the boys don't remember."

"Who?"

Martin said, "Sammy and me have visited to these people. Sammy many times. He saw and he knows."

"They take this memory-juice," Sammy told them. "First you remember every single thing in the world, then you don't remember a-tall. Zip. Nothing. Nada," he added in what was evidently a polite attempt to get the point across.

"They have a big ceremony, lot of days long, when it's time to—" Martin pointed at Fiskadoro's crotch and sucked the breath through his teeth.

"Subincision," Mr. Cheung said. He drew the sheet back up to the boy's chin.

"Horrible. Horrible. Horrible," Park-Smith said.

"What they do," Sammy said, "they take the boys supposed to get cut up like this, and they recite out a whole lot of things to say—these old men recite it out at the boys all day long. Then sundown every day they take all this stuff and grind it up with *something*—blood, Jesus, I don't know *what*-all—"

"Mushrooms," Martin said, "and a one blue pill."

"—and when these boys drink it down, Sir, I swear they recite it all back, remember every word." The small man's white face was amazed. "I mean it takes *all night* to get it said, and these little—brown kids, they don't never miss a beat. Next night it's the same thing, only different speeches to learn. Three, four nights running they've got them out there in a clear spot by the village, cleaning out their brains, is how I'd say it, and then they get crazy and, Sir, I ain't lying, those young boys rip up their own peckers with a jagged rock. I ain't lying. Couple days after that, these same boys can't tell you their own name, plus I hate to tell you what they sound like every time they go to piss out a drink of water." He looked at the mother. "They heal up after a while," he told her.

"You saw this take place?" Mr. Cheung asked.

"Seen it three times. But I don't remember much."

"You drank the memory-juice?"

"*Hell* no. You don't think I'd wipe out thirty-two years of my life just to satisfy a load of niggers? Well, you know," he said quickly to Martin and William Park-Smith, "them *are* niggers—about the low level of them burros go hauling the carts around these islands. What it was, they kept me up two days straight and had me looking in a fire, till I couldn't've told you was I dreaming or was I real."

"I think," Martin said, "all what they have to remember back for the ceremony, es a lotta trash. Not important. The old fathers just only want the boys to forget. When es all done finish, the boys don't even know they name."

"Got a totally blank screen there," Sammy told them, "just like if you unplugged their heads."

"Do they know how to talk?" Park-Smith asked.

"They talk, they eat—everything, like anybody else," Sammy said. "But first of all they blank out every two seconds. Couple weeks they're regular again, but they never do get back the memories that happened before all that craziness, and the cutting."

Mr. Cheung had never heard of this. "Incredible."

"Horrible," Park-Smith said again.

"But if a person found out the source," Martin said.

"These swamp-people are the source," Park-Smith said. "That's obvious."

"But I think of the blue pill," Martin said, "and I wonder where does it come out of?"

"*Now* he puts a mark down on the map," Sammy said. "I was wondering what we come here about."

"The source of this kind of blue pill," Martin said. "A lot is interest me about a problem like that."

He lay flat under a sheet. There were men around him. Over his face a black face came down and said, "You met the Quraysh. You know who these Quraysh are? Mohammed's family, exact. Mohammed's tribe from over there."

"Over there happens to be half the world," a small one, scratching his big belly, interrupted with disgust. "You have a private history, a religion—privado, it's your own, all your own."

The black one's sense of wounded dignity was so powerful it seized the air like a color. "I studied it in the Koran, The Human Bible, The Book of Mormon—"

"The *Holy* Bible."

"The *Human* Bible. It's new in Deerfield." The black man disappeared. "Lookyer. Attende. I got it all in my bag."

The one with the big belly disappeared. There was a doorway now, beyond which, in another room, sat a woman. Desire moved inside him and stung him between his legs.

A small man with a big belly appeared, holding books in either hand. "Where did you get these sacred books?"

A black man snatched the books away from him. "Deerfield is the middle of civilization, not Cuba. Cuba ain't. Deerfield machines *print* books. See?" The black one raised up a book. "Human Bible aqui. Cuba makes a big secret, but Deerfield gone print for everyone."

The other man rubbed his face with his hands. "The world is repeating itself. The story of the world is happening again."

"You call me I'm a trash-man. But I bring books. I travel knowledge."

Fiskadoro attended their exchange carefully, understanding and remembering nothing.

When Park-Smith elected to sleep on Martin's boat, Mr. Cheung went along with the idea, against his better judgment. The motion of water was soothing to him—he felt he'd developed an immunity to seasickness—but there was no telling how many of the things around him on this vessel were poison. His half-brother had lamps, a kerosene stove, fresh canvas, thousands of pre-End matches in tiny wooden packages, no shortage of rope or diesel fuel. He was called a "traveling man," or a "trash-man," the respectful and disrespectful terms for a pirate of the land, a scavenger and purveyor of radioactive goods. Only a few of them operated below Key Largo, wearing their protective suits as they gathered and transported various useful items just like the ones on this boat, taking off their suits and risking contamination long enough to barter their goods away without arousing the anxiety of the head-men, town councils, and Societies who bought them. But Mr. Cheung didn't know, absolutely, that Martin sold contamination. He knew very little about his half-brother. "You're a ghost, aren't you?" Mr. Cheung guessed, watching Martin light his stove to warm some coffee. "You deal between the two worlds."

"Es expectable. I'm a half-and-half. Like the boy."

"Why did they take him?"

"Remember they losted a boy on West Beach?"

"The subincised boy. The one who drowned, yes."

"Well well," said Martin, who knew all about trading, "now they made a trade."

"But they didn't keep Fiskadoro. He couldn't have come by himself. Why do you think they let him go?"

"What they gonna worry where he live? He belong to them now."

"It makes a little sense," Mr. Cheung admitted. "Not much."

The coffee was warm. Martin turned off the stove and gave him a cup.

"This will keep me awake," Mr. Cheung said, looking with distaste at his coffee in its metal mug. He sipped of it; he didn't like coffee, particularly when it might be radioactive, but he would rather have been contaminated than impolite. He held the mug between his knees and watched the brown liquid keep its level against the boat's subtle rocking. "You've been among those people?"

"The Quraysh," Martin said. "The original first tribe of Mohammed."

"They aren't the Quraysh. That's your fantasy."

"I believe what they told to me. They told to me, We are the Quraysh."

"What happened to you when you went visiting? Is this your trouble I've heard about?"

"What you heard?"

"Nothing. Only that you had some trouble up north."

"I got the wafer. The other traders wanted it, but the elders said no more trading after me."

"And now they don't want you up in North Deerfield," Mr. Cheung said.

Martin smiled falsely and swirled his coffee in its mug. "Be a lotta business right here to keep me. I tired of the north."

It was a familiar story. Mr. Cheung withheld comment.

Martin sat down across from him on the edge of the other bunk in the small cabin, their knees almost touching. "I have some of the wafer."

"Wafer?"

"First they making a liquid, the memory-juice. When es dry, they got you call him a wafer. I have one. I traded to them."

"Will it work? Will it make me remember?"

"You?"

Mr. Cheung was surprised he'd said it. But he wanted to remember his previous lives.

"We give it to the *boy*," Martin said. "Maybe he have memories where to find the blue pill."

Mr. Cheung felt desire turning him into someone else. "Give it to me!" He ached for want of it. He was angry.

He half-woke in a dark place, lying on his side. He started to turn over and the pain woke him fully. He stood up through the pain, moving in search of an end to it. He found a person, a child. He found a woman and got near to the smell of her, touched her leg in the dark, found her knee, and slid his hand up higher. She moved a little and opened her legs. He felt of the hair between her legs and moved his fingers in it, looking for something. She woke up and closed her legs with great strength, and slapped him around the head. He felt how she kept her wrist loose, in a way that was familiar, so that the fingers whipped hard against his ears, his nose—one caught the corner of his left eye. He fell back and the pain struck him again between his legs. "Fiskadoro—you can't sleep here no more." It was dark. He didn't know who she was. Or who he was.

Martin took his brothers to Twicetown on his boat the next day. The weather was as expected for this time of year, cloudy and offering rain by the afternoon. Mr. Cheung told himself he'd come back here soon, but right now he'd had enough excitement. He didn't even want to see the boy.

He wanted to avoid the mother, too, but Belinda waded out to the boat through the high tide to have a word with him.

She looked up into his face, and knocked on the side of the boat as if she thought he couldn't see her. And in fact, he'd been behaving as if he couldn't: though it was time to say goodbye, he hadn't yet said hello—he still resented Belinda for denying him the clarinet. "How are you?" he said.

"Oh, about in a middle," she said. The engine throbbed deeply. It was hard to make out her words. She squinted up at him. "I got a trouble in my tit, Manager. Dureza."

Now he wished he'd shown her more kindness. "I'm very sorry."

"Es a medicine on that boat he fix me?"

Mr. Cheung shrugged his shoulders and showed her the empty hands of somebody who couldn't help.

"Seem like getting bigger," she said.

"Often these things are nothing," he told her. "Cysts, we call them. They don't grow."

"Not today," she said.

"Sí. Not today."

"No medicine?"

"I'm very sorry."

"Okay. No problem." She didn't leave, but stood hip-deep in water with one hand flat on the side of the boat. He waited while she looked back at Sammy, the bodyguard, in the dirt before her house. In what Mr. Cheung felt must be an uncharacteristic display of good humor, the little white man was down on his haunches, copying every motion of the little boy Mike. The boy was getting annoyed. "The last night," Belinda said.

"What is it?"

"Fiskadoro, the last night. The last night he bothering me."

"Last night?"

"*Yeah*," she said. "He bother his own mother."

He really didn't know what the woman meant. "Fiskadoro is very—sick." He wished for another word, but it was the only word that came. "He'll get better. Not now, but in a few days, a few weeks. I'll look in on him. I'll come often," he promised.

"Keep touch," she said, and turned and waded back toward her house.

One night in the middle of the night, just before he forgot it all again, Fiskadoro remembered a lot of what had happened and where he'd been. And he remembered the people he'd been among.

It was no struggle for them to live, but it took all day, they thought. They thought they had everything they needed—some plants, some huts, some ceremonies. They never appealed for help to the ghosts of their friends and neighbors. They thought the soul was a blank and empty thing that did nothing all day long, and as far as they were concerned there weren't any ghosts living in their village. But they were wrong: their air was unbreathable because it was turned into syrup by the cries of ghosts, the presences of ghosts, the secrets of ghosts.

On sunny days the snakes lay out on the trail soaking up the light, and they took any snake with two heads, except for the venomous coral snakes, and instantly ate it alive in order to swallow its strangeness and power. In the case of two-headed coral snakes, these they fed with frogs stuffed with mushrooms, and when the rapto came over them, the two heads would start quarreling until one head struck the other and the snake killed itself. And the tattoo so many of them wore, the line with a loop at one end, like the empty outline of a spoon, was the snake trying to swallow its first head with its second mouth.

It took him a long time to learn these things about these strangers. Even to see them took him a long time, because they weren't his people. At first they resembled nothing, because he didn't know this place.

Once he'd come over the dunes, whatever he knew about the world was useless. He had to start over. Each day he learned something that was obvious.

He learned something each day, but he had no thoughts. Every time he started to think about something, there came another overpowering idea—he was hungry, hungry, hungry. Muddy hands offered him plants dangling filthy leaves, and he really didn't know they expected him to bite into these things. They tore open big bugs with popping eyes that lived in the water like fish, and held the pale meat in his face, and he cried. They showed him how to eat. He knew how to eat, but he didn't know these plants and bugs were food. They knew the plants and bugs were food, but they didn't realize he knew how to eat. All of it was raw. They had fires in their village, but they didn't seem to believe these fires were meant for cooking anything but potions. He couldn't learn to like this food, but he learned to use it like medicine to cure his hunger. His head cleared and he looked around himself.

Fires sat on humps of earth in a swampy region and lit up the undersides of cypress leaves. Among the fires and trees there were small huts made of twigs, and he sat in the doorway of one of them. The ground dampened the seat of his pants.

In his mind he saw himself climbing over the dunes in pursuit of a girl from these swamps, but he didn't know how many days ago this had happened. He thought of the places he'd left behind—West Beach, the steel music and dancing, and the Army. It came to him he didn't want to be here. But it didn't occur to him that he might leave, that he could travel. He assumed that he was dreaming and that he'd get out of this place only by waking up.

Swamp-people went in and out of the huts or squatted before the fires. A lot of them looked like desechados—humpbacked, or armless, or moving carefully in a way that said they were blind or drunkenly in a way that said something was missing in their heads. Fiskadoro shut his eyes hard, tensed the fibers of his body, and told himself to wake up. He shouted out loud and slapped his own face. When he opened his eyes, he was still sitting in the hut's doorway and he was still surrounded by desechados moving through firelight under cypress trees that hung down out of a roof of darkness.

He couldn't hear the Ocean, only the wind in the trees. He didn't see any dogs or cats. Bugs and frogs made sounds that blended together into a great engine of noise. There was someone—more than one—inside the hut, looking at his back. He moved out of the doorway, backed up against the structure's prickly wall, and put his arms around his shins and his forehead down on his knees. Believing that if he slept in this world he'd wake up in the one he'd left, he relaxed as much as he could.

The next morning the air was so cool and grey and wet that

it made him cough to breathe it. A woman who had no arms or hands, only fins like a fish, came and watched him. A couple of little boys came around later and had a look at him and laughed. For a while he was alone, and then two men who seemed to think they were important people, who weren't desechados but were nevertheless of a very small size, came and talked to him. In the usual way of dreams, he couldn't hear them and they couldn't hear him, but they managed to communicate. He made them understand that he was cold and thirsty. They gave him water in a plastic canteen just like the ones at home and a muddy blanket with a hole in it that he could put his head through. They told him he was not like other men.

By the morning's end the air was a little warmer. Things got more visible, but the roof of branches overhead was so thick he never got a look at the sun. All day people came and watched him for a while as if he were a show. His stomach burned with shame, fear, and disgust. One little desechado boy had eyes on either side of his head, almost where his ears were. Turning sideways, he watched Fiskadoro with one eye for a while, and then he turned and watched Fiskadoro with the other one.

After the day had gone on for longer than most days in Fiskadoro's experience, the two small men showed up again.

At first the two small men didn't talk. A woman who had no nose, only two large nostrils in the middle of her face, brought a hollow log, like a tiny boat, with more leaves and more bugs riding in it. The two men cracked the bugs open and started eating the meat. When they offered a bug to Fiskadoro, he took it and cracked it open. They offered him water from a plastic canteen.

He asked the two men to tell him how to wake himself up.

They told him he'd changed a lot. He wasn't anything like the person they used to know.

He said that didn't make any sense. He ate some more of the bug's fishy meat, which might have been tasty if cooked up with some spices.

They asked him if he'd taken on the body of another person.

He told them he didn't think so. It looked like the same one to him.

Then why, they asked him, was he no longer like other men?

He insisted he was the same. It was everyone and everything else that had changed.

This was something they wanted to ponder. They left him alone for the rest of the afternoon, while desechados and other swamp-people came and watched him, all of them with thick helmets of mud caked on their heads and holes in their ears dangling knots of colored string, bits of metal or bright pebbles. He didn't leave his place next to the hut—he was afraid that if he moved around in the dream, he'd find himself in the wrong place when he woke up. He was already so far from the Ocean in this dream, so distantly removed from the real world, that there wasn't any sunset here. At the end of the day the shade just got larger and more ominous and moved up from under the trees and into the sky.

The longer he stayed here in this dream, the more people and things it produced. The floor of it, which had been only a dull rug with warts of huts and humps of fires, changed and yielded up its details: ground-running vines of various thicknesses, tiny grassy plants so low their round leaves were nearly imbedded in the dirt, beetles and ants on their errands along the reach of vines and underneath the fuzzy saw-toothed leaves of another kind of plant that was also everywhere underfoot. The dream's undistinguished grey walls turned out to be a congestion of cypress and, in the wet hollows, mangrove and some other trees he couldn't call by name, all woven together with slender green vines and barred across by frail dark ones. Out of this swamp-growth the patchy clearing of fires and huts had been hacked and burned, leaving too many trees, just the same, to let the day down. Faces came and went, and he started recognizing some of them. He saw also that the times for doing things were regular. They had three meals a day here, as in real life, and about three hours after dark everybody went quiet and slept through the night, and arose in the grey light to get together around the fires and look out of their sleep-blankened faces until they were wide awake and there was something to do. It was the first dream he'd ever peed in. They all, Fiskadoro too, did their business in pots behind the huts, and every morning people took the pots and dumped them out somewhere beyond the dream's living walls.

The two men came to see him each day. One was Zeid, with a face impossible to look at, it was so much like an animal's: black and furry, and as flat as if a heavy rock had been set down on it one day. The older and more presentable one was Abu-Lahab, who was in charge of all the fires—nobody was allowed to tend them but Abu-Lahab. Sometimes they talked about nothing, asking Fiskadoro to tell them about his life in the Army and to explain, as best he could, what had happened to change him. But as far as Fiskadoro knew, he hadn't changed at all, not since the day he was born, and he couldn't understand the question.

One afternoon, in order to explain themselves a little better, they took Fiskadoro out behind his hut and asked him what he thought he looked like.

He told them he didn't think he looked like anything.

But down here, they wanted to know, down here where he peed, down here where he was a man? What did he think he looked like down here?

He told them he didn't know what to tell them.

Zeid wore a denim skirt. He lifted the hem of it and showed Fiskadoro that there was something wrong.

Fiskadoro didn't know what to say. He felt sorry for Zeid, but there was nothing he could do about whatever had happened to make the old man just as ugly between his legs as he was in his face.

Abu-Lahab talked to Zeid in frustration. Finally Abu-Lahab also lifted the hem of his own skirt. There was something wrong with him, too.

Did Fiskadoro understand what they were getting at?

I see there's something wrong with you, Fiskadoro said. Your penes are all banged up.

We're like other men, they told him. And you're not.

Throughout the rest of the day, until the somber afternoon turned black and Fiskadoro couldn't see them anymore, Zeid and Abu-Lahab brought other men around who lifted the hems of their skirts or unhooked the flies of their pants, and showed him. Fiskadoro discovered that they were telling the truth. He wasn't like these other men.

A couple of days after Fiskadoro had recognized this fact about himself, Abu-Lahab came along to Fiskadoro's hut and sat down beside him. Was he feeling all right? was the first question he asked, and Fiskadoro told the old man that he was feeling fine, but got cold at night. Abu-Lahab was delighted with this answer. Did the boy know that he was the keeper of fires here, and that his name, Abu-Lahab, meant Father of Flames? He promised to start making the fires a lot higher and hotter.

Fiskadoro thanked him, but Abu-Lahab didn't leave right away. Instead he began clearing his throat and shifting around as if the ground were alive and he'd sat down on it by mistake, and told Fiskadoro that a long time ago there was a village where the young men and women grew restless. People from far away kept visiting their village and spreading all kinds of lies about a place where everyone was always happy, where a party went on day after day without stopping, where everybody danced, ate food, drank liquor, and made love. As soon as they'd had a little time to think about this never-ending party, the young people wanted to go. One morning before anybody else was awake, they all held their breath so they wouldn't make a sound and left the village together. It took them several days to reach the place, and when they arrived they found out that these lies they'd been hearing were almost true—people were dancing, getting drunk, making love. But nobody knew them there. To gain courage among strange people, the youngsters drank too much wine and one of them got drunk and fell in the sea. The others ran home to their elders. The whole village felt terrible. The youngsters were ashamed because they'd been tricked by lies and had lost a friend. But the trouble with a lie is that it's easier to believe than the truth. After a while the same young people forgot what had really happened, and one morning they all left again when there was no one awake to stop them. They went back to the party, saw once again that they'd only tricked themselves, saw that they'd always be strangers at this gathering, and started back home. In a little while they noticed that the friend they'd lost was with them, traveling along some distance behind. It was the same person, the same soul, and they recognized him. But a soul has no name and has nothing to say. Forever and ever, a soul is like a baby who hasn't been born, to whom nothing has happened yet. And so a soul with a new body has a new face and a new name, and remembers new things. Their friend's soul didn't remember who it was supposed to be. It began crying and talking the wrong language. To keep it from running away, its friends had to beat its new body with their hands until it was quiet. Then they carried the soul of their good friend, which was now inside a completely different body and remembered completely different things, back to its home. But the soul's new eyes had never seen its old home, and it never remembered. Still, still, still, Abu-Lahab insisted, it was the same soul.

Fiskadoro said nothing, because he felt only contempt for this idea. There were ghosts everywhere who had the same names, the same memories, and the same friends and relatives that they'd had when living. The kind of soul Abu-Lahab talked about wasn't any kind of soul at all. Their twisted notions about these things explained why they didn't see any of the ghosts among them, walking around their village, sitting beside the fires, wandering in the dark. These swamp-people were concerned only with the future, with things that would happen at some later date—Zeid and Abu-Lahab talked about it all the time—a ceremony to be held soon, in which Fiskadoro and some younger boys would be changed until they were like other men.

When he saw the white trader visiting various huts around the village and heard him say, "North Deerfield," Fiskadoro recognized the words and thought of Ernest Bodine, the horrible white gambler, talking to Cassius Clay Sugar Ray in the North Deerfield. But the trader didn't look at all like Cassius Clay Sugar Ray's depiction of a North Deerfield person. He had no fangs, and wasn't much bigger than Fiskadoro. He wore tall slick boots that kept his feet dry, and a canvas belt with a gun and a canteen hanging off it, but otherwise he looked like anyone.

The villagers didn't seem to mind that this white man walked around the place bothering everybody. Nobody traded with him, but they were all happy to pass the time and accept his gifts. He ate their food, slept in a hut, went out on the trails with the men looking for two-headed snakes, and generally seemed to be having a friendly visit out here in the muddy swamp. Now and then he rested with his back to the warmth of a fire and watched the people go by, looking for somebody to answer his questions.

Eventually the trader came to ask Fiskadoro the same two questions he asked everyone.

"You like candy, boy? You know where they get them little pills, boy?"

The man said his name but it came out without sound, "———." He smiled out of a small and innocent face, hunkering down where Fiskadoro sat against a tree and offering him a red ball of sugar candy.

Fiskadoro took the candy and put it on his tongue. He closed his eyes and floated away on its sweetness.

"Where you get all the stuff goes in the juice? Stuff they dry down to the wafers. Got to come out of some sort of hospital, right?"

Fiskadoro shook his head and shivered.

"Or maybe like a science laboratory, someplace like at."

The man waited a minute without getting an answer.

"Someplace where it ain't all bombed out."

Fiskadoro didn't know what this man called ——— was trying to say. Fiskadoro himself said nothing because he didn't talk in this part of the dream.

Later, when they came on one another as they both paced the village with nothing to do, Fiskadoro told the trader, "Cassius Clay Sugar Ray. Cassius Clay Sugar Ray say you take me West Beach."

The trader looked at him in surprise. "I could take you as far as Key Largo," he said.

"When?"

——— unhooked the canteen from his canvas belt and took a swallow. "I could take off about any time after the ceremony," he told Fiskadoro. "Whenever your business here is done with. How's at sound?"

When he heard these words, and saw the look on the white trader's face, Fiskadoro understood that his whole purpose in the dream was to go through the ceremony and make himself like other men.

While these people didn't see any ghosts, Fiskadoro considered himself a ghost among them, one of the waking world, and he took to wandering the village like the other less visible ghosts —a few hundred meters from end to end, a path that took him past the dark entrances of huts, through clouds of smoke and a mist of voices speaking a language that made no sense. The children liked him and sometimes followed him around, trying to touch his crotch or give him bits of food. A lot of the time he felt heavy and lifeless, and he started worrying that this wasn't a dream at all, but the real thing. Now in the evenings Abu-Lahab built up the fires so they leapt and flared, and the stormy light yanked at the shadows so that the branches, vines, and huts seemed to cower back and then suddenly stand up and dance. The children began staying up late, drumming with sticks on hollow logs. When one night the drumming went on for hours past dark, Fiskadoro retreated into his hut and wouldn't come out, although he never slept inside it and hardly ever let himself be found under its roof and in its smelly darkness. The two people who lived there were nowhere around. He stayed inside, hunched in a ball on the floor of rotten grasses, and cried. A little later, Zeid appeared and called him out of the hut. Zeid was alone. His face was covered with orange clay that looked green in the odd light. Fiskadoro sat before the hut and saw Abu-Lahab moving from fire to fire, scattering handfuls of powder from a bag at his waist. Violet, red, and sky-blue smoke rushed out of the flames. Meanwhile Zeid knelt beside Fiskadoro and caked the boy's head with mud, using tender motions and speaking soft words, and then without warning he drove something sharp into Fiskadoro's earlobe. Shivering and crying, Fiskadoro waited while Zeid moved to his other side and drove the thorn or needle through the flesh of the other ear and then tied strings through each hole. In a way that was comforting, he took Fiskadoro's hand and told him that Mohammed lived a long time ago. The Sovereign Lord, the Lord God, the Mighty One, the Most High, gave Mohammed half His power and said, It isn't for you to keep. Give this power to the people, some to the men and some to the women. It will save them when Hell is brought near. Mohammed went to the people but most of them didn't believe he had any power. Show us your power, they said. Mohammed moved a whole mountain from one place to another, but the people said, That mountain has always been where we see it now. Show us again. This isn't a power to move, tear down, or raise up, Mohammed told them. It's the power to go on living after Hell is brought near, the power to make babies and keep generations living on the Earth. We already have that power, the people said, and left Mohammed alone. As they were leaving he said, No!—but when the Earth is beaten into dust, and your Lord comes down with the angels all around him, on that day you'll remember your mistakes, but what good will it do you to remember? Only one man believed Mohammed, and that man believed him only a little. When Hell was brought near, this was the only man who stayed upright. Everyone else was dead. The man stood on a mountain looking for a woman to make babies, but everyone else was dead. He called his dog, but his dog was dead. Then he heard Mohammed calling him: Are you dead? No, I'm alive, the man said. If I call you as you called your dog, Mohammed said, will you come? I'm coming, Mohammed, the man said. He crossed a valley and went half-way up a mountain to Mohammed's cave. He went inside but it was dark, and there was nothing there but a two-headed snake who talked to him with both heads at once. I am Mohammed, the snake said. You aren't Mohammed, the man said. No, but I'm a man, the snake said. You aren't a man, the man said. No, but I'm a part of a man, the snake said. You aren't a part of a man, the man said. No, but I can be part of a man if a man wants the power to make babies, the snake said. Eat me where you find me. Where I go between your legs, make yourself like me. Thus sayeth Mohammed, the snake said, and he was gone. The man looked all day for the cave's door and almost died of thirst before he found it. When he got outside he went to a stream and drank from it for half the night, and slept beside it for half the night. When he got up in the morning he opened his pants to relieve himself, and he found the two-headed snake there.

This is the man we, the Quraysh, all came from.

Fiskadoro didn't know what Zeid was talking about.

As the little man led Fiskadoro outside into the noisy village, boys were throwing firecrackers into the flames, howling and screaming as the explosives went off amid the sound of drums and tore apart the fires and tossed coals and brands at their feet. Older boys joined the two of them as Zeid led him wherever they all were going, the boys also driven along by painted men like Zeid. Some of the men carried a massive head, covered with sparkling beads, that wobbled above their ambling procession along the trail out of the village and looked back at the boys with jutting, outraged eyes.

For two days and nights the men fed Fiskadoro and the other boys only cookies tasting of dried mud, and made them learn speeches, longer and longer ones. They recited the speeches to the boys; and in unison, to their amazement, the boys recited the speeches back.

By the end of the first day Fiskadoro felt as if he'd run down a beach until his eyes were blind and his legs were numb and had leapt into the sea to find it full of words. The tide of them rose above his chest and throat and spilled into and out of his mouth.

Fiskadoro was the first to go. The older men hemmed him around, breathing and groaning in a way that would have scared him if he hadn't been senseless with exhaustion and hypnotized by fire. Words were said over him, and magic gestures accompanied the lowering of the big head down over his own. Through the glassy eyes of the head the brightness of the fire was shattered and magnified painfully. They knocked on the head with sticks and half-deafened him, but he managed to hear the rhythm of drums in the village blurring into one repetitive signal and the voices of women and children singing songs that made no sense.

He couldn't see straight, his neck was tired, his voice was loud and hollow in his ears when he spoke, and he had to breathe the same air over and over. By the time the ceremony began, although he remembered everything he was supposed to remember, he'd forgotten he was wearing another head, forgotten his voice hadn't always been huge and dark, forgotten what it was like not to be dizzy. He believed now that his head was outside of him, all around him, and that all around his head were his dreams and thoughts. He was inside-out. The wild tempo of the village percussionists cut through the trees and found his ears. The languid song of voices fell down like rain over the clearing.

"*The Sovereign Lord,*" Zeid said, shiny and orange across the fire, blasted by Fiskadoro's glass vision into a dozen of himself, "*the Holy One, the Giver of Peace, the Keeper of Faith; the Guardian, the Mighty One, the All-powerful, the Most High; the Creator, the Originator, the Modeler; the Unbecome, the Unborn, the Unmade; the Dissolver of Space and of Time, the Weaver of the Web of Appearances, the Inbreather and Outbreather of Infinite Universes; the Formless, Non-existent, Imperishable, and Transcendent Fullness of the Emptiness; the Voidness; the Eternal God.*

"Who has the power to mystify, how did he get it, how does he keep it?"

Fiskadoro said something but couldn't hear his own answer.

"Does there not pass over a man a space of time when his life is a blank?"

Fiskadoro knew the answer and said it.

"You touch the people and they dissolve. There is nothing left but you. And you will not remember."

But at this moment Fiskadoro remembered everything except his own name. He spent the next several minutes talking and talking and knowing just what to say. It was the right answer.

"On that day we shall ask Hell: 'Are you full?'"

Fiskadoro said, *"And Hell will answer: 'Are there any more?'"*

Then it was Fiskadoro's time. His mouth moved. He remembered every word they'd told him and he said them all at the proper times. Fiskadoro said, *"No! But when the earth is crushed to fine dust, and your Lord comes down with the angels, in their ranks, and Hell is brought near—on that day man will remember his deeds. But what will memory avail him?"*

He spoke for hours. Every word was in his mouth, and in his mind was his whole life. In his head a long tunnel had been opened, down which he could see all the way back to the moment he'd been born in hunger and fear onto a wall of light, and had awakened in this world between the mountainous thighs of his mother Belinda, and had been carried in her hands as if by two great clouds through an otherwise empty sky toward the comfort of her breast. He saw his father handing a china plate, a shawl, and a jug of brandy to the midwife. He smelled his father's hair and his parents' bedding, and recalled their conversation as they stood above him the first night he slept away from them on his own blanket, in a box.

All this time he held a sharp rock in his hand, waiting until the moment he wanted to make himself like other men. *"When the two keepers receive him, the one seated on his right, the other on his left, each word he utters shall be noted down by a vigilant guardian.*

"And when the agony of death justly overtakes him, they will say, 'This is the fate you have striven to avoid.' And the trumpet shall be sounded." He talked and talked. Toward the end he said stranger and stranger words, such words as "ephod," and "teraphim."

"And the going up to it was eight steps," he said.

He couldn't wait any longer.

"I will go down now!" he said. *"And see whether they have done altogether according to the cry of it, which is come unto me!"*

He couldn't see anything below the level of his shoulders, and even then could see only his own orange and black fire-blindness, and so Zeid had to guide his hand, the one that held the rock, when he cut himself.

After he cut himself with the rock, nothing happened for a long minute. People only breathed. *"We shall surely die,"* two voices said, *"because we have seen God."* But then there was only more breathing.

Someone took the head from his shoulders and led him by the hand back to his hut. Except for the fact that the fires seemed a little brighter than usual because he'd been so long in darkness, the swampy village of huts and people looked the same.

Fiskadoro lay in his hut with songs rising and falling outside it through the whole night. He was delirious. He didn't know who came to him at some point in the evening to pierce the tops of his ears, or who appeared later to bathe his forehead and bandage the wound between his legs with a dressing of pungent glue and boiled leaves. In the morning he was stiff all over and felt like a sack of wet, chilly sand.

He was very let down, because everything had been heading toward this, and it was nothing. His head was a blank, he felt no pain. Now he was like other men.

When the white trader named ———— was making ready to leave, he came to Fiskadoro and said, "You about set to take off?"

As far as Fiskadoro knew, he'd never seen this man or this place in his life before. Every time he looked at something, it came up before his eyes for the first time, unexplained and impossible to understand.

"They'll let you go, if you're ready to go," ———— told him. "You ready? You feel okay?"

"I fix now," Fiskadoro assured this man, whoever this man was. But he was lying. He wasn't at all well. He had a fever and couldn't keep food down and hurt, every minute, between his legs.

———— said, "Walk behind of me," and took Fiskadoro with him to the water.

People Fiskadoro had never seen before stood in a place he'd never been before and waved to him, whether hello or good-bye he didn't know, because only a minute after his words with ————, he'd forgotten whether he was coming or going.

"I don't set foot on that road," ———— said. "I go by the canal."

As Fiskadoro stepped onto the raft after this stranger, his memories suddenly returned to him for a minute. He remembered that he was asleep in a dream and that his memory had been coming and going, as it generally seemed to do in dreams.

They traveled on a raft along a channel like a long tin roof between two oceans of mangrove that stretched to the horizon and appeared to be the whole world. Alongside the channel ran a road. For a long time Fiskadoro lay on his side with a groin of fire while ———— pushed them forward with a pole.

Fiskadoro sat up when they came to a patch of dead grey mangrove. Another dead patch followed; and suddenly they were in a lifeless place. The branches were bare as far as he could see. He thought that he must have fallen from one dream into a deeper dream, and he panicked inside without moving, because he was getting farther and farther away from waking and might never get out.

"Miami ef el ay," ———— said.

For a long time, as Fiskadoro looked at it, he thought it was a storm of clouds, and then he assumed it was a big boat bearing down on them and he wondered what these people did when a boat was about to crush them. And then he realized that it was far away, it was made of houses, and then he began to understand that these houses were too far away to look at, that he was able to see them from this distance only because they were bigger than his mind could grasp.

Fiskadoro wept and trembled. "Was I ever see this before?"

"I couldn't say," ———— said.

Alongside them even the dead mangrove was gone. There was nothing but brown and silver ash streaked black in places. There was no end to it.

"Am I see it now?"

"I couldn't say," ———— said. "But I'd guess you were."

———— walked back and forth slowly on the raft, pacing out kilometer after kilometer across its brief length, pushing them toward the vision with his pole.

Fiskadoro saw that today was the day. Just by saying the words he'd made it come true. The earth had been crushed to fine dust. Someone had come down to see whether they had done altogether according to the cry of it, which was come unto him, and crushed it to dust. Fiskadoro put his arms around himself as the tears fell down his face. Today he would remember his deeds.

Ahead, on the road alongside the channel, tangled black autocars made a breakwater of wreckage, behind which, as far as Fiskadoro could see down the diminishing road, stretched a motorcade of burned-black cars and trucks, every size and shape, with their tires melted into the road's ash. He'd never seen so many. He didn't know where they were all going.

Every car—as the raft moved alongside them toward the clouds of buildings in the east—was being driven by a person made of brown bones who didn't shift or flicker or turn his head, but Fiskadoro knew they were all aware of him. There were riders in every car, big and little, twisted into different shapes, all made of brown bones. Now he understood that his purpose in this dream was to die. He was sobbing so hard now, and with such shame, that he couldn't make a voice to ask ———— what the death-ceremony meant by "Deeds."

"They got stuck here while the whole Everglades burnt up around them," ———— said.

There was a police car, with the red light on top. Even the police were skeletons.

"They couldn't get outa them cars, and they couldn't stay in."

Fiskadoro felt the deep echo of these words, as if he heard them spoken from another place, from tomorrow, when he would be awake. He waited for the two keepers to receive him, and the vigilant guardian to note down each word, and the trumpet-sound. He bawled out loud for his lost life. His memory left him and he looked up at the giant desolation in grief and amazement once again, but also for the first time.

When, in just a few minutes, he had forgotten all these things again, Fiskadoro was glad. He lay in his bed in the midnight listening to the Gulf wash and wash the hem of the island and remembered the act of remembering those experiences, and that was bad enough. Then, as if the burbling permutations of the water were carrying it away, his ability to remember anything at all was gone again. In the darkness his eyes were directed up toward the thatched ceiling, but as he didn't know the ceiling was there his sight reached on beyond it indefinitely toward nothing.

I think we should go out in the yard," Mr. Cheung told Fiskadoro.

"Why?"

"The odor." Mr. Cheung made a face. "Forgive me, this is your home, but it doesn't have a pleasant odor for me."

Fiskadoro made no objection and followed his teacher out into the yard before the quonset hut.

In the yard the boy looked here and there with some curiosity, because, Mr. Cheung guessed, he didn't remember the outhouse, the three fenceposts without a fence, or even the Gulf of Mexico from ten minutes earlier when he'd stood in the doorway and watched Mr. Cheung pass between these fenceposts, with this outhouse and that Gulf behind him, and walk up to the broken steps and say, "I'm Mr. Cheung," a name the boy had also probably forgotten. "Sit down," Mr. Cheung told him now. "Do you know who I am?"

"Who?" Fiskadoro wondered.

"I'm your teacher, Anthony Cheung. I'm going to show you some things I have in my bag." He jiggled the pillowcase he was carrying so that its contents clinked and rattled. "Please, let's sit down," he said, trying, himself, to get comfortable on the ground.

The boy sat down on the sand and leaned back on his elbows with his legs stretched out straight and his ankles crossed and seemed to think it was a joke when Mr. Cheung reached into his bag for an amethyst and said, "What is this?"

"Es a rock."

"Yes, all right. A rock, a stone." Mr. Cheung decided to limit this study to a very few objects, since most of those in his bag were all minerals from his collection—each with a different name, it was true, but to the boy, as he should have expected, one rock was like another rock. He set the amethyst on the sand between them. "Whatever you want to call it, that's fine," he said with some disappointment.

"Bueno, I gone call him a rock," Fiskadoro said.

"And this?"

"Es a thread thing," the boy told him.

"A spool. You're right, we put thread on it. We wind it around like so—ah? Yes. Spool."

"Espool," Fiskadoro said.

Now Mr. Cheung closed up the spool inside his fist. "What do I have here?"

"Espool."

"Have you heard that word before?"

"Yeh. Sure. Alla time."

Mr. Cheung set the empty spool down next to the amethyst and reached into his bag. "And this is a chicken."

"Naw!" Fiskadoro uncrossed his legs, leaned forward to take a better look. "Es a knife you know. Es ain't a chicking."

The teacher lay the clasp-knife down beside the spool. "I'm just testing you."

He drew out a small brass bell, many decades old, very valuable, from China, and dangled it from his fingers and let it ring softly.

"Es a bell."

"Right. Tell me all four things now. Point." Mr. Cheung showed him. "A bell, a—what."

"Es a bell, un espool, you got a knife, you got a rock."

"Very good. Okay, close your eyes now, put your hands—" Mr. Cheung showed him, and the boy covered his eyes with his hands. "Can you tell me what I have now?"

"Bell. Espool. Knife. Rock."

"Excellent. All right. I'll put them back in my bag. My bell, my spool, my knife. There—my rock—all in the bag."

"Sí," Fiskadoro said.

"Do you know who I am?"

"No," Fiskadoro said.

"Do you know where we are?"

The boy rubbed his face and suddenly looked frightened and ill. "Maybe. I think about it. Ask to me later."

"No, I won't ask you," Mr. Cheung assured him. "It's not at all important." He was wary of exciting the boy. He'd thought about this, about what it might be like to move from one day to the next, maybe from one hour to the next, and even, as looked possible in Fiskadoro's case, from one minute to the next, without taking with you any recollection of the previous one. Surely it would break a person. Surely it would maim the soul.

But then again—if he had no memory of having once had a memory?

In such a case, where was the soul at all—had it been erased? This boy's seriously ailing mother had to lock herself away from him at night: he crept after her with no more compunction than a little dog or a tomcat because, like a dog or a tomcat, he didn't know who his own mother was beyond that she was female. But even a dog behaved as if there were people, places, and things it recognized—did that kind of behavior mean it remembered them? If so, then this boy's soul lacked even the proportions of a dog's.

"What do I have in my bag?" he asked Fiskadoro.

"Some thing you got."

"Could you please tell me what things? Tell me four." He held up four fingers.

Fiskadoro shrugged. "A few thing. Whatever you need."

"Do you remember when I put them in my bag?"

"Sure. One time I remember."

"When?"

"Long time ago." Fiskadoro pointed with his chin at the distance.

"One time when you were a little boy?"

"Yeh. Before that maybe, I think."

By Mr. Cheung's estimation, not five minutes had passed. "What is your name?" Mr. Cheung asked him.

"My name Fiskadoro." He never failed to remember his name. But everything else got away from him.

"Let me take you back inside, Fiskadoro. And then I have to walk. It helps me think." He led the boy back toward his completely unfamiliar home to be given his lunch by the mother he'd never seen before. "There's a woman in there. She's not for you. Please don't bother her."

The day was unseasonably crisp. With the noon sun directly overhead the water was a blackness, not a liquid. His hands clasped behind him and his head bowed, he walked in under the Army's high ceiling of palm leaves, and as he continued on the path he perceived beneath his feet an alternation of light with shadow. Would Fiskadoro see it? Looking down at his feet in a spot of brightness, would he remember his feet in the shade? Would Fiskadoro, in fact, looking down at his feet, even remember the rest of himself—his hands, his head? If he didn't remember the inside of his house when he was out-of-doors, did he also forget the out-of-doors, even the *fact* of the out-of-doors, when he was inside? And if he were blindfolded a few minutes, would he forget what it was like to see—would he forget there was such a thing as "seeing"?

In the clearing around the well, the sweaty-faced neighbor-women were gossiping and cleaning rice, tossing handfuls of it in the air over straw mats and letting the wind seize away the dust and chaff. Respectfully they silenced themselves as the thinker passed.

He'd been assured by Martin and Martin's companion Sammy that Fiskadoro's memory would come back to him in a while—though they didn't seem to think he'd ever remember his past—but, for now, each time the boy witnessed the sunrise he saw it for the first time.

There was something to be envied in that. In a world where nothing was familiar, everything was new. And if you can't recall the previous steps in your journey, won't you assume you've just been standing still? If you can't remember living yesterday, then isn't your life only one day long?

Mr. Cheung unclasped his hands from behind him and gestured in the air. He was walking in circles around a date palm over and over through the same few regions of light and dark. He couldn't have explained why suddenly he felt such panic.

Over the next couple of weeks, Fiskadoro got back his ability to remember current events. But his memory for the past, for the time before he'd come back home, was gone forever. His earliest recollection was of lying in the darkness and remembering the village of swamp-people; as far as he knew his life reached back no farther than that moment when he'd lain in bed and remembered that he had died.

There was something real about him that came out of the memory and wouldn't go away. It was slowly healing, but still he screamed every time he peed. Every day when he woke up, it was still split open at the end, like a fish just cleaned.

In the dream, his first purpose had been to go through the ceremony and make himself like all other men, because he was different from all other men in the dream.

Now he was awake, and he was different from all other men who were awake. Now he didn't have to go through the ceremony, but it was too late.

They all told him he'd been alive before, in another world very much like this one. Why couldn't he remember it?

Mr. Cheung didn't want him just to learn the clarinet music. Mr. Cheung wanted him to eat the wafer, remember things, and tell Cassius Clay Sugar Ray where the blue pills were found. "I don't know where the blue pills come," he kept telling Mr. Cheung.

"But the wafer will help you remember."

"I not gone remember, Manager, because of I don't know."

"But how do you know you won't remember, if you don't remember what you know?"

"I remember that I don't know."

Talking about it made them both crazy. Mr. Cheung was strong, and he worked hard to move through all the words, but he kept bumping into the same ones over and over. "You'll remember who you are."

"I don't wanna remember who am I. Es me already, right now today. If I remember, then I gone be somebody else." During these conversations Fiskadoro's head hurt and his thoughts went around and around, but the thing that words couldn't change was that in between his legs he wasn't like other men, and so nobody could make him do anything: because when they talked to him they were talking to a person who was partly in a dream. They were sending their voices into another place. They were uselessly calling out to where the words of their own place didn't work.

Eventually Mr. Cheung gave up trying to get him to take the wafer of memory. Cassius Clay Sugar Ray traded the wafer to someone in Marathon, and whatever that person found, by swallowing it, belonged to that person. Nobody knew what had returned to that person, what knowledge of things that were lost.

Mr. Cheung had insisted, "You must take the drug again to remember who I am, who you are, and who this woman is."

But he'd refused the drug because he already knew that this was Anthony Terrence Cheung, his clarinet teacher and Manager of The Miami Symphony Orchestra. And he already knew that he himself was Fiskadoro. And Fiskadoro already knew who this woman was—his mother. He knew she wasn't for him, and he wasn't supposed to bother her at night. He understood, but didn't remember, that in the world before his dream and his death his mother had been everything to him, that she had gradually become only a part of the world, but the biggest part, and had turned eventually into just one person in the world, but the person he loved the most. Fiskadoro didn't mind knowing about this, but he didn't want to remember it. His mother was sick. She was getting smaller and smaller. After she closed her eyes there would be a hole in the air where she'd been, and then nothing where she'd been, only the air. He didn't want to eat the wafer. He didn't want the hole in the air to be a hole in Fiskadoro. He didn't want to remember what he was losing.

Fiskadoro was proud of himself because he was really learning to play the clarinet—Mr. Cheung said that he'd forgotten how *not* to play. The notes on the page flowed into his eyes and out of the instrument and into the world as music. And he was a much better reader of words now, too. Sometimes, but not all the time, when he read to Mr. Cheung from one of the books the teacher brought around, instead of marks on a page Fiskadoro saw images in his mind.

Sometimes, when his brother Drake came around, Fiskadoro told him about reading and tried to interest him in a book, but Drake was a fisherman. He liked boats, not books. People said Drake looked just like their father. Mike, the youngest brother, didn't look like anybody yet. He didn't mind being read to, but he didn't seem to listen very carefully. He spent most of the time with the neighbors, because Belinda was getting too weak to take care of him. Fiskadoro spent very little time with either of his brothers.

Most of the time he spent healing. Belinda had taken the

strings out of his ears, and the holes where they'd been were closed to dots now. His groin was well, but he would always be different from other men.

Being different from other men sometimes sent him walking far down the beach, down among the huge green flies and the stink that rose off the garbage pit and the hooting gulls that never seemed to mind the stink or eat any of the flies. Belinda's ashes would be thrown away here after her body was burned.

The gulls argued with him as he came too close to their nests in the weedy sand near the pit. They rose in flocks, their shadows whirling all around him on the beach. Farther up-shore he always saw them walking in little groups, ignoring each other, wise and smug, looking at nothing. They reminded him of Mr. Cheung.

More than once he saw others here, also different from other men: ghosts who had appeared out of the sea—from the shipwrecks, from the End of the World, from the plagues, from the cold time, from the kill-me—drowned sailors and frozen children, young maidens bleeding down their legs, sick old men and women and cancer-wasted fish-wives who seemed to wander hopelessly near the place of their burning; but all of them were smiling and no longer touched with pain.

The days were cooler, generally grey or sometimes overhung with tremendous white clouds whose shadows traveled the Gulf, and yet the dust on Towanda's breasts and shoulders was mapped with perspiration when she came to see Belinda. Towanda carried a penny jug of potato brandy, a crumpled aluminum can faintly bearing a bleached design.

Belinda didn't get up from her chair. Her eyes were sunk deep in brown circles, and the rest of her was the color of stale fish-meat.

Towanda smiled at this sick woman and nodded in an encouraging way. But when Belinda had swallowed some brandy and was passing back the can, her struggle was so great and her movements were so weak that Towanda gave up trying to look happy and just sat there wishing everything would go away.

Belinda noticed how her neighbor wiped the mouth of the can with her thumb before taking a swallow.

"You-all gone have to burn me up," Belinda said.

Towanda's face was twisted and her voice came out in whispers and squeaks. "Yeah," she whispered. "You got it."

"I on fire already sometime," Belinda told her. "Sometime he run down me like letric, sometime he coming up *shoosh*, like kerosene."

"You hurting alla time yet?" Towanda whispered.

"Sometime, not alla time."

"Es ain't over yet."

"Oh, no," Belinda said. "I got a little time. Nothing gone happen today."

"But he getting a little worse and a little worse?"

"Oh, yeah," Belinda said. "He getting worse." Suddenly the salt tears poured out of her eyes. "He taking me all the way, Towanda!"

"Oh, God, Belinda!" Towanda wiped her eyes and nose with the back of her hand. "We gone have to burn you up!"

"Got to," Belinda said. Her head shook with weeping.

"Yeah. Got to. Real life," Towanda agreed.

They passed the can of brandy. Belinda coughed and

started laughing, even as she wiped her own tears away. Towanda couldn't help laughing too.

"Make me feel stupid be laughing," Belinda said. "I don't know why I laughing now." She laughed harder.

"Me too, you know!" Towanda shouted, and they were both taken so relentlessly by laughter that they could hardly draw a breath.

She at first prayed and then gave up praying to Atomic Bomber Major Colonel Overdoze, the most powerful loa of all. Fiskadoro didn't understand, and he didn't care. He just wanted to be right there with her, seeing whatever she was seeing. She got wild in her talk eventually: Major Colonel Overdoze did what he wanted. Major Colonel Overdoze gave back her son, but all cleaned out inside like a baby. Major Colonel Overdoze wasn't controlled by shrines— he could set the shrines on fire if he wanted. Major Colonel Overdoze didn't take away the tumor, he made it bigger, and gave it children, and set them all on fire. The tumors covering her body hurt so much that Belinda was too surprised to yell. She tried to find a comfortable position, but the sensation, which she said sometimes ached and other times seared her bones, kept after her. She twisted and turned to get away from it, covered herself up to hide from it, flung herself around in the bed to shake it off, but it held her like hooks, rolled over her like water, fell down on her like sparks. She said it never stopped. Atomic Bomber Major Colonel Overdoze kept turning it up higher, until she knew she wasn't feeling *it*, but seeing *him*, closer and closer, brighter and brighter, and she couldn't close her eyes. Major Colonel Overdoze didn't need a plane to fly, or bombs to burn away the shrines that tried to control him. Without any hands or fingers or eyes, without even a mind, he could turn it up higher and higher until it couldn't be anything, not darkness, not light—it could only be him.

When the neighbor-ladies started bringing her potions to drink for the hurt, they told Fiskadoro the time was getting near. She didn't scream or cry about the pain anymore, but she looked out from farther and farther back inside herself every day and didn't seem to believe any of what she saw.

Fiskadoro kept watch by her bed and held her hand. He didn't care if he caught it, and sometimes he hoped he would. He was aware he was getting a little crazy about it. People did that in this situation. He cried a lot, and he got mad enough to kill. But the whole time there was something about it, as if he and the woman were going through all this right in the middle of the sun and not being burned. When she died it was the middle of the night; his brothers were asleep, the village was asleep, but the sea was awake and Belinda was awake, and her oldest son was awake, holding her hand as he sat beside her bed.

The sweat began pouring off her. She asked for the pan several times but then discovered she didn't have to make water. "Jimmy! Jimmy!" she said. She started talking to others who'd gone there first—her mother and father, her older brother. "I don't hurt no more," she said. She took a deep breath; and then she died.

SEVEN

On the day the Israelites came for him, Mr. Cheung was ready with a hundred objections, and he seriously planned, as soon as he saw them, to start listing the many good reasons why he couldn't go with them today, or ever.

Flying Man and the two young savage boys flanking him in Mr. Cheung's doorway were smiling and serene—much, much more calm and contented than he'd imagined possible.

"News come," Flying Man told him right away.

"I thought so."

"Dat news when say today."

"Yes," Mr. Cheung said, completely terrified. "I thought so."

"Bear good. Bear bear good." Flying Man clasped his hands above his head. His goodwill and happiness were overpowering.

In Mr. Cheung's view the chief obstacle was that his wife Eileen was at the vendors, and he couldn't leave his aged Grandmother Wright at home alone. "Most of the orchestra can't come, I'm afraid. But Fiskadoro will be here soon, any minute." He wrung his hands. "But I don't think it's a very good idea. My grandmother is here. She can't be left alone." He looked from one man to the next, over and over, in the weak hope of finding a face that shone with some small light of comprehension.

"Oxra," Flying Man told him. "Yah! News come."

Beyond them, Mr. Cheung saw several others, all striped with paint and hung with feathers, standing in the dirt street in front of his house.

It wasn't so much a fear of their wrath as a deep reluctance to make ripples in the pool of their contentment, finally, that kept Mr. Cheung from refusing their wishes.

He'd made no preparations for this day, hadn't mentioned it to the others of The Miami Symphony Orchestra, hadn't said a word about it to anybody. The fact that Fiskadoro was coming here today was just a lucky coincidence—it happened to be the boy's lesson day.

Mr. Cheung hoped there wouldn't be any kind of tragedy. He profoundly hoped that this ceremony didn't involve the eating of raw meat, or sexual perversion, or some manner of blood sacrifice.

"I think I would like my grandmother to come along, too," he said. "Could we carry her?" He demonstrated by joining his hands together as if rocking a baby.

Fiskadoro took the beach route down to Twicetown, clutching the briefcase called Samsonite to his chest. To his left was nothing but the beach and a thin strip of lowland tangled with cypress and brush. Beyond the brush, parallel to his progress and hidden by the growth, was the road to Twicetown. He was late, but he failed to hurry. He walked on the wet sand near the water, and kept turning around to see what his footprints looked like getting smaller and smaller behind him.

Eventually he came to the place where paths led away from the Gulf over crude bridges of heaped rocks through the bog and into Twicetown. He'd walked this road with Mr. Cheung for one of his history lessons. His teacher had told him that the town—and in many ways, although several sections of it were lifeless now, it remained a town—had been known, in the other age, as Key West. But during the End of the World it had been saved twice and had earned itself a new name. A missile blew up like a firecracker, but a dud missile only brought good luck.

Mr. Cheung had explained these things to him, but he hadn't yet told Fiskadoro where he was—if this was the land of death, a land that came after the land of death, or some other place entirely.

After Twicetown's more desolate section he passed along the edge of commerce and entered a gauntlet of vendors. They had a lot of things for sale, but Fiskadoro hadn't been told yet if he was entitled to have any of them.

At one table he recognized a boy named Sanchez, but he couldn't remember the rest of the name. Before him on his collapsible table Sanchez showed off a pile of valuable items— scuba knives, combat boots, tennis shoes, watches, a set of three kitchen pans, one resting in another in another—waving over them the wand of a geiger counter that obviously had no power and counted nothing. People stayed away from him. Only a few allowed themselves to show interest, slowing down a little but not stopping.

In this life Fiskadoro had seen Sanchez twice before—once

on a morning after a party celebrating a baby's birth into the Army, when he'd found Sanchez sleeping on the dirt of a path with sand crusted in the corners of his mouth and his nostrils ringed with dried blood; and another time, at the party celebrating Belinda's burning, when this Sanchez had peed on the fire in front of everybody, and later fell in the sea and had to be pulled out. Sanchez's mother had cried, and his father had driven him away and told him never to come back to the Army.

Fiskadoro stood looking down at Sanchez and trying to remember his whole name.

"Yeah," Sanchez said, in a slick way that Fiskadoro disliked listening to.

"You looking better today," Fiskadoro told him. "Face ain't dirty."

"Es ain't what I ask you," Sanchez said. "I ask you what you want, how much, and come on make a move."

Fiskadoro freed one hand from the task of holding the briefcase and knocked on the table as at a door. "What's you name in the real situation?" he demanded.

Obviously Sanchez recognized him. He was sober now, and a look of apology passed over his features. "My name Harvard Sanchez," he said, and then, recovering some pride, he added, "relate to *Los Desechados* Sanchez family, even Leon Sanchez. He my father, Leon." Harvard Sanchez looked at Fiskadoro, squinting his eyes as if Fiskadoro were down at the end of the street. "I don't remember you too good," Harvard confessed.

"That's because of I eat something make everybody forget me," Fiskadoro explained.

"Es ain't what I ask you. I got buttons. How many you want?" He was referring to radiation-sensitive badges that made travel possible through the contaminated regions. He waved the wand of his geiger counter over a small pile of them that glittered like so many coins.

Fiskadoro just didn't like the way this man talked. He seemed to be issuing some kind of challenge. "I be going in someday. Not today," Fiskadoro said.

"Not to*day*," Harvard Sanchez said contemptuously. "Today 'bout the last day. Quarantine end any minute. Bob Marley gone coming, Jah gone coming, everybody coming. Buy now."

"I mean it what I say. Soon." Fiskadoro wished he was going into the contaminated regions tomorrow, so he could show this man just who, out of all these people, was ready for danger. He knew that anyone who saw the City became a great person. "Even tomorrow," he said suddenly. "I be go tomorrow."

"Mañana!" Harvard Sanchez said. "Then you need buttons. How many? Come on. Everybody going la beach now. Big time today. Let's go. Can't wait. Buy now." He gestured at the people going past. Everybody seemed to be headed in the same direction. All along the street the vendors were packing up their tables.

"I got buttons mi casa. I *got* buttons," Fiskadoro said, moving on quickly, almost against his will.

He felt completely defeated when Harvard Sanchez shouted after him, "Fish-man!" Not least of all because it was his name.

When Fiskadoro reached his teacher's house he found a whole lot of Israelites, black people with painted faces and wild shiny black braids of hair—feathered and animal-skinned Israelites who didn't know how to talk—carrying Mr. Cheung's grandmother away in her red rocker. Mr. Cheung was directing and encouraging them cautiously. Fiskadoro stood in the street.

His teacher noticed him and came over. "Fiskadoro," he said.

"Sí," Fiskadoro said.

His teacher clasped his hands together over his belly, and then unclasped them and flung his arms wide. "These Israelites are going to have a ceremony. I've agreed that we'll play some songs for them."

"We got the music," Fiskadoro said.

"Exactly, exactly. You understand." Mr. Cheung looked a little ashamed of himself.

The Israelites moved past them carrying Grandmother Wright in her red chair, three on each side. Grandmother looked straight ahead. Her feet hung down in thick blue socks.

"We go *play* para tu," Fiskadoro told the Israelites. He and Mr. Cheung followed along behind.

The six Israelites carrying Grandmother Wright in her red chair didn't seem capable of tiring, but after the group of them had passed beyond Twicetown, with the old woman floating in their midst and Mr. Cheung and Fiskadoro trailing them closely and nearly every vendor following also in a spontaneous parade, the Orchestra Manager found space for his grandmother on a mule-cart, and they put her aboard.

Grandmother faced out the back of the cart, rocking to and fro with each step of the burro, and she clutched the arms of her chair as she had clutched the side of the bunk on the boat that had saved her from the waves nearly ninety years before, as she had clutched the metal side-rails of the stretcher on which she'd been unloaded from the boat, and as she had clutched the higher railings of the bed she'd failed to sleep in at the naval infirmary at Sangley Point in the Philippine Islands.

Today was one of her clearer days. She was recalling these things on purpose—flinging herself onto these memories as onto a solid place while wild men followed her onto the beach —because the Ocean's smell and the sounds of water were too much for her. It was better to recall in her mind a terror that was finished than to face, in some confusion, these salt waves and their very doubtful intentions.

The Israelites knew the proper place. It was only a few hundred meters downshore from their tiny village, a miscellany of lean-tos surrounding their wrecked vessel. They stepped hard, three or four of them, on the rear of the mule-cart and tipped it toward the sand, taking hold of the rocking chair. They set down Grandmother Wright with a thump before the mud flats some distance from the action of the waves.

There were more people here than Mr. Cheung had ever seen in one place at one time. Possibly, everyone was here. His wife Eileen had come along with the mob of vendors who'd left their tables behind and hurried here to watch and sell nothing. Eileen gave him a kiss and wandered off. At one point or another he saw every member of The Miami Symphony Orchestra, but they all pretended they didn't see him. At least two dozen fishing boats sat where the outgoing tide had beached them, all in a row with their anchor lines sprouting from the mud, and most of the Army population seemed to be present. Fiskadoro's two little brothers were here, the smaller one riding the shoulders of the larger. Mr. Cheung thought he saw Fiskadoro's mother, but then remembered that she'd passed on. The bodyguards employed by his own half-brother,

Martin, appeared and disappeared on the edges of the crowd; and Martin himself, and Park-Smith, also avoiding the two clarinetists, convened and dispersed in various corners of the gathering.

Only Mr. Cheung and Fiskadoro played for the Israelites. But far from being disappointed in the ensemble's size, these savage people were all enthralled. They came around and for once stood quietly in one place, tipping their heads, closing their eyes, and listening as if this music came from far away, or as if they were remembering it fondly from a time in their lives more sensible and beautiful than this one.

The Orchestra Manager and his pupil played improvisations based on the *Sidney Bechet* exercises. Fiskadoro played better than his teacher: as soon as he tasted the reed with his tongue, he forgot himself and turned into music. The tide lay far out, and their songs flew over the mud flats and died above the small waves. After an hour, as they took a break and Mr. Cheung cleared the spit from his mouthpiece with a bit of cloth, he said to Flying Man, "Tell me, please, what this is all about."

Flying Man nodded his head and danced two steps, shaking all his feathers. "Bobbylon all over now. Time nex' planet now—planet Israh-el!"

Mr. Cheung saw that Grandmother Wright's forehead was veiled with perspiration. He wished he could wipe it away, but all he had was the rag he'd already used to clean his mouth-piece. The town behind them was desolate, he was sure not a soul remained there. Still, he felt bad about bringing her here into the elements. He hoped his grandmother would be able to survive this experience.

Grandmother was remembering the flight from Vietnam, and the crash that ended it.

When the helicopter crashed into the sea the Lieutenant was the first, of those who surfaced, to go down, because he hadn't taken his shoes off soon enough—he'd wanted to protect his feet from sharks. He'd exhausted himself trying to stay afloat with his feet in canvas combat boots with heavy soles. By sundown he'd gone under and untied the laces and let them go, willing at that point to lose his shoes, and his feet, if necessary, to live another minute, to draw a few more breaths. But it was too late to get any strength back, and before sundown he'd begun slipping under the waves, coming up coughing, moving his arms and legs around as eventually Marie had done at the end—not to swim, but to find a purchase, the solid place that was certain to be around here somewhere—and going down more and more often, until the new energy of panic was exhausted and he slipped away and didn't come up. They saw him surface face-down some meters off, and Marie saw the body only as something she might grapple with to help her stay afloat, but she didn't have the strength to go after it. He'd wasted his energy trying to keep his shoes—but it wasn't his pair of shoes, or his fear of sharks, that killed him. He died because he wasn't saved.

He'd been bent on improving his chances, and he'd almost gotten out a life jacket as they'd crashed—as soon as Captain Minh spoke to him and smacked the faces of the helicopter's dials and instruments with alarm, the Lieutenant had turned in his seat and managed to move people off the service locker, ordering them at gunpoint to squeeze themselves impossibly against the others as he stood up, and Marie knew she had to move or he would shoot her, so she did her best to crush the bones of the people behind her to give him room. He had the locker's lid raised ten centimeters and one hand caught in its open mouth and touching a canvas life jacket, his revolver in the other hand, when the craft descended, very slowly, to the water's surface.

They were raised once by a wave, and Marie was beginning to wonder how long they would float here before they were rescued or starved to death, when Captain Minh leapt from the door, which now, only two seconds after their touching down, was filling with water. Marie waited, while her heart beat twice, for the people between her and the door to jump also, and then she clawed and broke her way through them and into a sea which was suddenly up to the level of her throat.

She swam away, and when she turned around, treading water, the helicopter was gone.

Upturned heads floated around her in a green waste. Between the blasts of wind rolling over it, there wasn't a sound but the water. The shock of being here was no greater than the shock of being defiled by this filthy secret, the noises the ocean made all alone in the middle of itself. Its infinitesimal salt bubbles hissed and breathed, and the surface water turned over and licked along itself and coughed softly.

Under these circumstances the China Sea looked like nothing. Here was the difference between something big—as seen from the craft, horizon to horizon—and something enormous, engulfing, mind-erasing, seen only in series, swell after swell, too absolutely filled with itself to admit any mercy, to know its name or take any thought. It was as if, having found herself all wet, she'd taken an astonished breath to say, "Look what happened!" but was stalled in the astonishment and couldn't exclaim, or even exhale.

In a moment another head popped up streaming with water, eyes closed, black hair plastered to the scalp, and drew a deep breath, like a baby being born. She didn't know this one—but it was the Lieutenant, unrecognizable, somehow, having lost not only his beret, but also his rank, his name, his personality. The Lieutenant had no life preserver, and no revolver.

Her skirt and blouse were heavy. She let herself go under

while she tore her blouse open, kicked upward, broke the surface, went under as she took off the blouse, thrust to the surface, lost the world of air while she pulled at the button on the side of her skirt and yanked the garment down over her hips, and came back to the possibility of breathing again as she loosed her knees from its girth and kicked it from her ankles. She didn't think. She only wanted a place to stand, rest, and eat and drink the air.

She kept her head up among the other heads, losing and regaining sight of them when a swell lifted and dropped her.

At first they all treaded water, not caring how the exertion drained them. Within a few minutes Marie was more tired than she'd ever been, and then she didn't think anymore, except to wish she could lie down.

Captain Minh was the first to go over on his back. The others did so right away. It gave them a style of rest, more breath, and more time; and though it exposed their backs to a huge world of liquid and somehow, therefore, wracked their nerves, it took their eyes off a sea higher than themselves and showed them something bigger—the sky.

The sky was a major discovery, holding an element of hope that charged among them and got them talking. Marie said some things in English, and then in French, just to be heard. The others answered importantly, with interest, though no answers were required of questions like "What time is it?" and they asked each other questions of their own—"Where do you think we are?"—in French, and said other things in Vietnamese, and gave opinions and looked at the sky. Captain Minh organized an effort to stay together, getting the others to take off their clothes and link themselves like a chain by clutching shirtsleeves or pantlegs. The Lieutenant wouldn't contribute his pants because he didn't want to take off his shoes. Some of the others warned him against this, in French, and Captain Minh argued with him in Vietnamese. The Lieu-tenant, already breathless, shouted, "Fack you, body boy!"

The talk gave over to the work of breathing, and they were voiceless now except to gulp air or clear their throats. Marie answered the others only briefly, and asked only, "Où êtes vous?" and occasionally turned her head, looking for anyone. People talked only to locate themselves among others, and now it appeared they were nine. The center of the group were a man and his wife, who called to each other often and said, Marie supposed, "Here I am!" and "I see you!" Because these two signaled themselves the most, the others took them as markers in the ocean and stayed near, keeping their chain of laundry slack so as not to have to fight each other's drift. Marie used the man and woman angrily, let them do the work of crying out, and saved her own strength for keeping her face turned away from the swells that broke over her head if she didn't lift it slightly out of their heaving approach.

The effort this kind of floating required wasn't too great, but her neck ached and soon the back of her skull felt flat and numb and her spine burned, all from the repeated task of lift-ing her head. The surface that had seemed so black and heavy from above, whose motion had seemed so blubbery and incidental, now proved active, populous, and resourceful, throwing up generations of fingers that clawed her face, worms that raced across her nose and mouth and choked her, small whirling mouths that swallowed and abandoned her hair. It was windy. The whitecaps that had seemed so widely separated now came relentlessly, their froth blasted by small gusts into rainbows. Their mist strangled her. Her lips were chapped and raw with salt, her eyes stung, and before long her face hurt as if she'd been beaten. She began to cry. She'd already passed the point of thinking that she might swim until she got out of here to continue the business of life, and had come to the point where she swam because it was, in fact, life's business, the thing to be carried on until she died.

They watched the Lieutenant go down. He let go of their improvised lifeline and struggled to give up his shoes, and then his pants. He struggled again as he went under repeatedly, and he begged the others for some kind of help, but soon he was paralyzed and wordless and all alone, although he was right there among them, and then he was gone.

Before nightfall the wind blew gentler, the swells were born smaller and more courteous, and life got better. But then night fell, and there was no more seeing in this life.

In the dark they stayed near each other, fought to keep near when one lost hold of the lifeline, though clinging to one another was fatal, and they called to one another and answered —there was never any talk about why. It was understood that they would stay together, though Marie had forgotten by now who they were, how many, what they looked like. Hands were sought, voices chased with precious strength, the touch of hands slipped away, voices were lost. People went silent, gasped and choked. It occurred to her that these people were falling asleep. Her own changeless condition was a paralysis that somehow found a way to move when the water lapped her nostrils and she panicked, snorting and coughing, and sculled again. She passed beyond waking, but she didn't sleep. And yet it was hard to tell the difference. For a while there were some stars, and a blurred half-moon, but they disappeared without her noticing and then there was only herself in a floating dark of no particular dimension but full of soft aimless noise. Uniformly, infinitely, and permanently it hissed, and along the fabric of this sound it burbled and squeaked, it flushed and spat. In the action of water it trilled and sang. It spoke; it rolled words over words. It knew—and, in a kind of shock, it ceased; in the water of it it reconsidered; it cleared its mind and opened its eyes and saw itself.

Her ears were filled with water, her tongue so swollen she could hardly shut her mouth on it, but still she tasted the ocean, and she heard it. Her nostrils were closed tight and she couldn't tell if her eyes were open or not. She realized the stars might not have gone away, but that the salt might have blinded her.

At some point in the dark two hands clutched and held her, someone trying to stay afloat. She poked their eyes and bit the fingers digging into her arms. She kicked their stomach and tore herself away. A little later, as she began to let herself sink, finding no difference in her mind anymore between the blackness of air and the blackness of water, something frond-like touched her cheek, and something more solid bumped her shoulder—a person—and she grabbed at the neck, held on to the collar of an undershirt. There was no resistance; the person was dead. The body went under a ways, but she was able to use it to help keep herself above the water a little longer. She rested with her head on its back, until it went under deeper, and she kept it near, straddled it a while and finally stood on it for a second at a time, keeping her chin above the swells, while it washed downward and came up again to give her feet its slight support, until she lost it.

When the sun came up the first day, its light was unbelievable. There was strength in it. Marie felt saved. The time in the water now seemed longer than all her life before. Her life before had been a preparation for this water, and the sun finally becoming a whole circle and clearing the surface, flying out of the water into the sky, paid for and explained everything. She laughed and felt powerful. Her stomach ached and the thirst, as the sun touched her lips, was all of a sudden more fateful than the need for air. She drank some water. Her throat was swollen nearly shut, and her tongue had forced itself halfway out of her mouth. She was hardly able to swallow.

Captain Minh was nearby. A man and a woman floated between them. Nobody else was in sight. The sea lifted, kept,
and released her over and over.

The woman tried to keep the man's head above the water
when he passed out. She kicked the water, launching herself
as high as her shoulders repeatedly, and slapped him, but he
didn't come around. She cupped his chin in her hand and
tried to drag him along behind her, her face, smashed and
puffed-up like a beating victim's, turned up toward the sky.
After a while he slipped away from the woman. The water
flowed into his mouth with a sucking noise as he went under.
The woman floated on, looking at the sky. Marie turned her
own eyes up to the sun.

It clouded over slowly and then began to rain.

The rain, which was a hard one, fell down on her face and
tongue with great force. The water on her tongue was new,
and the purity of it on her eyelids brought her to life. Then
she felt the fresh water reaching the cells of her stomach as
if each one were being stabbed. She let her feet drop, kicked
once, and lifted her head to look around.

She was alone. The rain drove up a low fog from the
ocean's surface, and she couldn't see very far, she thought, but
had no idea how far she was seeing where there was nothing
to see. A swell coming toward her broke into two shapes, and
one was another corpse that came right to her arms. It was
the man who'd gone under some time ago, she didn't know
how long. She clung to the body and rested piecemeal as she
had before, until the effort to find its lowering support was
greater than the effort to float alone. The rain passed over,
and now she was rested enough to know, at least, that she was
here.

But in just a few minutes she was gone again, without
strength enough to think, without mind enough to know if

she was above or below the water. If she didn't have a thought, still she had a sense that she'd been in this life for a day and a night and a day, that this was all there was, or ever had been, of this life, and that she had somehow reached, by floating, the bottom of everything. But she was wrong.

The stamp of endlessness driven down onto her mind was erased, washed away, the first time she passed out and slept, as the others had, and slipped beneath the waves. She might have been anywhere as she woke up with water in her mouth, disbelieving and startled, charged with the responsibility of taking a breath. The shock of finding herself here where she'd always been was like a birth. It became the common torture of her existence to sleep, choke, wake, and come back to the slave-labor of floating. She began to experience the process less and less as trying to stay afloat, and more and more as trying to stay in the air, trying to keep from crashing to the ground. Then it came to her that the ground was where she wanted to be, the place to lie down and breathe; and then she woke up, drowning.

The idea of lying down on the earth to take a deep breath seemed so wonderful it could only be put off; it was something worth waiting for, something to enjoy a moment from now, and then a moment from now.

Breathing was living. It was a living accomplished by no one, but a living that this No One had to accomplish on purpose, willingly, because she could not both sleep and breathe. She could not forget herself without dying. Nevertheless she forgot herself.

She left herself and drifted with a sense not of the water, but of something that was in it, a perfect and invaluable presence, a rubble of treasure growing up from the bottom of the world how many countless fathoms beneath until it touched and lifted her, bringing her face up to feel the air; and then it abandoned her and declined away into its origins so that she sank down again, not into water but into black, sharp, unconsolable pity. But it came back, growing out of nothing from the floor of life, and lifted her. It wasn't just the most priceless fact and thing; it was her breath; it was the sole fact and thing.

By sunset she was only a baby, thinking nothing, absolutely adrift, waking to cough and begin crying, drifting and weeping, sleeping and sinking, waking up to choke the water from her mouth and whimper, indistinguishable from what she saw, which was the grey sky that held no interest, identity, or thought. This was the point when she reached the bottom of everything, when she had no idea either what she'd reached or who had reached it, or even that it had been reached.

The heavens looked huge today, as if their blueness rocketed out beyond the edge of everything and even beyond time itself, because their infinite spaces easily entertained great clouds like monsters that moved through them living their oblivious, prehistoric dreams. But Mr. Cheung wondered who it was who watched and who it was who slept. Behind the clouds, in the south, a clear patch was growing larger, and pretty soon emptiness would have the sky. That was the way, a dream of days followed by emptiness, the huge water turning over the grains of sand, neither one knowing which was big and which was small. Mr. Cheung was uneasy and sad. He would have to die, and the quiet knife of this fact wasn't dissuaded by the interplay of milkiness and inkiness in the textures of the Atlantic under these clouds of October, or by his prayers, best wishes, or sorrow. His mood swelled and the action of the wind over the beach seemed full of power.

. . .

Since the death of his mother, Belinda, Fiskadoro was confused. If everyone in this world around him had died once, as he himself had died, then where had Belinda gone when she died the second time? How many worlds were there?

As a way of approaching these questions, he confided to Mr. Cheung, "I saw those skeleton in the cars that won't go."

"You'll be a great leader," Mr. Cheung said.

Fiskadoro didn't know what his teacher was talking about, as he hardly ever knew what anybody was talking about.

"I'm not like other men," he reminded Mr. Cheung.

"No, I know that. You've been to their world and now you're in this world, but you don't have the memories to make you crazy. It isn't sleeping under the moon that makes a crazy person. It's waking up and remembering the past and thinking it's real."

"I saw the ashes driving the cars forever," Fiskadoro said.

"Something big is happening today. I wish it was yesterday," Mr. Cheung said. "I wish it was five minutes before this minute, when I went around wishing it was a hundred years ago. You know," he said, "in this past I long for, I don't remember how even then I longed for the past."

This talk was only taking them away from what Fiskadoro wanted to ask. With some anxiety about being so direct, he got right to the question. He pointed off toward the northern horizon as far as their vision would carry, and brought his finger around in an arc through the chambers of the sky over the Ocean and held it out to the south. "I don't know what es," he said.

His teacher seemed to understand. "I don't either," he told Fiskadoro, "but we're here."

"You don't remember?"

"I never knew."

"Anybody know?" Fiskadoro asked him.

"Possibly my grandmother," Mr. Cheung said.

. . .

The Lieutenant was lost. Small children were lost. The husband and wife who'd persevered and stayed afloat a long time were lost and still falling, probably, through the water toward the bottom, and everybody was lost who had flailed in panic, while their lives clung to them unreasonably, through the fields and barricades and over the faces of other people equally rabid to live. Marie was the last of three to be taken out of the water—Captain Minh and one other woman had been saved, and now the young girl Marie. Saved not because she lasted, not because of anything she did, or determined in herself to do, because there was nothing left of her to determine anything; saved not because she hadn't given up, because she had, and in fact she possessed no memory of the second night, and couldn't believe, to this day, that she'd spent twenty hours staying alive, breath by breath, without knowing enough to desire it; saved not because she'd held out long enough, because there was nothing to say what was long enough; saved because she was saved, saved because they threw down a rope, but she couldn't reach her hand up now to take hold of it; saved because a sailor jumped off the boat, his bare white feet dangling from the legs of khaki pants, and pulled her to the ladder; saved not because her hands reached out; saved because other hands than hers reached down and saved her.

Mr. Cheung stood on the beach holding his clarinet in one hand. He and Fiskadoro were standing, as a matter of fact, between two civilizations, standing together at the southern edge of the crowd of people and at the northern edge of the crowd of seagulls, who'd come around to see what was happening through eyes too tiny to hold any questions. The seagulls walked back and forth at the border of water, all bellies and beaks, throwing out their chests with an air of flat assumption like small professors. Fiskadoro looked back and forth between these seagulls and Mr. Cheung, and Mr. Cheung guessed what he was seeing.

The Cubans will come, the Manager recited to himself, the Quarantine won't last forever. Everything we have, all we are, will meet its end, will be overcome, taken up, washed away. But everything came to an end before. Now it will happen again. Many times. Again and again. Something is coming and something is going—but that isn't the issue. The issue is that I failed to recognize myself in these seagulls.

On the boat she hung onto the bunk's right edge with both hands and never once let go of it. Each motion of rising and suddenly unsupported sinking shocked her awake.

In the hospital, each time she passed into sleep, she woke up immediately.

The last of it, the bottom she'd sunk to by staying afloat, would have meant nothing if she hadn't stayed alive. It only made sense when a person had a name, like Marie, and a body, like this wasted old one, and a place like this rocking chair, and a breath, like this one she was taking now.

By now all the clouds had passed them by, and the blue atmosphere looked thin enough that Mr. Cheung expected to see faint stars behind it. Though it was sunny, a haze came down over the water and made it seem the beach led down to the end of all thought. A few feet past the licking edge of water there was nothing. Sounds came out of it that made

no sense—a talking of horns, a shifting song of voices, and
something too low and too deep to hear which was still
much more definite than the other sounds. Everyone on the
beach was silent. Mr. Cheung was frightened.

One day the Quarantine would be lifted, and the Cubans
would come. If today was that day, then the shape of something, a white shadow framed by dull swords of light in the
place out there beyond the end of all thought, was a Cuban
fleet.

Ship or shape, it came in slowly as the tide.

One day they would all be dead. If today was that day, then
everything was clear. Now the sounds and visions and ideas
coming at them from beyond the end of all thought were real.
Now the white boat, or was it a cloud, came for the Israelites
out of the fog of their belief. In all likelihood it was a ghost-
ship, and the Israelites were ghosts, and the man standing at
the bow was a ghost who had come for them, it was clear in
the draw of this white, white vessel—unless the light happened to be playing tricks, it wasn't touching the water at
all—clear from the majesty of it, the sense that it floats in
the air and not in the waters of the world, floats in the
heart of Allah, the Compassionate, the Merciful.

Nodding down into a nap beneath the canopy of her memories, she jerked awake and saw the form again in the early

mist of the second morning and the third day—a rock, a whale, some white place to cling to, sleep, and breathe. And in her state of waking, she jerked awake. And from that waking, she woke up.

ABOUT THE AUTHOR

DENIS JOHNSON was born in 1949 in Munich. His first novel, *Angels*, was awarded the Sue Kaufman Prize for First Fiction in 1984 by the American Academy and Institute of Arts and Letters. His volumes of poetry include *The Man Among the Seals*, *Inner Weather* and *The Incognito Lounge*. He lives in Wellfleet, Massachusetts.

V I N T A G E
CONTEMPORARIES

"Today's novels for the readers of today."

—VANITY FAIR

"Real literature—originals and important reprints—in attractive, inexpensive paperbacks."

—THE LOS ANGELES TIMES

"Prestigious."

—THE CHICAGO TRIBUNE

"A very fine collection."
—THE CHRISTIAN SCIENCE MONITOR

"Adventurous and worthy."

—SATURDAY REVIEW

"If you want to know what's on the cutting edge of American fiction, then these are the books you should be reading."
—UNITED PRESS INTERNATIONAL

On sale at bookstores everywhere, but if otherwise unavailable may be ordered from us. You can use this coupon, or phone (800) 638-6460.

Please send me the Vintage Contemporaries books I have checked on the reverse. I am enclosing $ _____ (add $1.00 per copy to cover postage and handling). Send check or money order—no cash or COD please. Prices are subject to change without notice.

NAME _____

ADDRESS _____

CITY _____ STATE _____ ZIP _____

Send coupons to:

RANDOM HOUSE, INC., 400 Hahn Road, Westminster, MD 21157

ATTN: ORDER ENTRY DEPARTMENT

Allow at least 4 weeks for delivery.

VINTAGE
CONTEMPORARIES